The Museum of Dr Moses

Other OTTO PENZLER BOOKS by
Joyce Carol Oates

The Barrens

Beasts

Rape: A Love Story

*The Female of the Species: Tales of Mystery
and Suspense*

Joyce Carol OATES

The Museum of Dr Moses

Tales of Mystery and Suspense

AN OTTO PENZLER BOOK

Quercus

First published in Great Britain in 2008 by

Quercus
21 Bloomsbury Square
London
WC1A 2NS

ISBN (HB) 978 1 84724 179 5
ISBN (TPB) 978 1 84724 180 1

Designed by Linda Lockowitz

Printed in Great Britain by Clays Ltd, St Ives plc.

10 9 8 7 6 5 4 3 2 1

For Richard Burgin

Contents

Hi! Howya Doin!   1

Suicide Watch   7

The Man Who Fought Roland LaStarza   25

Valentine, July Heat Wave   85

Bad Habits   98

Feral   120

The Hunter   146

The Twins: A Mystery   165

Stripping   182

The Museum of Dr. Moses   185

The Museum
of Dr Moses

Hi! Howya Doin!

Good-looking husky guy, six foot four, in late twenties or early thirties, Caucasian male as the initial police report will note, he's as solid-built as a fire hydrant, carries himself like an athlete, or an ex-athlete, just perceptibly thickening at the waist, otherwise in terrific condition, like a bronze figure in motion, sinewy arms pumping as he runs, long muscled legs, chiseled-muscled calves, he's hurtling along the moist wood-chip path at the western edge of the university arboretum at approximately 6 P.M. Thursday evening and there comes, from the other direction, a woman jogger on the path, in her late thirties, flushed face, downturned eyes, dark hair threaded with gray like cobwebs, an awkward runner, fleshy lips parted, holds her arms stiff at her sides, in a shrunken pullover shirt with a faded tiger on its front, not large but sizable breasts shaking as she runs, mimicked in the slight shaking of her cheeks, her hips in carrot-colored sweatpants, this is Madeline Hersey, frowning at the wood-chip path before her, Madeline's exasperating habit of staring at the ground when she runs, oblivious of the arboretum though at this time in May it's dazzling with white dogwood, pink dogwood, vivid yellow forsythia, Madeline is a lab technician at Squibb, lost in a labyrinth of her own tangled thoughts (career, lover, lover's learning-disabled child), startled out of her reverie by the loud aggressive-friendly greeting *Hi! Howya doin!* flung out at her like a playful slap on the buttocks as the tall husky jogger passes Madeline with the most fleeting of glances, big-toothed bemused smile, and Madeline loses her stride, in a faltering voice *Fine, thank you* but the other jogger is past, unhearing, and now on the gravel path behind the university hospital, now on the grassy towpath beside the old canal, in the green lushness of University Dells Park where, from late afternoon to dusk, joggers are running singly and in couples, in groups of three or more, track-team runners from the local high school, college students, white-haired older runners both male and female, to these the husky jogger in skintight mustard yellow T-shirt, short navy blue shorts showing his chiseled thigh muscles, size-twelve Nikes, calls out *Hi! Howya doin!* in a big bland booming voice, *Hi! Howya doin!* and a flash of big horsey teeth, long pumping legs, pumping arms, it's his practice to come up close behind a solitary jogger, a woman maybe, a girl, or an older man, so many "older" men (forties, fifties, sixties and beyond) in the university community, sometimes a younger guy who's sweated through his clothes, beginning to breathe through his mouth, size-twelve Nikes striking the earth like mallets, *Hi! Howya doin!* jolting Kyle Lindeman out of dreamy-sexy thoughts, jolting Michelle Rossley out of snarled anxious thoughts, there's Diane Hendricks who'd been an athlete in high school, now twenty pounds overweight, divorced, no kid, replaying in her head a quarrel she'd had with a woman friend, goddamn she's angry! goddamn she's not going to call Ginny back this time! trying to calm her

rush of thoughts like churning, roiling water, trying to measure her breaths Zen-fashion, inhale, exhale, inhale, and out
of nowhere into this reverie a tall husky hurtling figure bears
down on her, toward her, veering into her line of vision, instinctively Diane bears to the right to give him plenty of room
to pass her, hopes this is no one she knows from work, no one
who knows her, trying not to look up at him, tall guy, husky,
must weigh two-twenty, works out, has got to be an athlete, or
ex-athlete, a pang of sexual excitement courses through her,
or is it sexual dread? even as *Hi! Howya doin!* rings out loud
and bemused, like an elbow in Diane's left breast, as the
stranger pounds past her, in his wake an odor of male sweat,
acrid-briny male sweat and an impression of big glistening
teeth bared in a brainless grin, or is it a mock grin, death's-
head grin? — thrown off stride, self-conscious and stumbling,
Diane manages to stammer *Fine — I'm fine* as if the stranger
brushing past her is interested in her or in her well-being in
the slightest, what a fool Diane is! — yet another day, moist-
bright morning in the University Dells along the path beside
the seed-stippled lagoon where amorous-combative male mallards are pursuing female ducks with much squawking, flap-
ping of wings and splashing water, there comes the tall husky
jogger, Caucasian male, six foot four, two-twenty pounds, no
ID as the initial police report will note, on this occasion the
jogger is wearing a skintight black Judas Priest T-shirt, very
short white nylon shorts revealing every surge, ripple, sheen
of chiseled thigh muscles, emerging out of a shadowy pathway
at the edge of the birch woods to approach Dr. Rausch of the
university's geology department, older man, just slightly vain
about being fit, dark-tinted aviator glasses riding the bridge of
his perspiring nose, Dr. Rausch panting as he runs, not running

so fast as he'd like, rivulets of sweat like melting grease down his back, sides, sweating through his shirt, in baggy khaki shorts to the knee, Dr. Rausch grinding his jaws in thought (departmental budget cuts! his youngest daughter's wrecked marriage! his wife's biopsy next morning at 7 A.M., he will drive her to the medical center and wait for her, return her home and yet somehow get to the tenure committee meeting he's chairing at 11 A.M.) when *Hi! Howya doin!* jolts Dr. Rausch as if the husky jogger in the black Judas Priest T-shirt has extended a playful size-twelve foot onto Dr. Rausch's path to trip him, suddenly he's thrown off stride, poor old guy, hasn't always been sixty-four years old, sunken-chested, skinny white legs sprouting individual hairs like wires, hard little potbelly straining at the unbelted waistline of the khaki shorts, Dr. Rausch looks up squinting, is this someone he knows? should know? who knows *him*? across the vertiginous span of thirty years in the geology department Dr. Rausch has had so many students, but before he can see who this is, or make a panting effort to reply in the quick-casual way of youthful joggers, the husky jogger has passed by Dr. Rausch without a second glance, legs like pistons of muscle, shimmering sweat-film like a halo about his body, fair brown, russet brown hair in curls like woodshavings lifting halolike from his large uplifted head, big toothy smile, large broad nose made for deep breathing, enormous dark nostrils that look as if thumbs have been shoved into them, soon again this shimmering male figure appears on the far side of the Dells, another afternoon on the institute grounds, hard-pounding feet, muscled arms pumping, on this day a navy blue T-shirt faded from numerous launderings, another time the very short navy blue shorts, as he runs he exudes a yeasty body odor, sighting a solitary male jogger

ahead he quickens his pace to overtake him, guy in his early
twenties, university student, no athlete, about five eight,
skinny guy, running with some effort, breathing through his
mouth and in his head a swirl of numerals, symbols, equa-
tions, quantum optics, quantum noise, into this reverie *Hi!
Howya doin!* is like a firecracker tossed by a prankish kid, snap-
pishly the younger jogger replies *I'm okay* as his face flushes,
how like high school, junior high kids pushing him around,
in that instant he's remembering, almost now limping, lost the
stride, now life seems pointless, you know it's pointless, you
live, you die, look how his grandfather died, what's the point?
there is none, as next day, next week, late Friday afternoon of
the final week in May along the canal towpath past Linden
Road where there are fewer joggers, looming up suddenly in
your line of vision, approaching you, a tall husky male jogger
running in the center of the path, instinctively you bear to the
right, instinctively you turn your gaze downward, no eye contact on the towpath, you've been lost in thought, coils of
thought like electric currents burning hot, scalding hot, the
very pain, anguish, futility of your thoughts, for what is your
soul but your thoughts? upright flame cupped between your
hands silently pleading *Don't speak to me, respect my privacy
please* even as the oncoming jogger continues to approach, in
the center of the path, inexorably, unstoppably, curly hairs on
his arms shimmering with a bronze roseate glow, big teeth
bared in a smile *Hi! Howya doin!* loud and bland and booming mock-friendly, and out of the pocket of your nylon jacket
you fumble to remove the snub-nosed .22-caliber Smith &
Wesson revolver you'd stolen from your stepfather's lodge in
Jackson Hole, Wyoming, three years before, hateful of the old
drunk asshole, you'd waited for him to ask if you'd taken it,

were you the one to take his gun that's unlicensed? and your stepfather never asked, and you never told, and you lift the toy-like gun in a hand trembling with excitement, with trepida-tion, with anticipation, aim at the face looming at you like a balloon face up close, and fire, and the bullet leaps like magic from the toylike weapon with unexpected force and short-range accuracy and enters the face at the forehead directly above the big-nostriled nose, in an instant the husky jogger in the mustard yellow T-shirt drops to his knees on the path, al-ready the mustard yellow T-shirt is splashed with blood, on his belly now, brawny arms outspread, face flattened against the path, fallen silent and limp as a cloth puppet when the pup-peteer has lost interest and dropped the puppet, he's dead, *That's how I'm doin.*

Suicide Watch

"If you could tell me where Kenny is."

It was a matter of trust. He wanted to believe this: he was to be trusted. A father, a son in trouble. A father anxious to help a troubled son. A father with obvious resources. A father in his midfifties, with resources. A father who'd terminated a business trip to Seattle to fly to Philadelphia to help a troubled son. A father saying, "It's a matter of trust. If you could tell me where Kenny is."

Careful not to say *If you could tell us.* For *us* would imply that the father was speaking on behalf of others. *If you could tell me.*

"And where Christa is."

Kenny, the missing grandson, was two years, three months old. He was missing in the sense that no one (including the son?) seemed to know where he was. The missing mother, Christa, wasn't a daughter-in-law because she and the son, Seth, weren't married. Seth was twenty-eight, Christa was a year or two younger. He, Seth's father, who shared a last name with the troubled young man, ran these facts, this litany of bare and somehow desperate statistics, rapidly and repeatedly through his mind.

Human relations: riddles. You tell them to yourself to decipher their meaning but you don't know (how can you know?) if they have any meaning that can be deciphered.

"Seth? I mean, if there's any need for trust. If you are in danger . . ."

Danger. Almost the father had stumbled and said *trouble*.

In fact, the father knew that the son, Seth, was in trouble. The son certainly was in trouble: the two-year-old child missing, the mother of the child missing. The condition of the wrecked house.

Slowly the son shook his head. Slowly his eyes lifted to the father's eyes. There was something wrong with the son's eyes: set deep in their sockets, bloodshot, with a peculiar smudged glare like worn-out Plexiglas. The son's soot-colored hair was disheveled and matted and his jaws were covered in stubble. The father took comfort in the fact that the son wasn't handcuffed, or shackled to the table.

None of the other inmates/patients in the visitors' lounge, so far as the father had noticed, appeared to be restrained. Several were very large men. Like these, the son was wearing prison-issue clothing: pebble gray shirt, gray sweatpants with an elastic waistband. The son was allowed to wear his own shoes, rotted-looking running shoes, minus laces. The son had been taken, "forcibly," into police custody and remanded to the Philadelphia House of Detention for Men, the psychiatric ward, for a minimum of forty-eight hours of observation, evaluation, round-the-clock suicide watch.

Suicide watch. For the son's forearms had been crudely slashed and bleeding when he'd been taken into police custody, and it hadn't been clear from his dazed and incoherent account if he'd inflicted the wounds himself.

Both forearms, wayward gashes that hadn't severed any arteries. The father had been informed: in a normal state, an individual probably couldn't slash both arms in such a way, but in an abnormal state, drug psychosis, mania, it could be done.

There were also minor burns on the son's fingers, the backs of both hands, his ankles. These were unexplained, too.

The father tried not to stare at the son's bandaged arms. The father tried not to stare at an open sore on the son's upper lip. The father heard himself saying, calmly, "I mean, if there's danger in your immediate circumstances. Anyone who might want to hurt you, or . . ." The father wasn't sure what he was saying. He might have meant that the son might be in danger inside the detention facility, or would be in danger when he was released. The father might have been speaking not of the son but of the two-year-old grandson, and of Christa. The father was distracted by the son's breath, fetid as liquidy tar in which something had died and was decomposing.

"Hey Dad: who in hell'd want to hurt *me*?"

The son made a wheezing noise like laughter. The son was picking at the sore on his upper lip. Thumped one of his bandaged arms against the edge of the table, soiled white gauze looking as if it was leaking blood.

At least the son was speaking coherently. And the son had decided to speak to the father.

For the father had been warned by the resident psychiatrist that the son might not make sense, or might refuse to speak at all. The son was joking, the father supposed. The son had, since childhood, cultivated a style of droll deadpan joking to entertain, confound and dismay selected elders. The kind of joke that depended on an expression of mock innocence. The kind of joke that hurts to tell (you had to assume) and hurts to hear. In this case the father interpreted the son's joke to mean: who in hell'd want to hurt *me*? I'm past hurting.

Or: who in hell'd want to hurt *me*? I can do that myself.

Or: who in hell'd want to hurt *me*? I'm shit.

Of course it was his grandson, the two-year-old, of whom the father was thinking. On whose behalf the father was anxious. His only grandson, missing. But believed to be in Philadelphia. Very likely, South Philadelphia. Two-year-old Kenny, whose name the father could scarcely speak without faltering. Halfway thinking Kenny was his own son.

His son. As his son was meant to be.

". . . a matter of trust, Seth. You know you can trust me."

For Seth had been questioned by police officers, and Seth had said repeatedly that he had "no idea" where his son was, where the son's mother was. "No idea" why neighbors on Forty-third Street had called police to report what appeared to be a domestic disturbance. Why he'd been "forcibly" arrested at three o'clock in the morning, shirtless and barefoot and covered in blood from gashes in both his forearms, outside the brownstone row house on Forty-third Street, where he'd been living with his son and the young woman named Christa.

Nor had Seth any idea of what had happened inside the house. The overflowing tub in the bathroom on the second floor, water so scalding hot its steam had caused paint to blister and peel off the ceiling and walls, plastic fixtures to melt. On the landing outside the bathroom, on the stairs, scalding-hot water had done more damage, and in the kitchen raw garbage floated in puddles. Police officers reported drug paraphernalia, broken glass and broken toys, sodden clothes. Bloodstains, vomit. Cockroaches.

Where was the two-year-old child amid the wreckage? Where was the child's mother?

"Missing."

Painful for the father to utter the name: Kenny.

"Seth, if you could tell me. Where Kenny is. If . . ."

Seth he could utter. *Niorde, Seth M.* He'd become accustomed to *Niorde, Seth M.* as a name that might require being stated in the way that you might state the name of a recurring illness, a chronic condition. At the reception desk stating the purpose of his visit. *Niorde, Laurence C. Father.* Eager to provide a driver's license, a passport. For the father was a businessman-traveler who carried his passport with him much of the time because he traveled frequently by air. Domestic flights, transatlantic. More convenient for such travelers to keep their passports close at hand than to file them away between trips.

Mr. Niorde, wait here. He'd waited.

He wasn't shown the police report but he was informed of its contents, which seemed to him confusing, inconclusive. He'd been shown Polaroids of the interior of the row house at 1189 Forty-third Street, and he'd been stunned by what he saw. Evidence of his son's madness. Sickness. In one of the photos what appeared to be a small, lifeless body broken like a toy amid the watersoaked debris.

"Oh my god. Oh."

Of course, it wasn't. Looking more closely he saw that it was just twisted, sodden clothing, possibly a child's.

Still, the father had been badly frightened. He had not expected to be so badly frightened, so soon.

Telling himself *It's just beginning. This journey.*

He was led through the security checkpoint. He smiled, he was eager to comply. It wasn't so very different from airport security, to which he was accustomed. He tried not to observe that he was the only white man in view. Tried not to note how brusquely he was ordered to empty his pockets, turn his pockets inside out, remove his shoes and pass through a metal detector. And to be frisked by a frowning guard who avoided eye contact. He was a man not accustomed to being treated without deferential smiles, courtesy. In his professional life, often quite exaggerated courtesy.

But never had he entered such a place: the Philadelphia House of Detention for Men.

Psychiatric ward.

This was a fact: *Niorde, Seth M.* had been a patient at several drug rehabilitation clinics (Hartford, New York City). But the father had not visited the son in these places. The mother had visited him; that had seemed sufficient at the time.

In the visitors' lounge he was escorted to a small table and told to wait, and so with increasing anxiety he waited. Here, too, *Niorde, Laurence C.* was the only Caucasian in sight. He was fifty-seven — a youthful fifty-seven — but he was the oldest individual in the room. In his businessman clothes, he was weirdly dressed. He was perspiring and short of breath and not so immaculately groomed as he'd been fifteen hours before in another time zone. Still, you had only to glance at him to recognize *a man with resources. A man with investments, properties.* He had residences in Fairfield, Connecticut; Wellfleet, Massachusetts; Boca Raton, Florida. He was a man not inclined to shift in his seat nervously, to tug at his shirt collar, wipe his forehead with a wadded tissue. A man not inclined to glance up anxiously at strangers.

The son, Seth, looking like a stranger! Though of course the father recognized the son immediately.

Now there were two Caucasian males in the room.

A guard was bringing the son to the father, bypassing other guards, visitors. The father stared at the son's bandaged arms held stiffly at his sides. The son's sallow slack face and scratched-glassy eyes. How weak-limbed the son appeared, like an elderly man negotiating a tilting floor.

"Oh god. Seth."

With a twitchy smirk-smile the son acknowledged the staring father. "'Sme."

It wasn't clear what the son had mumbled. *It's me?*

Like a load of damp sand falling off a shovel, the son sank into a grimy vinyl chair. The father's nostrils began to pinch, immediately he smelled something dank, tarry, fetid, rotting. So the visit began. Like a small rudderless boat being tossed in the waves of a river too vast to be seen, so the father felt himself dazed, desperate. He had only one question to ask. But he dared not ask his question too quickly. Too emphatically. Too obviously. He assured the son, or anyway tried to assure the son, who might have been listening, that he would arrange for a lawyer for him, by noon tomorrow. He would post bail. He would insist on private medical care. As soon as the son was released . . . The father was distracted by a large glaring clock on the facing wall. Visiting hours in the facility ended at 9 P.M., he hadn't been escorted into the lounge until 8:35 P.M. The father was distracted by the busyness and commotion of the place. Tables spanned the breadth of the overheated, low-ceilinged room, and most of these tables were being used. Visitors were facing inmates — blacks, Hispanics — some of them speaking loudly, excitedly. The father hadn't been prepared for so many others. Having to raise his voice to be heard and then uncertain if he was being heard. The father was not dressed appropriately, he'd become itchy-warm and so felt the need to remove his suit coat and hang it on the back of his grimy vinyl chair. The father was speaking to his mostly unresponsive son in a lowered voice not meant to sound anxious. Not wanting to sound as if he was begging.

Each time the father glanced up at the glaring clock the minute hand had leaped forward. Twenty minutes remained, it was 8:40 P.M.

The father hadn't booked a hotel room in Philadelphia for the night. Beyond 9 P.M., the father hadn't allowed himself to think.

"Can I! How'd I know that, Dad?"

What was Seth saying? The father hadn't exactly heard. The father wasn't sure if the son was responding to something the father had said, belatedly; or if the son was saying something unrelated, in a slurred mumble. The son was partially hiding his mouth with his hand, his front teeth were stained the hue of urine. And there was the fetid breath, of teeth rotting in the son's jaws.

"Trust me? Of course you can trust me. If you know where the boy is . . ."

It seemed urgent to touch the son. Touching by visitors and inmates/patients was not forbidden. Yet the father could not bring himself to touch the son, though the son was slouched in his chair only two or three feet away: one of the son's hands hovered at his mouth, the other was a scabby-knuckled fist on the table.

Impossible to close your fingers in a gesture of sympathy around a tight-clenched fist.

"Seth? If Christa has him, if you know where Christa is . . ."

"Told you, and I told *them*. Don't know where'n hell Ch'ista went."

"But — did she take him? Kenny?"

The father had managed to speak the grandson's name: Kenny.

A small trusting face, luminous eyes. The father had not seen the grandson in months, which had been a mistake he didn't recall having made, as in a dream in which something has gone terribly and irrevocably wrong but the dreamer can't recall what it is, still less how to grieve for it.

"Must've. I told them. Must've told you, I told *them*."

The father wondered if *them* meant police officers. The father didn't want to risk inquiring.

Important to keep the son speaking. To keep eye contact. To appeal to the son. Yet not to beg, for begging had never seemed to work.

The father had vowed last time, and the time before that, he would not beg the son again. He would not.

"See, what it's like . . . It's like cement, in your gut."

"Cement? What is like cement?"

Seth yawned. Suddenly, a luxuriant yawn. The terrible rotting breath that made the father's nostrils pinch.

This time it was methamphetamine, the father had been informed. Previously it had been crack cocaine. In prep school, marijuana, cocaine. At a later time, heroin. Once the son had been a beautiful boy who'd taken clarinet lessons, had an interest in astronomy, a boy whose high grades came with a minimum of effort; this was official family history.

". . . trying to shit cement. In your gut. 'Time.' When it doesn't pass."

"Seth, what are we talking about? Are we talking about . . . I'm not sure, Seth, what are we talking about?"

Time. Talking about time. Time that doesn't pass. Or was it time passing too swiftly. The father leaned closer, elbows on the table. The father tried not to glance up at the glaring clock face, where another time the minute hand had leaped forward. The father had to fight an impulse to lunge at the son, grab the son's slumped shoulders and shake, shake, shake. Slap the gaunt stubble-cheeks. Shout in the son's face instead of trying to keep his voice calm, measured, fatherly warm, sympathetic and yet not outwardly pleading.

"Seth? Try not to fall asleep, will you? If you could just tell me where you think Kenny might be, or Christa. Is there someone she might have gone to, with Kenny? If she didn't have a car, where could she have gone on foot . . . ?"

The father had been cautioned: whatever his addict-son told him, if the son told the father anything, would very likely be confused and incomplete and possibly inaccurate, for the addict-son might not know what had happened, or might not remember. The child had been missing for at least forty-eight hours but possibly longer. The child might have been gone before Wednesday. Neighbors on Forty-third Street who'd called police were not certain what they'd seen. They thought they'd seen Christa leaving the residence at about 11 P.M., running out into the street, into a nearby intersection, alone. But other neighbors had reported a child crying. A child, half-carried and half-dragged by a young woman. Except it wasn't clear when this had been: Wednesday night, or another night? A day earlier? Two days earlier? Residents of the 1100 block of Forty-third Street gave police conflicting information. The father learned that twice in the past six weeks Philadelphia police officers had responded to domestic disturbance complaints at 1189 Forty-third Street.

Officers had spoken with the adults at that address. No arrests had been made.

"Seth? Tell me about Christa. Were you quarreling with her, is that why Christa took Kenny away? And where would —"

The father hadn't ever felt comfortable speaking the name: Christa.

A wanly attractive girl, very thin, slouch shouldered like the son, sulky-quiet, at least in the father's presence, something smudged and sly about the eyes. She wasn't a daughter-in-law and she wasn't a girl whom Seth had seemed especially to care for, yet somehow it happened that Christa was the mother of Seth's child, which made her the (improbable, undesirable) mother of the grandson, Kenny, whose name the father can scarcely utter. The father had given the son money, from time to time. Not for drugs (of course!) but in behalf of Kenny (that was the hope, the plea), but it hadn't been as much money as the son had wanted and in recent months he had stopped giving him money altogether. The father had met Christa only three times, he had no idea who her family was, if Christa had a family, if there were adults, parents, people like himself who were providing money, however intermittently. The father had not exchanged more than a few perfunctory words with Christa and never, he'd later realized, apart from the son's presence. In his father's household, the son had exuded a slovenly and unexpected glower of sexuality, laying hands on his female companion, stroking his female companion's straw blond hair, kissing the sulky mouth, with the father looking on.

The father hadn't known whether to believe what the son had told him: he and Christa had first met in an economics class at Penn. That Christa had been a scholarship student at Penn. That Christa had remained in school for a final semester after Seth had dropped out, after they'd begun living together in an apartment off campus.

The father hadn't known with any certainty that Christa was the girl's name, in fact. He hadn't known her last name. She hadn't referred to him by his name, that he could remember.

The son had had high SAT scores, somehow. The father had wanted to think *He takes after me.*

". . . know her name, Dad? Never met her."

"Never met Christa? Is that what you're saying? Seth, of course I've met Christa."

". . . or him, you met *him*?"

"Kenny? My grandson? Of course I've met Kenny. You must know that."

"You know his name? Ken-ny."

The son's mouth began to quiver. The eyes were rapidly blinking. A look of something like hurt, tenderness, regret came into the son's face.

"See Dad, I called you. Never called back."

"Called me? When?"

"When? That night."

"Which night?"

"*That* night. That it happened."

"What happened?"

"You should've called, Dad. I told you."

Maybe this was so. The father was having trouble recalling. The father had not always called the son back. The father had sometimes seen *Pennsylvania* on his caller ID and had not picked up the phone. The father had more than once erased the son's rambling message midway.

In a loud aggrieved voice Seth was saying, "She took him! Fucking junkie, know what she did? Wrapped him in this stuff like a mummy shroud. Wrapped him in tinsel like Christmas. Like, you shake this stuff, it shoots sparks. *I* never wanted to, it was her." The son's outburst was so sudden, one of the guards approached him. Without glancing around, instinctively Seth hunched his shoulders and lowered his head, protecting himself against a blow. He crossed his bandaged arms tightly over his chest and clamped both hands beneath his armpits rocking forward in his chair. The guard told the son to keep it down and told the father visiting hours were almost over but the guard did not touch the son. The terrible minute hand in the wall clock leaped forward. The father dared to reach out to the son, hesitantly touching the son's arm at the elbow. The son was hunched over, breathing heavily. "Seth? What are you saying? 'She took him' — where?" and the son shivered, and said, "I said to her, she's a bad mother. And she's trying to get past me and open the door. I told them this. And there's steam coming out from under the door. There's this steam from the tub. The bathroom. I wasn't high, I hadn't been high all day, my mind was clear like glass. The thing is, the kid isn't in the bathroom. He'd shit himself, puked and shit himself, and she never got around to cleaning him. She is such a bad mother! No matter what she tells you, she is such a failed mother!

Should've called the cops myself. What I did was, I hid him
out in the back, the car. My car, I had. I hid him in the backseat. I know I did. I said, 'It's a game, we're playing with
Mommy. You stay here and keep your head down, and if she
calls you don't look up, okay?' and Kenny says, 'Yes Daddy.'
He's a smart kid, he always trusted his daddy. Couldn't trust
his junkie-mommy but trusted his daddy. It's a responsibility,
a kid like that. How the world keeps going, the human race,
it's like cement in your guts you have somehow to shit, how
the human race keeps going is a riddle. So she comes in, this
woman, she's been out and she's high and she comes in, I'm
waiting for her. And right away she says, 'Where is my baby?'
and I'm like, 'Your baby is in the tub having his bath, that you
should've done last night,' and she says, 'I want to see Kenny,
let me past,' because I wasn't letting her past me, had hold of
both her wrists like these little sparrow bones you could break
like snapping your fingers. I'm like, 'You can't, he's having his
bath,' and she's excited saying, 'If you hurt him, I'll call the
cops,' and I said, 'Call the cops, the cops are going to fucking
bust you,' and now she really gets excited, all this while the
steam is coming out beneath the door, I was sleeping in the
front room and it must've been the tub got filled and the damn
hot water keeps pouring out and there's water condensing on
the walls even downstairs and dripping from the ceiling and
hot water starting to come down the stairs, it's a wild scene,
and she's screaming, 'Get him out of there, open the door,' the
door was locked from the outside, this berserk woman on the
stairs and clawing at me, and the bathroom door is hot like
fire, the doorknob so hot you can't touch it, all this steam all
over everything, I'm sweating like a pig, and somebody's
screaming, you'd think it was Kenny screaming 'Daddy!

Daddy!' but it can't be Kenny, I know this because Kenny is outside hiding in the car, and Christa's fighting me, Christa gets the door open, the steam is burning us, and I'm waiting for you, Dad: for you to call. And you don't call, and you're not here." And the father said, "Me? Waiting for *me*?" and the son said, "It was a test, Dad. To see how long it would take you to get here," and the father said, slowly, "I don't understand, Seth. You were waiting for me here, in Philadelphia?" and the son said, "You had your chance, Dad. Hell of a lot of times I called you, left a message and now it's too late," and the father said, "But I'm here now, where is Kenny? If he was in the car, where is the car? He wasn't in the bathroom but in the car, was he? Seth, please tell me," and the son said, "Hey Dad: *you* tell *me*. You're the one with all the answers, I thought," and the father said, trying not to beg, "You didn't hurt him, did you? Did you hurt his mother? Where are they, please tell me," and the son said, "Her, how in hell'd I know where she is! Damn junkie you can't trust behind your back. Him, I told you: he was in the car. Sleeping in the backseat. I was telling her: he isn't in the bathroom, he's in the car. She's clawing at me to get past me. She's got the bathroom door open and there's this cloud of pure steam, and hot water on our feet, our ankles, it's burning us, there's noise from the water rushing from the faucet, now the water's coming out like a flood, what I do is grab a chair to stand on, would've been scalded if I hadn't. And Christa is on the stairs, and she slips and falls, and she's screaming, the water is so hot. And there's so much steam you can hardly see. And there's the kid, there's Kenny in the water! There's Kenny in the bathroom, on the floor. Kind of wedged under the sink. These pipes under the sink, he's kind of wedged there. It's hard to see in all the steam, I'm thinking it isn't him, I'd been sleeping downstairs and wakened by her coming home and making so much noise, it's like a dream, I'm thinking it's some other thing under the sink that crawled in there, a squirrel, like, or a dog, size of a Pekinese, the fur is scalded off this poor thing, it's got to be dead, boiled dead, the skin is all red and blistered and coming off in my hands and the eyes are popping. I'm thinking somehow the kid got past me and hid up in the bathroom. Why'd he do that? and locked the door behind him! He was naked, like somebody was giving him a bath but went away and the water got too hot. So I'm thinking maybe Christa did it, somehow. When I was asleep. *I know this:* I left Kenny in the car. It had to be her, it wasn't me. Think I'm going to call 911, try to explain to the cops or anybody, like hell they'd believe me. They would not believe me. The hot water ran out, finally. So it's cold water so the steam wasn't so bad. So I got the faucet off. So I tried to help Kenny but it's too late. Splashed cold water on him but anybody can see, it's too late. I picked him up, he was so hot! His little body, the skin was all red, and peeling off on my fingers, and his face red and wizened like a little old man, it was a terrible thing. Must've been calling me—'Daddy! Daddy!'—but there was so much noise from the water, I couldn't hear him. Christ I'm feeling so bad about this, what happened to Kenny, it's like . . . Like there are no words . . . Later, we're downstairs, and there's water here, too, we've got Kenny on the kitchen table and Christa is crying over him, wrapping him in cold-soaked towels, ice cubes from the freezer, thinks he's breathing but he is not breathing, then she wraps him in some stuff like gauze, and tinsel paper that's sparkly that she said would preserve him from decay for a while at least. And it's my idea, to send him to *you*."

During this torrent of words, the father was staring at the son. Pulses beating in his ears, barely could he hear the son's terrible words. It seemed crucial to watch the son: the mouth. The smirk-smile, the sore on the upper lip. The father laughed suddenly, a sound like fabric being torn.

"None of this is true, is it? Seth? You're making this up, are you? My god."

"Fuck, I'd be jiving about my own son! Not like you, Dad, that doesn't give a shit about your son." Seth spoke shrilly, like a hurt child. He continued to rock in the vinyl chair, hands clamped in his armpits. "So — we got high, we were so stressed. And Christa says, 'We will bury our son ourselves. A decent burial.' For Christa saw the folly of summoning help, any kind of help, as I did, and have always. And I'm like, 'We can send him to my father. *He* can bury him.' So we got some garbage bags from out in the alley that our neighbors had put trash in, and dumped out the trash, and we put this little tinsel mummy, that hardly weighed more than a cat would weigh, in the bags, more than one bag for safekeeping. Then we wrapped it all tight with wire. Then, there's cardboard cartons in the cellar, we bring one of them up and put Kenny inside, it's a tight fit. And we wrap this all up tight, and secure, and what I can remember of the address in Boca Raton is just Prudhomme Circle. So I make out the address label to L. NIORDE, PRUDHOMME CIRCLE, BOCA RATON, FLORIDA, and lock the box in the car trunk and next morning I take it to the post office and mail it parcel post. And the guy behind the counter says, 'Are the contents breakable?' and I say, 'Yes. The contents are breakable.' So he stamps it FRAGILE like they pay any fucking attention to FRAGILE at the fucking P.O., don't bullshit *me*. However long it takes for the package to get to

Boca Raton, I don't know. Might be a week. I figure, it's time that's stopped. For me in here, like for Kenny where he is. Because nobody knows where my son is. Because the damn package might get lost. And nobody's staying at the Florida place now, right? Not you, and not Mom. So Kenny is like, nowhere — no time." The son smiled a slow, sly, stained-tooth smile. "See, Dad: it's a test."

"A test . . ."

"You've been believing this! That's the test."

The father heard himself say, "I . . . I didn't believe you. As if I would believe such a . . ."

"Don't bullshit me, Dad. You believed it! You still do, I can see it in your eyes. That's the test, Dad."

". . . a terrible story, from my own . . ."

The father's feet were tangled in something. The suit coat had fallen to the floor from the back of the vinyl chair. Stooping to pick it up he felt his face pound with blood. His heart pounded strangely. The son was jeering at him, the son was on his feet preparing to leave the visitors' lounge. The father was pleading, "It isn't true, then? Kenny isn't . . ." It must have been 9 P.M., visitors were being asked to leave. There was a scraping of chairs, commotion. Loud voices, emotional farewells. The son was being led away by a guard and the father tried to follow after him but was restrained. At the doorway the son took pity on the father, called back over his shoulder, "Hey Dad: if the carton shows up where I mailed it, then you'll know. If not, you'll know, too."

The Man Who Fought
Roland LaStarza

1.

And in that instant the Armory is silent. Every uplifted face still, frozen. Overhead lights are reeling like drunken birds. Where my eye is bleeding there's a halo of red light. No pain! Never pain again! Only this strange, wonderful silence. A giant black bubble swelling to burst. It was the moment I died, and I was happy.

2.

This is not a very pretty story, and not just because it's about boxing. In a way, it's only incidentally about boxing. Its true subject is betrayal.

A story about the only person I've known, close to me, lodged deep in my memory like a beating heart, who took his own life.

Took his own life. These clumsy words. But words are what we say. We try our best, and words fail us.

Took his own life. This was said about Colum Donaghy, my father's friend, after he died at the age of thirty-one in September 1958. Colum would be spoken of in two ways depending on who the speaker was, how close to Colum and how respectful of his memory. To some, he would always be *the man who fought Roland LaStarza*. To others, he would be *the man who took his own life*.

My heart would beat in fury when I heard them speak of my father's friend in that smug, pitying way. As if they had the right. As if they knew. "Where'd he take his life to, if he took it!" I wanted to shout at them. "You have no right. You don't *know*."

In fact, no one knew. Not with certainty.

My own father, who'd been Colum's closest friend, hadn't known. The shock to him was so great, he never truly recovered. He would remember Colum Donaghy's suicide all his life. But it was rare for him to speak of it. My mother warned us children *Don't ask your father about it, you hear? Not a word about Colum Donaghy*. As if we required warning. You could see the hurt of it in my father's face, and the rage. *Don't ask. Don't ask. Don't!*

Colum's parents and relatives, especially the older Donaghys, could never accept that he'd shot himself deliberately, at the base of his skull. They were Roman Catholics; to them *taking your own life* was a mortal sin. No matter the evidence of the county coroner's report, the police investigation, no matter how circumstances pointed to suicide, they had to believe it was an accident, but they refused to talk about that, too. My father said it's necessary for the Donaghys, let them think what they need to think. Like all of us.

Forty years ago. But vivid in my memory as a dream unfolding before my eyes.

And now my father has died, just five days ago. Which is to say New Year's Day of this new era of 2000. "Outlived Colum by forty years so far," my father said the last time I visited him. Shaking his head at the strangeness of it. "Christ, if Colum could see me now! Older than his father was then. Old people made him nervous. But maybe we'd have a laugh together, once he saw it was me."

3.

"Know what? I'm betting on myself."

Colum Donaghy was a man who liked to laugh, and he laughed, telling my father this. Seeing the look in my father's face.

It was his Irish temperament, was it? Colum's first instinct was to laugh, as another man might steel himself against surprise. His eyes were pale blue like washed glass, and didn't always reflect laughter. There was a part of him held in reserve, calculated, wary. But when Colum entered a room it was like a flame rising, you couldn't turn your eyes away. He had a deceptively childlike face to which something had happened. Something with a story to it. A misshapen nose and scar tissue above his left eye, like an icicle, that seemed to wink at you. There was a pattern of tiny scars like lacework in his forehead. A scattering of freckles like splashes of rain on his pale coarse skin, and reddish blond hair, ribbed and rippled and worn a little long in the style of the day. And sideburns, which offended the elder Donaghy men and older boxing fans (except if you kept Billy Conn in mind, flashy Billy, as a model for Colum Donaghy). Colum had a rougher, wilder ring style than Conn, for sure. There were some observers who praised Colum for his natural gifts and for his "heart" but worried the boy had never learned to seriously box, that he was all offense and not enough defense; whatever strategy his trainer had drilled into him before a fight he'd lose as soon as he got hit, and started throwing punches by instinct. Colum was a natural counterpuncher, that look of elation in his face like flame. *Now you hit me, now I can hit you. And hit, and hit you!*

At the time of his fight with Roland LaStarza in May 1958 in the Buffalo Armory, Colum was thirty years old, weighed 187 compact, muscled pounds, and stood five feet ten-and-a-half inches tall. Colum was such a forceful presence in and out of the ring you were inclined to forget that he was a small heavyweight, like Floyd Patterson, like Marciano and La-Starza, and had shortish legs and a short reach, built powerfully in the torso, with the muscular stubby arms and smallish hands that in a later era, of Sonny Liston, Muhammad Ali, George Foreman, giant black heavyweights who have dominated the heavyweight division since, would have handicapped him from the start. And like most Caucasian boxers he bled and scarred easily; like his boxer friend in Syracuse he so admired, Carmen Basilio, with his wreck of a face, Colum wore his scars proudly as badges of honor. *If I wanted to stay pretty, I'd have been a ballet dancer.* Colum Donaghy was a natural light heavy, but there was no money in that division. And in the fifties, fighting in arenas and armories and clubs in Buffalo, Niagara Falls, Rochester, Syracuse and Albany; a few times in Cleveland; once as far west as Minneapolis; and in St. Catherines, Ontario, Colum Donaghy looked good. Even when he lost on points, he looked good. And in Yewville, where he'd lived all his life, where he was known and liked by everyone, or almost everyone, he looked good. That quick, easy boyish smile, the slightly crooked front teeth. His nose had been broken in an early Golden Gloves fight, rebroken in the navy where he'd made a name for himself as a light heavyweight, but it was a break that softened his hard-boned face and made you think, if you were a girl or woman and inclined to romance, that here was a tough man who wished for tenderness.

Like my father, Patrick Hassler, whom nobody called Pat, Colum was a man of moods. Gaiety, and sobriety, and melancholy, and anger smoldering like an underground fire. Maybe the moods were precipitated by drinking, or maybe the drinking was a way of tempering the moods. These were men you couldn't hope to know intimately, unless you already knew them; their friendships were forged in boyhood. If you hadn't grown up with Colum, you'd never truly be a friend of his, he'd never trust you and, as Colum had many times demonstrated, you couldn't trust him.

He confided in my father, though. Close as brothers they were, and protective of each other. My father was the only person Colum told about betting on himself in the LaStarza fight, so far as my father knew, though after Colum's death rumors would circulate that he'd owed money to a number of people including his manager who'd been advancing him loans for years. Colum surprised my father with the revelation that he wasn't just going to win the fight with LaStarza, he was going to knock LaStarza out. His trainer was preparing him to box, box, box the opponent but Colum sure as hell wasn't going to box a guy who'd managed to keep Marciano at arm's length for ten rounds in their title fight, made Marciano look like an asshole, for sure Colum wasn't going to pussyfoot with the guy but go after him at the bell, first round, surprise the hell out of him, get him into a corner. "Believe me, I know how," Colum told my father seriously. "You can bet on me. This time. No fucking up this time. Maybe a TKO, a KO. See, I can't risk going the distance and lose on points. So I'm going to win the smartest way." Colum paused, breathing quickly. He had a way of watching you sidelong, narrow eyed, cagey and alert as a wild creature. "Shortest distance between two points, see? I'm going to bet on myself."

My father was troubled by these revelations. He tried to dissuade his friend, not from winning the fight but from trying for a KO that might be disastrous; and from betting on himself if he was betting serious money. "You could lose double, man."

Said Colum with his easy smile, "No. I'm gonna win double."

4.

They were our fathers, we did not judge them.

The bond between them was: they'd been born in the same neighborhood in Yewville, New York, in the same year, 1928. Their families were neighbors. Their fathers worked in the same machine shop. They belonged to the same parish, St. Timothy's. Colum Donaghy and Patrick Hassler, high school friends who'd enlisted together in the U.S. Navy in 1949 and were sent to active duty in Korea the following year, there was that bond between them of which they had no need to speak. These were not men who were sentimental about the past: they survived it.

Of Colum's Yewville children (the rumor was, he had had others, outside his marriage) it was Agnes I knew. Or wished to know. She was a year behind me in school. With her father's fair, whitish skin that never darkened in summer, only burned. With her father's cold blue eyes that could laugh, or drill through you as if you didn't exist. For a long time Agnes was *the girl whose dad is Colum Donaghy the boxer* and she basked in that renown, then so suddenly she became *the girl whose dad took his own life* and her eyes shrank from us, all of the Donaghys were like kicked dogs. I was drawn always to Agnes, Agnes who was so pretty, but Agnes shunned me, hatred for me shone in her eyes and I never knew why.

Nothing so disturbs us as another's hatred for us. Our own secret hatreds, how natural they seem. How inevitable.

Colum Donaghy would say zestfully, "Before a fight, I hate a guy's guts. I just want to wipe him out. After a fight, I could love 'im to death."

Our fathers were young in those years, in their early thirties. They were of a generation that grew up in the Depression, they'd been made to grow up fast. Most of them had dropped out of school by the age of sixteen, were married a few years later, began having kids. Yet they would remain boys in their souls, restless, hungry for more life. "Boxing is a kid's game, essentially," my father said. "That's why it's deadly, kids are out for blood."

They were our fathers, we had no way of knowing them. We adored them and were fearful of them. Their lives were mysterious to us, as our mothers' lives and our own lives could never be. *I'm just a woman, what the hell does it matter what I think* I'd overheard my mother once saying, laughing wanly over the phone to a woman friend, and this did not seem a misstatement to me, or even a complaint exactly. No man would ever make such a remark. I knew that my father was co-owner of a small auto and truck repair and gas station, and I knew that Colum Donaghy supplemented his irregular boxing income by driving a truck, working in a local quarry, a lumberyard. I knew such facts without understanding what they might mean. None of us children had any idea what our fathers earned yearly. How much a boxer made, for instance.

A locally popular, much-loved boxer? Whose picture was often in the *Yewville Post* and the *Buffalo Evening News* sports pages?

Our fathers were to us their bodies. Their male bodies. So tall, so massive-seeming, like horses magnificent and dangerous, unpredictable. They were men who drank, weekends. At such times we knew to recognize the slurred voice, the flare of white in the eye sudden as a lighted match, nostrils quivering like those of a horse about to bite or kick—these were signs that alerted us, prepared us to flee, as the casual lifting of a hand at a window will send birds flying to safety in the trees. Young, we learned that the male body is beautiful and dangerous and not to be trifled with.

The safest time with these adult men was when they were drinking and laughing, maybe celebrating one of Colum's fight victories, and he'd be treating his friends to cases of beer in someone's backyard; it was a time of good luck and celebration and they'd smile to see a child appear, to be hoisted with a grunt onto a knee or onto shoulders for a piggyback ride. Grinning Colum Donaghy would extend his muscled right arm out straight from the shoulder, make a fist and invite a child to swing from his wrist, he was so *strong*. No other man so strong. If you were a little older, and if you were a girl, and even just a little pretty, he'd make you blush with flattery, your own dad would smile and it was a time of perfect joy rushing into your face like heated blood to be recalled forty years later. And your dad, Patrick, having to agree, yes, you weren't half-bad-looking, and Colum Donaghy fixing his sly blue eyes on you saying with a wink *This little girl takes after her ma not her pa, eh?* And all the men laughed, your dad the loudest.

When Colum Donaghy died the obituaries in the papers would end with *Colum Donaghy is survived by.* How strange those words seemed to me! *Survived by.* Only just close family members were named of course.

The friends who loved him were not named. My father, Patrick Hassler, was not named.

After Colum's body was found twelve miles from Yewville, off a country road near farmland owned by Donaghy relatives, Yewville police questioned Colum's male friends, and it was my father who'd had to admit to police that the handgun Colum used to shoot himself was one Colum had owned since Korea. It was an unregistered .32-caliber Smith & Wesson revolver of no special distinction and there were smudged fingerprints on it, and above these were Colum Donaghy's. He'd won the revolver in a poker game, my father said. No one in the Donaghy family admitted knowing that Colum had this gun hidden away somewhere, certainly his wife hadn't known. My father was sickened by having to give such testimony. He believed it was like kicking Colum when Colum was down, defenseless. It outraged him, to speak of Colum Donaghy to strangers.

My father believed that a man has a right to privacy, dignity. After death, as before.

5.

Patrick Hassler was two inches taller than Colum Donaghy, bigger boned, with heavy sloping shoulders and a fatty-muscled torso and long, sinewy arms, big hands, weighing well over two hundred pounds; you'd think of the two that he was the heavyweight boxer, not Colum Donaghy the smaller man, but you'd be mistaken. Size has nothing to do with boxing skills. You're born with the instinct or you are not. You're born with a knockout punch or you are not. When they were in their twenties Colum and my father sparred together a few times at the Yewville gym where Colum trained, both men in boxing trunks, T-shirts, protective headgear and wearing twelve-ounce gloves, and someone (my mother?) took snapshots of these occasions. My father marveled at how fast Colum was, it was impossible to hit him! Colum invited my father to hit him hard as he could, and my father tried, he tried, throwing wide awkward punches that, even if they landed, were merely glancing blows to be deflected by Colum's raised gloves or elbows, of no more force than a child's slaps, and within five minutes my father, who believed himself in decent physical condition, was flush-faced and panting and his eyes brimmed with hurt and indignation and frustration. Colum was no Willie Pep, not a graceful boxer, yet still he scarcely needed to move his feet to avoid my father's blows, without seeming effort he slipped blows thrown at his head, moving back then, and laterally, and everyone in the gym crowded around the ring cheering him in mock encouragement—"Get him, Hassler! Nail that mick bastard!" And Colum laughed and ducked and swerved back inside with a flurry of left jabs to Patrick's body gentle as love taps (he would afterward claim) that nonetheless left the larger man's fleshy sides flaming and his ribs aching for days. Patrick was panting, "Goddamn you, Donaghy, stand still and fight!" and Colum laughed saying, "That's what you want, Hassler? I don't think so."

Snapshots of these sparring matches were kept under the glass top of a cocktail table in our living room. For years. They'd been taken in the early fifties. So anyone visiting us who had not known of Colum Donaghy would ask who that was with Patrick, and the short reply was *an old friend of Patrick's, who'd once fought Roland LaStarza in Buffalo.* If my dad was present, there was no longer reply.

After Colum died my mother wondered if she should re-move the snapshots, how heartbreaking they were, my dad and his friend posed in the ring with their arms around each other's shoulders, grinning like kids. But she was afraid to ask my dad point-blank. Just to bring up the subject of Colum was risky. And who knows, it might set off my dad to discover one day that the snapshots were gone from the cocktail table, he had a quick temper and after he'd stopped drinking he was anxious and edgy as a spooked horse, so the snapshots re-mained there in our living room for years.

There were many more snapshots with Colum Donaghy in them, in our family photo album.

6.

Say there's this special place somewhere on Earth. Where the inhabitants know ahead of time when they will die. The exact hour, minute. Not only this, they know when Earth itself will end. The universe will end. How's their way of living going to differ from ours?

I'll tell you: they would measure time differently.

Like they wouldn't be counting forward from the past. No first century, second century, twentieth century, et cetera. Instead, they would be counting backward from the end. People saying, What's the date, the date is X. (X years before the end.) Somebody saying, How old am I? I'm X. (X years before he dies.)

And how'd these people get along, what kind of civilization would they have? I believe they would be good to one another. They would be kind, decent. Not like us! But they would like to laugh, too. Have good times, celebrate. Because, see, they wouldn't need to wonder about the future. They would know the future from the day of their births, they would be at total peace with it.

7.

Colum Donaghy was one to say strange things. He'd get this glimmering look in his face. After an out-of-town fight where he'd managed to win, but just barely; and took some hard punches to the head and body. A cruel welt on the underside of his jaw, fresh scar tissue in his eyebrow. Such a goddamned bleeder, Colum joked that he started to bleed at the weigh-in. Maybe it was funny? But a white man's face can get used up, hit too many times. What's being done to the capillaries in the brain, you don't want to think. Colum liked to say with a shrug *There's fights where even if you win, you lose.*

This was a fact nobody much wanted to know. Not in Yewville or Buffalo among Colum "The Kid" Donaghy's admirers. His trainer and his manager surely didn't want to know. It was nothing to be discussed. Like enlisting in the navy, being sent overseas to Korea, for sure you might get killed, you accept that possibility.

A kid just going into boxing, fighting in the Golden Gloves at age fifteen, fourteen, as Colum had done, he won't know it. A young guy just turning pro, he won't want to know it. And by the time he knows it, could be he's a legendary champion like Joe Louis, Henry Armstrong, it's too late for him to know it.

Even if you win, you lose.

You win, you lose.

And what of fixed fights, another fact of boxing in the fifties nobody liked to acknowledge? What of bribed referees and judges? A boxer wants to win, it's his life on the line; Colum used to flare his nostrils saying every time he stepped into the ring he was fighting for his life, but there are boxers who have given up wanting to win, their spirits have been broken, there's a deadness in their eyes and they know they're being hired to fight and lose, they're being hired as "opponents" to showcase another guy's skills, some hot young kid on the way up. Their paydays are about over, and they know it. So they will sign on, and go through the motions of fighting for four, five, six rounds, then suddenly they're on the ropes and the crowd is wild for blood, they're down, they're struggling to get up, on their feet, seeming dazed but with their gloves uplifted so the referee won't stop the fight, and the young kid rushes them with a flurry of hard, showy punches, and another time they're down, and this time counted out. And it isn't the case that the older boxer has been bribed, or the fight's been fixed, not exactly. But the outcome is known beforehand. Like a script somebody has written, and the boxers act out.

In the fifties, in any case. A long time ago.

If you rebelled, past a certain age, if you were a midlevel boxer who'd never made the top ten ranking in your division and your name no longer generated ticket sales, you were in trouble. It would begin to be said of you you're *washed up*. You're *on the skids*. If you persisted in being a maverick, your career was over, you were *out on your ass*. If you talked carelessly and word got back to the wrong people, you might be *dead meat*.

So Colum said unexpected things. Interviewed in the *Buffalo Evening News* after he'd won a locally big, moneymaking match when he was in his midtwenties, he'd said in reply to a reporter's question about alleged criminal connections with boxing that he'd fire his manager if he heard even that the man was taking calls from "those SOBs." (This was a time when boxers of the stature of Graziano, Zale, Robinson were being subpoenaed by the New York State Athletic Commission investigating bribe offers to fix fights.) A few years later, interviewed prominently in the *Yewville Post* before the La-Starza fight, which would be the biggest fight held in the Buffalo Armory since an aging Joe Louis came through in 1951, Colum promised the boxing crowd "exactly what they deserved." Which meant — what?

And with his friends Colum said even stranger, more enigmatic things that no one knew how to interpret. Saying he was a mick, he knew not to trust anybody at his back. Saying when his big payday finally came, he'd be giving money to the IRA back in Belfast, Ireland — "so those poor bastards can get some justice there." Saying he wasn't scared of anybody in the ring, white, black, spic, but anybody out of the ring, he was. My dad and the others never knew if they were expected to laugh, or whether all this was dead serious.

Like when after a few beers Colum got onto one of his subjects, which was time. *This special place on Earth where the inhabitants know ahead of time when they will die.* Talking so intense, excited. And his friends tried their best to follow. My dad said it was like some puzzle in the newspaper, Einstein and atomic physics and sending men to the moon. You could sort of follow it, but you only thought you were following it. Actually, you were lost. You couldn't repeat a word of it. And Colum was like that, talking faster and faster, and you'd be like trying to keep up with him in the ring. Quick as you might be, Colum was quicker. "See? A man would say, you asked him how old he is, 'I'm X years.' Like me, Colum Donaghy, might be five. By which it's meant, 'Five years till I die.' Instead of saying my age measured from when I was born, I'd say my age measured from when I would die, see? 'Five' means five years left to live."

Colum's buddies shook their heads over this logic. If it was logic.

Mike Kowicki pulled a face. "So? What the hell's that supposed to mean? I don't get it."

Otto Lanza, who was generally conceded as the most educated of the guys, he'd graduated from high school and owned a cigar store that also sold newspapers and paperback books, shook his head reprovingly. "Kind of morbid, ain't it? Thinking that way."

"It's the opposite of morbid!" Colum said. "It's what you call a hy-po-the-sis." Colum pronounced this word, which surely had never before been uttered at the Checkerboard Tavern bar in its history, with care.

My dad said, "What's the point, Colum? We're listening."

Colum said, like a child who's just discovered something, "The point is, see, if we could know how things turn out, how they end, we would experience time differently. We would count backward from the end, see? Like a boxer knowing how a fight was going to end, which round, he'd know how to pace himself, what kind of mind-set to go into it with. See?"

"Wait," my dad said, "he knows how it's going to end, what's the point of trying? If he's going to win, he wins; if not, he can't. Why'd he do anything at all? Why even show up?"

The others laughed. "Just collect his purse," Otto Lanza said sagely.

But Colum was shaking his head, annoyed. A slow flush came into his face. Maybe this was a factor he hadn't considered, or maybe it was far from the point of what he was trying to say; the reason he was so involved. "See, if we knew these things, we'd behave better. Like my last fight, I KO'd the guy in eight rounds, but I was pretty sloppy in the first rounds, I kept getting thrown off stride, I could've tried harder, looked better. See? I could've won with *style*."

"You won by a KO, so what? You don't get more money, winning with style."

Colum considered this. My dad said afterward that, for sure, Colum was thinking hell yes, you do get more money if you've got style, eventually you get a lot more money. Because you get matched with top contenders and your purses improve. But that was a subject of a certain fineness or subtlety

Colum wouldn't have wanted to acknowledge. The difference between "The Kid" Donaghy and, for instance, LaStarza, Marciano, Walcott. He said:

"See, if we *knew*, we wouldn't be *guessing*. Making mistakes. If you knew you were going to marry your wife, from the start when you first met her, you'd treat her a helluva lot better. Right? If you knew how you'd be crazy for your kids, once they got born, you wouldn't be, you know, scared as hell ahead of time. That's what I mean." Colum looked at his friends in his strange squinting way, as if daring them to disagree. And they were sort of conceding the point or anyway had gotten beyond a serious wish to contest it. What the hell? Let Donaghy talk. They loved The Kid when he was in his weird moods and insisting on buying rounds of beers, dropping ten-dollar bills on the bar like he had pockets of them, an endless supply.

"The crappy thing about dying is you only get to do it once," Colum added. "The second time, see?—you'd go with style."

8.

The man who fought Roland LaStarza, in Buffalo back in the fifties. Whatever happened to him?

A boxer who's going to be a champion is on the rise from the first fight onward. He's going to win, win, win. He's going to win his amateur fights, he's going to win his first pro fights. He's protected from harm or accident by a luminous light enveloping his body, like Athena protecting her soldiers in the Trojan War. He will not be seriously hit, he will not feel his mortality. He will not be matched with fighters who might beat him too soon. His career is a matter of rising, ascending. To him, it feels like destiny. It does not feel as if it's being arranged by human beings. Money changes hands, but it isn't a matter of money. Is it?

These boxers rise through their ranks undefeated. They win by spectacular KOs, or failing that they win on points. They win, consistently. The future champion is *one who wins*. If two future champions are fighting in the same division at the same time, their canny managers will not make a deal for them to fight too soon. Because the big payday is somewhere ahead.

Then there are the others: those who are not going to be champions.

They win, and they lose. They have a streak of wins, and then suddenly they lose. They lose again, and then they win. Their careers are what you'd call *erratic, up-and-down*. They do predictable things in the ring because their boxing skills are limited, like a small deck of cards. But they do unpredictable things, too, because their boxing skills are limited, like a small deck of cards. And sometimes there's a wild card in the deck.

This was Colum "The Kid" Donaghy.

He began boxing as a kid of fifteen, in 1943. He fought his last fight in September 1958.

Never would Colum Donaghy be ranked among the top ten in his division. In the navy, he'd been a light heavyweight winner and he'd looked good against that tough competition. In the places like the old Buffalo Armory, matched with men like himself, boxers with showy aggressive skills and little or no defensive strategies, he'd looked very good, crowds loved

Colum "The Kid" Donaghy. And grinning happily out at them, covered in sweat like cheap glittering jewels and an eye swollen shut, blood dribbling from a nostril as the referee held his gloved hand high amid a deafening roar of cheers, yells, applause, The Kid loved them.

There's these weird times, Christ! it's like I could bless everybody I see. Like I'm a priest or something, and God gave me the power to bless. My heart is so full, feels like it's going to burst.

Know what I mean? Or am I some kind of dope or something?

It's like I got to go through what I do, hitting, and being hit, hurting a guy, and being hurt, before I can bless those people? Before I can feel that kind of, whatever it is, happiness.

Next day, anyway it's gone. Next day I'm feeling like shit, can't hardly get out of bed and my eye swollen shut and I'm pissing blood and the fucking phone better be off the hook, fuck it I don't want any interference in the household.

9.

"That poor woman. I don't envy her."

So the Yewville women spoke of Colum Donaghy's wife, Carlotta. She was a brunette Susan Hayward look-alike from Niagara Falls. She hadn't any family in Yewville, and few women friends. A glamorous woman when you saw her ringside, and photographed for the papers beside her husband, but at other times she looked like what you'd have to call almost ordinary, shopping at Loblaw's, pushing a baby in a stroller and trying to hang on to a toddler's hand, to prevent him from rushing into the street.

"When he brought her here to live, she looked so *young*."

When Colum wasn't in training, it's true Colum did drink. Coming off a fight, whether he'd won the fight or lost, he'd start to drink pretty seriously. Because now it was normal life, it was the life of normal, average men, men who worked at daily jobs, in garages, in lumberyards, driving trucks, taking orders from others, trying to make money like you'd try to suck moisture out of some enormous unnameable thing, pressing sucker-lips against it, filled with revulsion for what you did, what you must do, if you wanted to survive. *These times, it's like I saw into the heart of things. The mystery. And there's no mystery. Just trying to survive.* It was known that Colum and Carlotta had married within a few weeks of meeting, crazy for each other but prone to quarrels, misunderstandings. Each was an individual accustomed to attention from the opposite sex. It was known that Colum loved his wife very much, and their children. If he lost his temper sometimes, if he frightened them, still he loved Carlotta very much, and their children.

Yet sometimes, specific reasons unknown, Colum would disappear from Yewville to live in Buffalo. He had many friends there, men and women both. Sometimes he'd only just move out of his house and live across town. Friends took him in, eager to make room for Colum Donaghy. Rarely did he pay rent. He'd stay in a furnished apartment in downtown Yewville near the railroad yard, which was also in a neighborhood of Irish bars where Colum "The Kid" was very popular, his boxing photos and posters taped to the walls. For a few weeks, or maybe just a few days, he'd live apart from his family; then Carlotta would ask him to return, and Colum would promise that things would be different, he loved her and the kids, he'd die for them he vowed, and he meant it. Colum Donaghy was a man who always meant the words he uttered, when he uttered them.

Sometimes it was Carlotta who left Yewville, took the children to stay with their grandparents in Niagara Falls. And it was Colum who went to bring them back.

"She's taking a chance. Him with that temper. And his drinking."

"What kind of woman would stay with him? You can't trust that kind of Irish."

Always there seemed to be women in Colum's life, so naturally there were misunderstandings. There were complications, crises. There were threats of violence against Colum, and occasional acts of violence. Scuffles in the parking lots of taverns, aggrieved husbands and boyfriends accosting Colum so he had no choice but to "defend himself," once breaking his fist on a stranger's jaw, so an upcoming fight had to be postponed. Another time, in a woman's house in Albany, police were called to break up a fight involving Colum and several others. "What can I do? These things happen." A man who's a boxer is attractive to both men and women, they want to be loved by him, or hit and hurt by him, possibly there's little difference, they only know they yearn for something.

When he wasn't actively in training, and in the rocky aftermath of a fight, never mind if he won or lost, Colum was restless and edgy as a wild creature in captivity; drank and ate too much, to the point of making himself sick; couldn't sleep for more than an hour or two at a time, walking the nighttime streets of Yewville, or driving in his car aimlessly; waking at dawn not knowing where he was, on a country road miles from home, having fallen asleep at last. He was happiest drinking with his friends, watching the Friday-night fights on TV, at a local bar. At such times carried out of himself in a bliss of excitement, subjugation. For he understood he was in thrall to boxing: to that deep rush of happiness, that blaze of life, that only boxing could give him. And he wanted even the yearning that swelled up in him as he watched the televised fights, broadcast from the fabled Madison Square Garden, the very center of the professional boxing world, where he'd been waiting, waiting, waiting to be called to fight, waiting so badly he could taste it. Colum Donaghy waiting for his turn, his chance, his payday. Though money had little to do with it, except as a public sign of grace. *A specially ordered canary yellow Buick convertible, he'd buy. A new house in a better part of town. Something for his parents, who deserved better than they'd gotten from life so far? A week in Miami Beach?* Colum "The Kid" Donaghy who wasn't getting any younger. Some of the kids in the gym, eyeing him. Maybe he's slowing down. Waiting for five years, waiting for eight years, ten years. But his manager, Gus Smith, was just a local Buffalo guy, in his sixties, near-obese, a cigar smoker with a goiter for a nose, goodhearted and decent but second-rate, unconnected, whom nobody in the boxing business owed favors, and the truth was Colum's record was not that impressive, he'd thrown away fights he should have won, thrown away opportunities because he had other things on his mind, like women, or Carlotta giving him grief, or he owed money, or somebody owed him, too many distractions, he'd become one of those wild mick brawlers the crowds cheer even when they lose, so losing was too often confused with winning. Like gold coins falling through his fingers, those years. There was the hot exhilarating rush of seeing the coins fall, and no way of guessing one day they'd all be gone.

So he was waiting, he was a hungry Irish kid waiting all his life. *If there's some other world, fuck it, I expect I'll be waiting there, too.*

10.

His record going into the fight with LaStarza in May 1958 was forty-nine wins, eleven losses and one draw. LaStarza's record was fifty-eight wins, five losses. But two of LaStarza's losses, in 1950 and 1953, were to Rocky Marciano, who would be the single heavyweight boxer in history to retire undefeated, and the second match with Marciano was for the heavyweight title. And LaStarza had mixed it up with Marciano for ten rounds before he was TKO'd in the eleventh.

Colum said excitedly, "That fight? LaStarza came close. If it'd been a decision, he'd of won. Shows it can be done, The Rock ain't invincible."

True, LaStarza may have been ahead on points through ten rounds of the fight but only because, and this is a big only, he'd boxed a cautious fight determined to keep the stronger Marciano at bay as you'd keep a coiled-up cobra at bay, if you were lucky, with a pole. But Marciano was relentless, always pushing forward. Always aggressive, maintaining a steady pace, not fast, but deliberate, dogged, knowing what he was going to do when he was in a position to do it. With Marciano as with Louis, the cagiest opponent could run but he couldn't hide. It was only a matter of time. "Like that story we read in school," my dad said, "a guy is caught between a pit and a pendulum, and it's only a matter of time."

Now Colum knew this, or should have known, but didn't want to admit it. He was eccentric like many boxers, he took contrary views that in oblique ways were satisfying to him if mystifying to others. Watching the Marciano–LaStarza fight on TV, in a bar with my dad and their friends, he was too restless to remain still, moving about excited, panting, calling out instructions to LaStarza as if he was ringside. "C'mon! Nail 'im! Use that right!" Each time the bell rang signaling the end of a round Colum would snap his fingers: "LaStarza." Meaning LaStarza won the round. When, in round nine, Marciano slipped to the canvas, Colum protested the referee should have ruled it a knockdown; and when, in round eleven, Marciano knocked LaStarza through the ropes and out onto the ring apron, Colum protested it was a push, a foul. Sure, Marciano threw a few low blows. His ring style lacked finesse. But the knockdown was a clean one and everybody knew it, just as everybody including LaStarza understood that LaStarza had lost that fight. If he'd kept on his feet for fifteen rounds with Marciano hammering away at him to the body, to the head, to the arms, practically breaking the man's arms and leaving them weltered in bruises like battered meat, LaStarza might have been permanently injured.

But Colum, stubborn and contentious, seemed to have been watching a different fight. This was years before the deal with LaStarza was even being dreamed of by Colum's manager, yet Colum seemed to foresee that one day he might fight Roland LaStarza, forget Marciano for now, it was his unconscious wish to build up LaStarza, the man who'd been a serious heavyweight title contender for years, and would be taking home a pretty decent purse from the night's fight, and Colum Donaghy three hundred fifty miles away in western Upstate New York is hungry for some of this, it's his turn, his time, how badly he wants to be fighting in Madison Square Garden in these televised Friday-night fights, broadcast throughout the entire United States, and people in Yewville and Buffalo crowded around their sets and cheering him on. "See? LaStarza came pretty close. It can be done."

My dad said when he heard this, he just looked at Colum, didn't say a word. Because already in Colum's imagination he was beyond LaStarza, he'd fought and beaten LaStarza and was ready to fight the legendary Marciano himself. That was the meaning of *It can be done.*

11.

"Oh, Colum! Come *on.*"

I'm remembering the time I came home from school, I was in sixth grade at the time, and my mom and Colum Donaghy were talking earnestly together in the kitchen. They were drinking beer (Molsons, out of bottles) and talking in rapid lowered voices, Colum in a freshly laundered white T-shirt, khakis, gym shoes, seated at the Formica-topped kitchen table, my mom leaning back against the rim of the sink, and in my memory she's wearing a cotton dress with a vivid strawberry print, short sleeves and a flared skirt, and her slender legs are pale and bare, and her feet in open sandals because it's a warm day in late May. And her hair that's chestnut brown is soft and curly around her face as if she recently washed it. And she's laughing, in her tentative nervous way. "Oh, Colum! Come *on*."

I wondered what they'd been talking about, my mother breathless and girlish. Where usually she's preoccupied, and two sharp vertical lines run between her eyebrows, even when her face is in repose.

It was vaguely known to me that my dad and mom had been engaged to be married twice; that something had gone wrong, some misunderstanding, in that murky region of time before my birth that both fascinated and repelled, and my mom had been "in love with" Colum Donaghy; and this love had lasted for six months, and had then ended; and again my dad and mom were together, and engaged, and married quickly. They were both so young, in their early twenties. They'd gone away from Yewville with no warning to be married by a justice of the peace in Niagara Falls, surprising and outraging their families. *Like it was something to be ashamed of, and not proud. Marrying that girl after she'd left him for Donaghy. Taking her back, after Donaghy.*

How I knew these facts, which could not have been told to me directly, I have no idea. I would no more have asked any relative about such things than I would have asked my proud, touchy father how much he made a year repairing cars and trucks and selling gas out on the highway. I would no more have asked my mother a personal question than I would have confided in her the early adolescent anxieties of my own life.

Had she left Donaghy, or had Donaghy left her?

This was not a question. This was a proposition.

My mother's name was Lucille, "Lucy." When I was a little girl and saw this name spelled out, I thought it was a way of spelling "lucky." And when I told my mom this she laughed sadly and ran her fingers through my hair. "Me? Lucky? No. I'm Lucy."

But later she hugged me, she said, "Hey, I am lucky. I'm the luckiest girl in the world to have *you*."

I was the oldest of Lucy and Patrick Hassler's three children, and the only girl. A daughter born within a year of their runaway wedding. If there were whispers and rumors in Yewville about who my father truly was, I did not know of them. And if I knew of them by way of my malicious girl cousins, I did not acknowledge them. I never did, and I never will.

Now my mother, Lucy, has been dead for nine years, and my father, Patrick, for five days.

That May afternoon was a delirium of wind! The air was filled with tiny flying maple seeds, some of them caught in my hair. I'd been running, I pushed through the screen door into the kitchen and there were Colum Donaghy and my mom talking earnestly together, and my mom was laughing, her nervous sad laugh, unless it was a hopeful laugh, which my brothers and I rarely heard, and my mom was wearing lipstick, which rarely she wore, and seeing me she quickly straightened her back, her startled eyes appearing dilated as if looking at me, her daughter, she saw no one, nothing. As if in that instant she'd forgotten who I was.

Colum Donaghy turned to me, smiling. If he was surprised at me bursting into the kitchen breathless, he didn't give a sign. He smiled:

"H'lo there, honey."

I muttered a greeting. I was very embarrassed.

They talked to me about nothing, my mother's voice was eager and bright and false as a TV voice trying to sell you something you don't want. I walked through the kitchen and into the hall and upstairs, my heart thudding. Out of a small oval mirror on my bedroom wall, a mirror my father had made for me framed in wood and painted pink, there glared my ferocious eleven-year-old face.

"I hate you. All of you."

A sensation of pure loathing rose in me, bitter as bile. At the same time I was hoping they'd call me back downstairs. I understood that I could not be a girl as beautiful as Colum Donaghy's wife, Carlotta, or pretty as Lucy, my mother; I understood, as surely as if my sixth-grade teacher had spelled it out in chalk on the blackboard of our classroom, that no man like Colum Donaghy would ever look at me as he'd been looking at my mother when I pushed through the screen door.

Still, the words echo in memory. So lightly tossed off, fleeting as breath. *H'lo there, honey.*

12.

After thirty a boxer's legs begin to go, and fast. If he's a brawler who hasn't taken care of himself, a crowd-pleaser who trades blows, confident the crowd will always adore him for holding nothing back, his legs will go faster. His punch he'll keep till the end. Maybe. But the legs, the legs wear out. Breath wears out. By the age of thirty-five you're an old man, by the age of forty you're unspeakably old.

Colum Donaghy was thirty years old by the time he fought Roland LaStarza in the Buffalo Armory. But LaStarza was thirty-one. Both boxers had been young for a long time.

Still, Marciano had retired undefeated two years before at the age of thirty-three, in his prime. Or nearly. So it didn't always mean that boxers beyond thirty were *old*. That their lives were speeding by like landscape glimpsed from a car window.

"It isn't a matter of old, young," Colum argued, "it's got nothing to do with calendar age. Look at Willie Pep, Archie Moore. Look at Walcott, thirty-eight when he won the fucking title."

My father said, "So you got plenty of time, you're thinking, eh Donaghy?" The men laughed, listening.

Colum said, "That's right. If it happens soon."

13.

Then in the late winter of 1958, the deal was made.

How much negotiating had gone into it, how many calls between Gus Smith and Roland LaStarza's manager, what the exact payment would be for each boxer and what sort of promises were made that were not in the contract, no one except a very few individuals would know. Certainly the boxers would not know. But a deal was made at last, and the media was notified: a match between LaStarza and Donaghy was set as the main card for a Saturday evening of boxing, May 20, 1958, in the Buffalo Armory.

The most exciting local sports news of the year! Colum Donaghy, the popular heavyweight who'd never moved away from his hometown, Yewville, was scheduled to fight a major heavyweight, an Italian glamour figure who'd "almost beaten" Marciano for the title and who was still a highly regarded contender and a TV favorite. (Or at least he'd been before his year of inactivity and losses to obscure fighters in places like Cleveland, Akron, Miami Beach.) How'd it happen, such a coup?

Gus Smith, interviewed locally, had a terse answer to this question: "It happened."

Colum called my father to tell him the good news before it broke. My father said, "This is great news, Colum. Congratulations." Trying to keep the dread out of his voice.

"Fucking fantastic, ain't it?"

"Colum, it is."

"Me and Carlotta, we're going out to celebrate tonight. At the Top Hat." The Top Hat was a well-known glitzy nightclub in Buffalo where individuals known in the media as *sports figures*, and their noisy entourages, often gathered on weekends. "You and Lucy want to join us? My treat."

"That sounds good, Colum. Let me check with Lucy and get back to you."

"Hey." Colum caught the signal. "Aren't you happy for me, Hassler?"

"Sure I'm happy for you."

"You're thinking—what? I can't beat LaStarza?"

"No."

"You're thinking I *can*?"

My father paused just a little too long. Colum said angrily: "I'm going to win, fuck it! I can beat LaStarza."

"Right. If anybody can, you can, Colum."

"What's that supposed to mean? Fucking condescending!"

"You can beat LaStarza, sure."

"You don't exactly sound overjoyed."

My father would recount how he'd been tongue-tied. Almost shy. Sweat breaking out on his forehead, in his armpits. Damned glad Colum couldn't see him, he'd have been madder than hell. "Colum, sure I am. It's just a surprise. It's— terrific news, what we've been waiting for, but—a surprise. Isn't it?"

Colum muttered, "Maybe to you, man. Not to me."

"Colum, it's just that I wonder—"

"Save yourself the effort, okay? *I'm* not."

Colum slammed down the receiver, that was that.

Patrick would wonder *What was happening, and what was going to happen?*

Because there was something fishy about the deal. Something in the evasive way Gus Smith talked about it that wasn't characteristic of the garrulous old man. And there was something in the vehement way Colum kept insisting, as the weeks passed, that he was going to win the fight, not on points but by a knockout; he'd give LaStarza the fight of his life, Colum boasted, and make the New York boxing crowd, those bastards, take notice of him. "It's my turn. I always deserved better." Colum confided in my father he wasn't going to follow his trainer's instructions, boxing LaStarza in the opening rounds, he was going to go straight at him, like Dempsey rushing out against Willard, or tearing into Firpo. Like LaMotta, Graziano. "LaStarza's manager looks at my record, thinks Donaghy is a pushover. Sure. It's a miscalculation in my favor. They see a fucking lousy draw in St. Catherines, Ontario! To a Canuck! So why should LaStarza train hard? This Donaghy is a small-town punk. I saw in the paper, LaStarza isn't in the best condition, after a year off. You hear things. Marciano almost broke his arms, shredded the muscles, he could hardly lift them afterward. And money he owes. It's just a payday for him, up here. But me, I'm fighting for my life." Colum grinned, showing his crooked teeth. "See? *I can't lose.*"

You never knew how Colum meant these words. He couldn't lose because he was too good a fighter, or he couldn't lose because losing this fight was unthinkable?

14.

The fight that ended in a draw in St. Catherines, Ontario?

Until the LaStarza fight, this had been the worst luck of Colum Donaghy's career. When he'd been twenty-seven, working in the Yewville stone quarry to support his young family, forty backbreaking hours a week, therefore goddamned grateful for any fight Gus Smith could arrange, anywhere, Colum would fight guys who outweighed him by twenty, even thirty pounds, for five hundred dollars. For four hundred. Three-fifty! Sure he'd take a chance, fighting in some place he didn't know, across the border in Ontario with a boxer he'd never heard of except he liked the name: O'Hagan. Between the Canuck O'Hagan and the Yank Donaghy they'd sell out the house, right?

A dozen or more of Colum's Yewville friends, including my father, drove to see the fight, and ever afterward it would be one of their tales, of outrage and sorrow, goddamn how Colum had been cheated of a win. It was an eight-round fight and Colum had won at least six of those rounds, beating up on his fattish thirty-six-year-old opponent who'd lost his mouthpiece in the last round, but managed to stay on his feet so the fucking local judges wouldn't allow the local favorite "Irish" O'Hagan to lose, declaring a draw. A draw! The judges had slipped out of the arena when the referee announced the decision, there were cheers, and a scattering of indignant boos, but the cheers drowned out the boos, and O'Hagan, looking shamefaced (both eyes swollen shut, nose broken), waved to his fans even as a sullen-faced Colum Donaghy climbed out of the ring indignant, like a rejected prince, and stalked away. Sports reporters for every U.S. paper agreed it had been a shameful episode. The New York State Athletic Commission was going to investigate, though it had no Canadian jurisdiction. Local headlines made Colum a hero, briefly: HEAVYWEIGHT DONAGHY CHEATED IN CONTROVERSIAL ONTARIO DECISION. In interviews Colum made it a point to be good-natured, philosophical. "At least they didn't stiff me, loading O'Hagan's gloves with buckshot." He laughed, on WBW-TV, showing his crooked, slightly discolored teeth, the shiny scar tissue winking above his eye. "What can you expect from Canucks? They don't have a democracy like we do."

15.

All I thought of was him. Him standing between me and what I wanted to make my life perfect.

The eight weeks Colum was in training, he avoided his old friends. He saw my father only a few times, when my father dropped by the gym, and he barely saw his wife and children. Long hours each day he spent at the gym, which was in downtown Yewville near the railroad yard. Often he slept and ate at his trainer's house, which was close by, his trainer was a soft-spoken monkish Irishman in his seventies, though looking much younger, never married. Each morning Colum got up at 4:30 A.M. like clockwork, to run deserted country roads outside Yewville, six miles before breakfast, and each night by 9 P.M. he went to bed exhausted. On Fridays he made an exception, stayed up to watch the TV fights. He ate six meals a day, his life had become almost purely his body. It was a peaceful life in its obsessive, narrow way. A monk's life, a fanatic's life. As a fighter he was focused exclusively on the coming fight and on the figure of his opponent who was no longer merely another man, human and limited, vulnerable and aging, but a figure of demonic power, authority. Like a monk brooding on God, so Colum brooded on Roland La-Starza. Pummeling the heavy bag, throwing punches whack! whack! whack! in a dreamy trance. *Him! Standing between me and what I want.*

In the past Colum had not liked training. Hell, no! Sure, he'd cheated. The random drink, even a smoke. Slipped away for a night with his friends. A night with a woman. This time there was none of that. He'd vowed. *What I want to make my life perfect, I can taste in my mouth like blood.*

Each day, the drama was sparring. Yewville men and boys dropped by to watch. Women and girls drifted in. They were crazy for Donaghy, there was an atmosphere of arousal, anticipation. The smell of male sweat, the glisten of bodies. In the background as in a film slightly blurred the walls of the old gym were covered in posters of bygone fights in the Buffalo Armory, some of them, faded to a sepia hue, dating back to the forties when the gym had been built. Most of the boxers' names were unknown, forgotten. Colum took no notice. He was fierce and alive in the present, in his vision he was climbing into the ring to confront LaStarza, he took little notice of his immediate surroundings for they were fleeting, insubstantial. In the ring, his body came alive. Where he'd been practicing his robot-drill, now he came alive in a quite different way. Each of his sparring partners was a vision of LaStarza. Each of them must be confronted, dealt with. Colum performed, and the onlookers called out encouragement and applauded. The bolder girls asked to have their pictures taken with Colum, and sometimes he obliged, and sometimes no. He was quirky, unpredictable. A good-natured guy except sometimes he was not. You dared not expect anything of him. A promise made one day, sure he'd be happy to oblige, next day — "No." That was the way with boxers of his temperament. Sometimes his trainer shut the doors against visitors, no one was welcome, not even Colum's friends. No one!

In the ring, in Colum's familiar safe place. In the ring protected by ropes. In the ring in which there are rulers, manners. No absolute surprises. He was shrewdly letting his sparring partners hit on him, his chin, his head, his body, to prepare him for LaStarza's hammer-blows that had knocked out twenty-four opponents so far and had visibly shaken Marciano. A wicked left hook to the body and a right cross to the chin that were almost of Marciano's caliber.

But I can take it. Anything he's got.

It was as if Colum knew, his trainer would afterward say, that this would be the last time he'd train so hard, he meant to give it all he had. Colum Donaghy never held back, his trainer would claim of him, even in the gym.

By the week of May 20 the odds were nine to one in favor of LaStarza.

16.

"What the hell, it's my advantage. I'm betting on *me*."

He confided in Patrick Hassler, but no one else was to know: not Colum's manager, not his trainer, not his wife. My father dreaded to ask Colum how much he was betting, and Colum told him: "Three thousand." My father laughed, out of sheer nerves. "Why three thousand, man?" Colum said frankly, "That's the most I could borrow." He laughed at the sick look in my father's face.

"Colum, my god. Are you sure?"

"Sure what? I'm going to win? Yes. I'm sure."

"Are you sure it's a good idea, to bet? So much?"

"Why the fuck *not*? It's like seeing into the future, you can figure backward what's the smart thing to do. Say I didn't, I'd be kicking myself in the ass afterward."

That was true, my father had to concede. If Colum was certain he was going to win. Why then, why not bet?

Colum said, "Nine-to-one odds, fan-tas-tic. *You* should bet, if you're smart. Three times nine is twenty-seven thousand, not bad for a night's work, is it? Plus the purse."

He spoke dismissively of the purse for it wasn't the big payday he'd long envisioned. LaStarza was getting $25,000 for the fight, and Donaghy was getting $11,000. So the newspapers said. Exactly what Colum's purse was, my dad didn't know. Public announcements of purses were always inflated. And Colum wouldn't see more than 60 percent of whatever it was, in any case. His manager took a big cut, his trainer, his cut man, his sparring partners and others. And then there was the IRS.

Colum, are you sure, man? This bet? You don't want to be making a mistake here.

Look: best you mind your own business, man. You think you do, but you don't know shit about me.

And that turned out to be true.

17.

We drove to Buffalo for the fight, a crowded carload of us. Dad and some of the Hassler relatives. I was the only girl. My mom stayed home.

These weeks, my mother had refused to read about Colum in the papers. Even his smiling photo on the front page of the *Yewville Post* she thrust away from her with a pained look. To my disgust I overheard her tell my father, "I don't think she should go with you. It isn't a healthy environment for a twelve-year-old girl. All those men! Such ugliness! You know what boxing is. Even if Colum isn't hurt, she will remember it all her life. And if—he gets hurt . . ." My mother's voice trailed off. My father said only, "She wants to go, and she's going."

She wants to go, and she's going!

Sharp as pain, the happiness I felt hearing this. For I had not expected my father to say such a thing. Like Colum, my father was an unpredictable man. You could not plead with him, you could not reason with him, he made decisions as he wished, and they were inviolable.

At that time in my young life I'd begun to hate my mother as always I had loved her so.

I hated her for wanting to keep me a girl, weak like her. I loved my father for taking me into his world, that was a man's world. There, weakness was not tolerated, only strength was valued. I could enter this world only as Patrick Hassler's daughter but I wanted nothing more, this was everything to me.

Driving to Buffalo my dad and the others talked only of the fight. Everybody wanted Colum Donaghy to win and was anxious about what would happen. What my dad must have known of Colum he would not reveal to these men, he spoke as if he knew Colum only at a distance. "It would be Donaghy's break of a lifetime, if he wins. But he's got to win. His manager says he's being 'looked at' for Madison Square Garden, to see how he'd perform on TV, but Colum is thirty years old, let's face it. He's fighting LaStarza, and LaStarza is still a big draw. He's on the skids, but still tough. You have to figure nobody in the boxing business wants LaStarza to lose just yet. Which means nobody in the boxing business wants Donaghy to win. Which means they don't think Donaghy can win, or will win."

One of my uncles said, incensed, "This wouldn't be a fixed fight, would it? Jesus."

My father just laughed.

"What's that mean? It's fixed, or—what?"

My father said, annoyed, "I don't know what it will be. I hope to Christ Colum survives it."

From the backseat I asked him if Colum Donaghy *could win*. I wanted almost to cry, hearing him say such things he'd been saying.

He said, "Sure Colum could win. Maybe he will. Maybe what I'm saying is bullshit. We'll hope so, yes?"

18.

"Ladies and gentlemen, our main event of the evening: ten rounds of heavyweight boxing."

The vast Armory was sold out, thousands of spectators, mainly men. In tiers of seats rising to nearly the ceiling. The smoke-haze made my eyes sting. The sharp sound of the bell. Sharp, and loud. Because it had to be heard over the screams of the crowd. It had to be heard by men pounding at each other's heads with their leather-gloved fists.

The ring announcer's voice reverberated through the Armory. My teeth were chattering with excitement. My hands were strangely cold, the palms damp. I felt a tinge of panic, that I had made a mistake to come here after all. I was twelve years old, young for my age. My heart beat light and rapid as a bird's fluttering wings.

God please don't let Colum Donaghy lose. Don't let him be hurt.

Beside me my father was quiet. He sat with his sinewy arms folded, waiting for the fight to begin. I understood that no matter how calmly and dispassionately he'd been speaking in the car, he felt very different. He was fearful for Colum's sake, he could not bear it that a man he loved like a brother might be publicly humiliated.

Injury, defeat, even death: these would be preferable to the abject humiliation of a boxer knocked down repeatedly, knocked down and knocked *out*.

At ringside in the row ahead of us there was the brunette in a showy electric blue velvet costume, the bodice spangled with rhinestones, her face heavily made-up: Carlotta, Colum Donaghy's wife. Tonight she was glamorous indeed. Her curled hair was stiff with spray, she wore rhinestone starburst earrings. She was seated with Colum's Buffalo friends whom my father did not like, and did not know well. Always she was glancing over her shoulder, seeing who might be watching her, admiring and envying her, she was Colum Donaghy's wife, his fans were eager to see her and there were photographers eager to take her picture. She smiled nervously, laughing and calling out greetings, her mascara-rimmed eyes bright and glazed. She saw my father, her eyes snagged on him, where we were seated in the third row a short distance away. Carlotta Donaghy staring at my father with an expression of— what? Worry? Pleading? Seeming to signal to her husband's friend *Well! Here it is, here we are, nothing will stop it now.* Quickly my father raised a hand to her. *Nothing to worry about, Colum will give him hell.*

I would see Colum's wife and another woman suddenly rise from their seats and leave the Armory by the nearest exit, midway in the fight. The tension was too much for her, her nerves could not bear it.

In his white satin robe Colum Donaghy was the first to enter the ring amid deafening applause. And how pale Colum's skin, milky pale, set beside the other boxer's olive-tinted skin. Roland LaStarza! Abruptly there he was. In black satin robe, black trunks. A pelt of dark hairs on his torso, arms, legs. He weighed only a few pounds more than Colum Donaghy but he looked heavier, older and his body more solid. His face was impassive as something carved from wood. His eyes were veiled, perhaps contemptuous. Wherever this was he was, this ring he'd climbed into, this drafty crude hall filled with bellowing and screaming strangers, he was LaStarza, the TV LaStarza, a popular heavyweight from the Bronx, he was

in western Upstate New York on business. He had no senti-
ment for the occasion. He knew no one in Buffalo, he had not
gone to school in Buffalo, there was no neighborhood here to
claim him. The Italians adored him, but he was LaStarza
from the Bronx, he could tolerate their noisy adoration, but
nothing more. His trainer had no need to talk to him earnestly
as Colum Donaghy's trainer was talking to him, trying to calm
him. LaStarza would do what he had to do, to defeat his opponent. He would not do more, and he would not do less. In
his career of more than ten years he had rapidly ascended the
heavyweight division in the way of a champion-to-be, he had
basked in victory, in praise, he fought for years before losing
his first fight and that had been no disgrace, for he'd lost to
Marciano, and still a young boxer he'd fought Marciano the
champion for the title and again he'd lost, he'd ascended the
glass mountain as far as his powerful legs would carry him. He
knew: his moment was behind him. Now he was in Upstate
New York, this was not a televised bout. His manager had
younger, more promising boxers to promote, another rising
champion-to-be, LaStarza would have to accept this deal, he'd
turned down similar deals in anger and contempt, but now he
had no choice, he was thirty-one years old. He'd never fully
recovered from the beating Marciano had given him. That
public humiliation, the terrible hurt to his body and to his
pride. He would win this fight, he would dispatch his opponent whom the morning before, at the weigh-in, he'd scarcely
acknowledged. One of those thin-skinned mick bleeders.
Their noses crumple like cheap aluminum cans, their eyes
bruise and swell. Their blood splashes like a tomato being
burst. At the weigh-in the men had been photographed together for local papers and for TV sports news, shaking hands.

Bullshit! The pose pained LaStarza, classy LaStarza, as a bad smell would pain him. He did not despise this Colum Donaghy; he had no thought for the man at all.

Colum Donaghy bounced about the ring in his white satin robe with gold trim. Shadowboxing, displaying himself to cheering fans. Almost shyly he smiled. A boy's smile, tentative and hopeful. He was one who knew he was adored yet could not entirely trust it, the adoration. He was one who required constant reassurance, nourishment from the crowd. For how milky pale he was: his torso and sides shone clammy white beneath fair-reddish hairs. The scar tissue in his face was obscured by bright glaring lights, his skin almost appeared smooth as a boy's. *Is it wrong that a boxer smiles before a fight?* I was very frightened for Colum Donaghy, and for my father seated grim and tense beside me.

I recalled Colum in our kitchen, a year ago. The lowered voices of adults. What had they been talking about so earnestly, why had my mother been laughing, what did it mean? I would never know.

The myriad small mysteries of childhood. Never solved. Never even named.

For all of the adult world is mystery, you will never comprehend it. Yet you must surrender to its authority. One day, you must enter it yourself.

The bell rang! That loud, sharp sound.

The first round began.

Colum Donaghy, fair skinned, in white trunks, moved swiftly to his darker-skinned opponent, and amid shouts and screams the long-awaited fight at last began. From the first, it was a surprise: for Colum rushed at LaStarza, throwing a flurry of punches, as LaStarza moved away, and to the side, raising his arms to ward off the fast pummeling blows, trying to use his jab. The boxers circled each other, Colum was pressing forward, always forward. He rode the wave of the crowd's excitement, he threw a right cross that swung wide of its target, he grappled with LaStarza and the men fell into a clinch. This was the pattern of the first rounds: Colum would push forward, LaStarza would elude him while catching him with quick sharp jabs, blows Colum seemed capable of absorbing, though a swelling began above his right eye. In the third round Colum came out fast and anxious and by apparent luck struck LaStarza a short, hard blow to the midriff, his powerful left hook he'd honed to perfection in the gym, and LaStarza reacted in surprise, in a flurry of blows pushing Colum back into the ropes. There was a scuffle and before the referee could break it up the crowd screamed, for LaStarza had slipped, one knee to the canvas, pushing himself up at once, and the referee didn't call a knockdown, which precipitated boos, and more aggressive tactics on Colum's part. The rounds were furious yet how slow time had become: the harder I stared at the boxers above me in their brightly lit pen, the more exhausted and unreal I felt. Everything was so much more vivid than on TV. The live fight was nothing like the TV fight, which was so small and flattened, in black-and-white images. And with broadcasters continually talking. In the Armory there were no broadcasters to explain what was happening. Much of the time I could not seem to see. My senses were overloaded. The thud of blows, the squeaking, scuffing sounds of the boxers' shoes on the canvas, the blood splattered on both men's chests and like raindrops onto the referee's white shirt, the deafening crowd noises and the referee's shouted commands — *Break! Break! Box!* — all were numbing, exhausting. Between rounds my eyelids drooped. My father and others shouted to one another, and shouted encouragement to Colum in his corner. I watched Colum Donaghy sitting in his corner as his seconds worked swiftly to prepare him for the next round. I saw his flushed, battered-looking face glisten with beads of water, a sponge squeezed out onto his heated head. Like an animal he seemed, a racehorse, purely physical, and strangely passive, so long as he was seated and these others labored over him. It had not seemed to me, maybe I had not wished to see, how Colum's eye was swelling shut, how his face was cut, but there was his cut man deftly treating his wounds, sticking something like a pencil up into his nostrils in a way to make me feel faint. I asked my father if Colum was winning, for it seemed to me as to the crowd that he was, yet I dreaded some more expert knowledge, and indeed my father frowning, said only, "Maybe. He's ahead." This was a mysterious answer for if Colum was ahead, was he not winning?

In the next rounds the boxers were more guarded, cautious. They were conserving their strength, covered in sweat and often breathing through their mouths. Colum's face was pinkened, as if flushed with health and excitement, LaStarza's was darker, heavy with blood yet still impassive with that carved-wood look. The older boxer was beginning to know that his opponent was going to give him serious trouble, the knowledge had sunk gradually in. A boxer wants to think that while his well-aimed blows are intentional, his opponent's are accidental and won't be repeated. But LaStarza saw that Donaghy was strong, clumsy and determined, a dangerous combination. The action erupted into flurries and then slowed into clinches. At the start of the seventh round Colum seemed to have regained his strength, and fought furiously, striking La-

Starza on the right temple, following with his left, and there was LaStarza, rocked back onto his heels. Screams on all sides, my father and his friends leaping to their feet, a wave of delirium, was LaStarza about to go down? But no. The moment passed. Yet the pace of the fight had accelerated. My eyes stung from the bright lights, the hectic action, a haze of cigarette and cigar smoke. Midway in the round Colum slowed, breathing through his mouth, and in that instant LaStarza swarmed on him, a right to the head that made Colum's eyes roll, a body blow like a sledgehammer. Yet Colum returned these with fierce blows of his own, and again delirium swept the crowd, for there was Colum in a frenzy pressing his opponent backward, relentlessly backward; yet unknowingly he lowered his left glove as he threw a right cross, and LaStarza, like a man trying to wake from a dream, swung blindly at him over the dropped left and struck him above the heart, a blow that might have killed Colum if LaStarza had had his full strength and weight behind it. The round ended in a flurry of blows and a repeated ringing of the bell as the fighters fought on unhearing.

The crowd erupted in applause for the fury of the fight.

Our way of thanking the fighters for — what? This mysterious gift of themselves they were giving us.

Daddy! Take me home, take me out of here. These words I could no more have uttered than I could have uttered obscenities.

It was seen that LaStarza, sitting slumped in his corner, was bleeding thinly from a cut above his left eye. It was seen that Colum leaned forward to spit into a bucket, and in the dazzling light that seemed magnified what he spat with an expression of disdain was tinged with red.

Another time I leaned over to ask in my father's ear if Colum was winning, I was desperate to know, but this time my father shrugged me away like a bothersome fly, frowning and indifferent. He was smoking a cigar, gripping the ugly dark glowing stub between his teeth.

At the start of the eighth round Colum came rushing to LaStarza as if bringing him something precious—a clumsy, downward-chopping blow to the head, which LaStarza only partly blocked. Next Colum pushed forward with head lowered, bull-like, taking punches even as he threw punches, of varying degrees of strength and accuracy. Already, at the start of the round, blood glistened in his nose. The deft assiduous labor of Colum's cut man had been outdone. There was LaStarza backed into a corner, now into the ropes, warding off Colum's wildly flung blows, which fell onto his arms and shoulders. LaStarza's ribs were reddened in welts. Colum swung and missed, another time swung and missed, but LaStarza's reflexes were slowed, he wasn't able to take advantage. My father said, as if thinking aloud, yet so that I might overhead, "This is the turn," and his face was somber, unsmiling. I wondered: what did *the turn* mean? One of the boxers wasn't able to fight back, to defend himself? Was the fight nearly over? *God please, end it now, please let Colum win.* I shut my eyes hearing the ugly whack! whack! of body blows. I had no idea who was being hit. I was dazed, sickened, the roaring of the crowd was so loud, I'd been pressing my hands against my ears without knowing. The referee struggled to pull the men apart. Their skins seemed sticky, adhesive. Again, again, again. Each man grappled, seeking advantage, hitting the other, short, chopping rabbit punches on the back of the neck. The referee's white shirt was now gray, soaked through with sweat as well as blood-splattered. His ridiculous bow tie was crooked. *Break! Box!* I would hear those shouted angry-sounding commands in my sleep. LaStarza seemed to be dropping by degrees out of the active fight, like a man observing himself at a distance; protecting himself, yet offering little offense now. It would seem that Colum had won most of the rounds — hadn't he? Colum "The Kid" Donaghy? His fans were cheering, inflamed with excitement. Both fighters had bloodied, bruised faces. LaStarza was clearly winded, yet like any experienced boxer he was dangerous, always dangerous, crouching in a corner, eyes glaring like a rat's. He would not go down, his will was unyielding. It was his opponent's will to send him down to the canvas but he would not, yet his knees buckled suddenly, the crowd again erupted. There was a palpable pressure, you could feel billowing waves of heat, that the fight must come to an end immediately, a climax, no one could bear it enduring any longer. Was this the knockdown? Colum struck LaStarza and LaStarza lurched forward into a clinch and amid deafening screams the bell rang signaling the end of the round. Colum continued pummeling blindly and the referee shouted *Bell! Bell!* He would deduct a point from Colum for hitting after the bell.

My throat was raw, I had not known I was screaming.

The last two rounds were very different. As if a flame had been burning higher and higher, but now a dampening wind blew on it, the flame lost its power, its luster. Colum tried to press his advantage as before but he'd lost momentum now. His legs were slower, sluggish. He threw combinations of punches intermittently, like a robot, LaStarza lashed out, yet both seemed to be losing their concentration. Now Colum, wrenching out of a clinch like a death grip, was the one to slip on the blood-dampened canvas and fall to one knee, and immediately pushed himself up with a grimace of pain. Had he injured his knee? The referee stopped the fight to examine Colum staring into his eyes, the crowd erupted in boos. Was the referee going to call the fight? award a TKO to LaStarza? *Was the fight fixed?* The crowd yelled its displeasure, the referee squinted into Colum's eyes in a pretense of concern but had no choice finally except to nod, to wave the men on, yes, the fight would continue.

Both men came out exhausted in the tenth and final round. Both men had difficulty raising their arms. It seemed now that LaStarza had been pacing himself more shrewdly than his opponent, yet still he had little strength left. He hit Colum with a combination of blows, none of them very hard, and Colum stood his ground, shaking his head to clear it. The men staggered like drunks trapped in some bizarre hellish ritual together. They had been together a very long time, neither would ever forget the other. It was possible to see both struggling men, near-naked and gleaming with sweat, as noble; and at the same time as defeated. Midway in the round LaStarza managed to hit Colum with what remained of his fearful right cross, and Colum countered with what remained of his fearful left hook, a short curving blow that looked more powerful than it could have been since LaStarza staggered but didn't collapse, grabbing onto his opponent like a drowning man. In the final ten or twelve seconds of the fight LaStarza seemed completely dazed and the crowd was chanting *Col-um! Hit him! Col-um! Hit him!* but Colum, who was the crowd's favorite, was too exhausted, his muscled arms hung by his sides like lead. He'd punched himself out, my father would say afterward. He had nothing left.

The bell rang.

19.

The moment I died, and I was happy.

20.

Following that fight of May 20, 1958, which would live long in ignominy in local memory, pervasive as the smoke- and chemical-tainted air of industrial Buffalo, Colum Donaghy would fight once more in September of 1958, in Syracuse. That fight, against an opponent of a very different stature than Roland LaStarza, he would win on points, narrowly. Five days later he was dead.

In the night Colum drove into the countryside. On a lane near his relatives' farm he parked, walked a short distance from his car and shot himself at the base of the skull. The county medical examiner stated he'd died instantaneously. He'd used a .32-caliber Smith & Wesson revolver, for which he had no permit. No one in the Donaghy family admitted to knowing of the gun's existence. But my father, Patrick Hassler, questioned by police, had to tell them Colum had brought the gun back with him from Korea. He'd won it there playing poker.

Had he been in the game with Donaghy? he was asked.

Not me, my father said. I don't play poker, I'm a man without that kind of luck.

Patrick was deeply ashamed to be questioned by police, for he understood that he was betraying Colum Donaghy simply by speaking of him as he did. Yet he believed he had no choice. Despite the ruling of suicide, there were questions

about Colum's death; there was a distrust of individuals asso-
ciated with professional boxing, and the LaStarza episode was
occluded by rumor, scandal. My father didn't volunteer to tell
police, however, that Colum had told him he'd borrowed
three thousand dollars to bet on himself.

Had Colum Donaghy ever spoken of taking his own life?
my father was asked.

Not to me, he told them. We never talked about that kind
of thing.

My father was stricken with grief at Colum's death. He
was stunned, he was baffled, he was ashamed. You could see
the vision in his eyes shrunken to pinpoints. You could see
he'd aged within days, his ruddy skin now ashen, tight. This
was not a man to speak of his feelings, this was not a man who
wanted sympathy. Like a dangerous sleepwalker he moved
among us, his family. My mother took care that we did not dis-
turb him. Sometimes he was absent for days. He'd go on
drinking binges. My mother wept in secret. Late at night we
heard her on the telephone downstairs, pleading. *Have you
seen Patrick? If you see Patrick* . . .

When Colum shot himself he'd knelt in the country lane.
In the darkness. He'd aimed his gun carefully. The bullet to
enter at the base of the skull, tearing upward through the
brain. Yet his hand must have shaken. It can't be so easy to *take
your own life* and throw it away like trash. He was missing for
two days before he was found lying on his side in the lane, the
fingers of his right hand curled stiffly around the revolver
handle. He was found by two teenaged boys out hunting.
They'd seen the car first, then found the body. They'd recognized Colum Donaghy, they said, at once. *The man who fought
Roland LaStarza.*

21.

That first terrible day at school. It was being said that Colum Donaghy had died. Agnes was called out of class, her mother had come to bring her home. Later it would be said that Colum had shot himself with a gun. He'd taken his own life, and that was a sin. A terrible sin. When we saw Agnes Donaghy again, two weeks later, it seemed that another girl had taken her place. Not so pretty, with eyes ringed in sorrow. Even her freckles had faded.

The cruelest among us whispered "Good! Now she knows."

Knows what?

How it is to be like everybody else. Not the daughter of Colum Donaghy.

In my father's face that was shut like a fist we saw the sick, choked rage. He would never speak of it. But sometimes he would say, "I hope they're satisfied now. The bastards." Meaning the boxing crowd. Gus Smith, too.

The judges had ruled the LaStarza-Donaghy fight a draw. A draw! Sports reporters had given it to Donaghy, clearly he'd won six or seven rounds. He'd punched himself out by round ten, but by then LaStarza was finished, too. The referee, interviewed, said evasively it had been a close fight, and a fair decision. One of the judges was from Rochester, the others were from New York City. No one could discuss the fight with my father. Colum refused to be interviewed afterward. He refused to see a doctor. A few weeks later he moved out of his home to live downtown near the railroad yard and the gym and the bars. He had a very young girlfriend from Olean, he spoke of quitting boxing. He complained of headaches, blurred vision. Still he would not see a doctor. He worked part-time at the quarry. He reconciled with Carlotta, and moved back home. Evidently he wasn't quitting boxing: Gus Smith signed him on for a fight in Syracuse, in September.

After that night in the Buffalo Armory, I never saw Colum Donaghy again. Though I would see his picture in the papers and on TV, often.

Sometimes when my father came home I was wakened, and listened for what I could hear. There was always wind, wind from the north, from Canada and across Lake Ontario, and the sound interfered with the sounds from my parents' bedroom. My mother's voice was anxious, lowered. "How could he, oh god. I can't sleep thinking of it, I can't believe it." And my father's voice was inaudible, his words were brief. My mother often cried. I wanted to think that my father comforted her then. As he'd comforted me when I'd been a little girl and had hurt myself in some childhood mishap. I wanted to think that my father held my mother in his strong sinewy arms like adults in the movies, that they lay together in each other's arms, and wept together.

Mostly I heard silence. And beyond, the wind in the trees close about our house.

22.

"I never wanted you to know how close to the edge we were in those days, honey. See?"

The edge. What was the edge?

He made a cautious gesture with the back of his hand. Approaching the edge of the table. It was not the Formica-topped kitchen table at which Colum Donaghy had sat, decades ago. A newer table, sleek and still shiny though my mother, Lucy, was not the one to sponge it down any longer.

The edge of things, Daddy meant. The edge of civilization.

At Christmas 1999, I went to visit my father in Yewville. He was living alone in the old house, stubborn and remote from his grown children. He lived in just two rooms, the upstairs was closed off, unheated.

He was seventy-two. His life, he said, had rushed past him without his exactly knowing.

He hadn't voluntarily seen a doctor since my mother's death nine years before, of cancer. He blamed the Yewville General Hospital for her death, or spoke as if he did. A malevolent *they* presided over such institutions. *Goddamned bloodsuckers.* A year before, he'd had a heart attack on the street and had been rushed to the emergency room of the very hospital that had killed his wife; he vowed he would never again return. He was subject to angina pains, he had bad knees, arthritic joints, yet he still smoked, and he drank ale by the case. He boasted to his children he kept "emergency medicine" in the house, for his private use when things got too bad. He would not be hooked up to machines as others had been. He would not be "experimented on" like a monkey. He laughed telling us these things, he gloated. Sometimes when we spoke of helping him sell the house and prepare for the future, he was furious with us, slammed down the phone receiver. But sometimes he listened attentively. It was "about time for an overhaul," he conceded.

His grown children took turns visiting with Patrick Hassler, when he would have us. Usually he was feuding with two of us, and friendly with the third. In December 1999, I was the one allowed to visit.

My father greeted me warmly, his mood was upbeat, his breath smelled strongly of ale. Seventy-two is not old but my father looked old. His skin was tinged with melancholy. His shoulders were stooped. He'd lost weight, his flesh seemed shrunken on him, loose and wrinkled like an elephant's skin. He wasn't a tall man any longer, he'd become a man of average height. A man who has punished himself? We sat in the kitchen talking. The subject was selling the house, and what to do next. We were sidetracked by reminiscing, of course. When I returned to Yewville always I was returning to the past. The city had not changed much in decades, it was economically depressed, frozen in the late fifties. The prosperity of subsequent decades in America had bypassed this region. Here, I was in Colum Donaghy's era. A thrill of something like panic, horror swept over me. For never had I understood. Why? Why that man so admired by so many had killed himself. He'd won his last fight. He had not lost the fight with Roland LaStarza, everyone knew. And he'd been only thirty-one years old.

I did not want to think that, at the age of thirty-one, a man's life might be over.

In Yewville, I stayed in a motel and visited my father for only a few hours each day. He seemed to want it this way, his privacy and his isolation had become precious to him. On the second day of my visit, he brought out the old photo album and we sat at the kitchen table looking through it together. I knew not to bring up the subject of Colum Donaghy and yet — there we were calmly looking at snapshots of him, and of my father with him, and of others, everyone so young and attractive, smiling into the camera. I was deeply moved by the snapshots taken in the gym, cocky-looking Colum and his friend Patrick in boxing trunks, headgear, arms around each other's shoulders, clowning for the camera. So young! Here were two men confident they had much life yet to live, and surely they had every right to think so. Except, seeing Colum Donaghy, and seeing that the date of the snapshot was February 1954, in that instant I was compelled to think of September 1958.

Four years, seven months to live.

My father said slowly, "It's like Colum is still with me, sometimes. I can hear him. Talk to him. Donaghy was the only person to make me laugh." Suddenly my father was confiding in me? He spoke calmly but I knew he was trembling.

So we talked of Colum Donaghy, and of those days. Forty years Patrick had outlived Colum, good Christ! That was a joke on them both. That was something to shake your head over. I said, "It was one of the mysteries of that time, Daddy. Why Colum killed himself. Just because he hadn't won that fight with LaStarza? But he hadn't lost it, either. He was still a hero. He must have known."

My father said, "Hell, I'm an old man now, I want to tell some things that couldn't be told before. Colum didn't kill himself, honey."

"What?"

"Colum Donaghy did not kill himself. No."

My father spoke slowly, wetting his parched lips. I stared at him in disbelief.

"Colum was killed, honey. He was murdered."

"Murdered? But—wasn't the gun his?"

My father hesitated, rubbing his eyes with both hands. His face was discolored by liver spots, deeply creased and fallen.

"No, honey. The gun was not Colum's. Colum owned no gun."

A chill came over me. A terrible subterranean knowledge like a quickened pulse. And my father glancing at me, to see how I was taking this.

He would tell me now, would he? An elderly man on the brink of the grave, with nothing to lose. Even his fear of God he'd long ago lost.

The thought came to me swift and unbidden. *He is the one who killed Colum Donaghy.*

I could not accuse him. Before this man, I would always be a stammering child.

He saw me staring at him. With a frowning, finicky gesture he smoothed the wrinkles in one of his shirtsleeves. The shirt had been laundered and not ironed, and fitted him loosely. "I had to tell the police what I did, honey. It would've been my life, too. I'd been warned. Gus Smith warned me. And Colum was gone, nothing would bring him back. Jesus, when he opened up like he did in the eighth round! It was a beautiful thing but—he was a dead man, from that point onward. See, they'd told him what to do. What not to do. They were paying him, and he'd agreed. He was to fight like hell but LaStarza was going to knock him out. All this I knew, but not directly. Colum hinted to me he was going against his manager and trainer, and LaStarza's backers, he'd even bet on himself to win. He'd intended all along to win. He was a—" My father's voice quavered. It was rare for him to speak at such length, and so vehemently. But now, words eluded him. "—so goddamned stubborn *Irish.*"

But I was left behind in this. I'd heard, but hadn't absorbed what I heard. "Daddy, I don't know what you're saying. Who killed Colum?"

"Who, exactly? Their names? Hell, I don't know their names."

"But—who hired them?"

My father shrugged. Shook his head, disgusted. "Some sons of bitches in New York, I suppose."

"But you told police—"

"Hell, you couldn't trust the police, either. Boxing was part of the rackets, there were payoffs, high-ranking cops and judges and politicians. I said what I said, I didn't have a choice. I had you kids to think of, and your mother. Yeah and I was afraid, too. For myself."

"Daddy, I'm just so—stunned. All these years . . . Colum was your closest friend."

"Colum knew what boxing was! Goddamn, he wasn't born yesterday. He wasn't any saint. Nobody forced him to sign on for the LaStarza fight, he knew what it was. LaStarza might not have been told, he only had to fight for real. But Colum! He thought he could win, and impress everybody, and everybody would love The Kid, and the New York promoters would sign him on. He could take LaStarza's place, he was thinking. Marciano's! But he'd underestimated La-Starza. That was his second mistake. He didn't pace himself the way a boxer is trained to, he punched himself out by the tenth round and couldn't KO his man so it went to the judges. They called it a draw. It stank, everybody knew it was rotten, but there it was. A draw, and nobody won. But Colum lost." My father spoke disgustedly, shoving the photo album away from himself.

"So the judges were bribed."

"Hell, those bastards wouldn't even need to be bribed. They'd have naturally done what was expected of them."

"Daddy, I can't believe this! You loved boxing."

"I loved some boxers. I loved watching them sometimes. But boxing—no, I didn't love boxing. Boxing is business, a man selling himself to men who sell him to the public. Christ!"

I was impatient suddenly. "And you never sold yourself, Daddy, I suppose?"

"For your mother and you kids, sure I did," he said. "I sold myself however I could. Just owning that garage that barely made a living, I had to pay protection to SOBs in Niagara Falls. If I hadn't paid them they'd have firebombed me. Or worse."

"You? Extorted?"

"Hell, it wasn't only me. Maybe it's different now, the police will protect you. But in those days, no. If I'd told anybody that Colum had been murdered, and the gun wasn't his—" His voice ceased suddenly, as if the strength had drained from him. He was rubbing his eyes in a way uncomfortable to see, as if wanting to blind himself.

"Daddy, I feel sick about this. I—don't know what to say."

"We sold ourselves however we could," my father said angrily, "and so have you kids, in your different ways. What the hell do you know?"

"It was all a lie, then? Colum never took his own life—his life was taken from him, and you knew, Daddy. And you didn't try to get justice for him."

"Justice! For who? What's that? 'Justice'—bullshit. I'd have been shot, too, or dumped in the Niagara River. You'd have liked that better?"

I was upset, revulsed. I stood and walked away. Suddenly I needed to escape this airless kitchen, this house, Yewville. My father reached for me but I eluded him. I fled outside, he followed me. The ground was crusted with snow that looked permanent as concrete. Our breaths steamed. My father said, close to pleading now, "I didn't want you, your mother or anybody, to know, how close we were to the edge in those days. It was Colum, it could've been me. I wanted to shield you, honey."

One day I would understand, maybe. But not then. I told him I'd talk to him later, I'd call him, but I had to leave Yewville now. Driving away I was shaken, stunned, as if my father had hit me. I was filled with a sick, sinking sensation as if I'd bitten into something rotten, the poison was activated in me, unstoppable.

The last time I saw my father alive.

23.

Not Colum Donaghy but Patrick Hassler, the sole person close to me who has taken his own life.

Taken his own life. But where?

My father died early in the morning of New Year's Day. He'd swallowed two dozen painkillers, washed down by ale. His heart, the medical examiner ruled, had simply given out; he'd never regained consciousness; his death was *self-inflicted.*

If I knew better, I told no one.

I would live with what I knew, and I would bear it.

He'd left behind items designated for us, his children. His survivors. There was a shabby envelope with my name printed

carefully on it, and inside were the old, priceless photos of
Colum Donaghy. One I hadn't seen before was of Colum and
my father and me, posed in front of a car with a gleaming
chrome grille. The date was 1950, I was four years old. Colum
and Patrick were each leaning against a front fender of the car,
and I was propped on the hood, smiling, legs blurred as if
I'd been kicking the instant the picture was taken. (By my
mother?) I was a blond curly-haired little girl in a pink ruffled
dress. Both men were holding me so I wouldn't fall. I saw that
a stranger, studying this snapshot, the three of us in that long-
ago time of June 1950, could not have guessed with certainty
how we were related, which man might be the little girl's
father.

Valentine, July Heat Wave

My calculated estimate is *Eight days should be about right.*

Not that I am a pathologist, or any kind of naturalist. My title at the university is professor of humanities. Yet a little research has made me fairly confident *Eight days during this heat wave should be about right.*

Because I have loved you, I will not cease to love you. It is not my way (as I believe you must know) to alter. As you vowed to be *my wife,* I vowed to be *your husband.* There can be no alteration of such vows. This, you know.

You will return to our house, you will return to our bedroom. When I beckon you inside, you will step inside. When I beckon you to me, you will come to me. You will judge if my estimate has been correct.

Eight days! My valentine.

The paradox is: love is a live thing, and live things must die.

Sometimes abruptly, and sometimes over time.

Live things lose life: vitality, animation, the pulse of a beating heart and coursing blood carrying oxygen to the brain, the ability to withstand invasion by predatory organisms that devour them. Live things become, in the most elemental, crudest way of speaking, dead things.

And yet, the paradox remains: in the very body of death, in the very corpse of love, an astonishing new life breeds.

This valentine I have prepared for you, out of the very body of my love.

You will arrive at the house alone, for that is your promise. Though you have ceased to love me (as you claim) you have not ceased to be an individual of integrity and so I know that you would not violate that promise. I believe you when you've claimed that there is no other man in your life: "no other love." And so, you will return to our house alone.

Your flight from Denver is due to arrive at 3:22 P.M. You've asked me not to meet you at the airport and so I have honored that wish. You've said that you prefer to rent a car at the airport and drive to the house by yourself and after you have emptied your closets, drawers, shelves of those items of yours you care to take away with you, you prefer to drive away alone, and to spend the night at an airport hotel where you've made a reservation. (Eight days ago when I called every airport hotel and motel, to see if you'd made the reservation yet, you had not. At least, not under your married name.) When you arrive at the house, you will not turn into the driveway but park on the street. You will stare at the house. You will feel very tired. You will feel like a woman in a trance of — what?

Guilt, surely. Dread. That sick sense of imminent justice when we realize we must be punished, we will "get what we deserve."

Or maybe you will simply think: *Within the hour it will be ended. At last, I will be free!*

Sometime before 4 P.M. you will arrive at the house, assuming the flight from Denver isn't delayed. You had not known you were flying into a midwestern heat wave and now you are reluctant to leave the air-conditioned interior of the car. For five weeks you've been away and now, staring at the house set back some distance from the street, amid tall, aging oaks and evergreens, you will wish to think *Nothing seems to have changed.* As if you have not noticed that, at the windows, downstairs and upstairs, venetian blinds seem to have been drawn tightly shut. As if you have not noticed that the grass in the front lawn is overgrown and gone to seed and in the glaring heat of the summer sun, patches of lawn have begun to burn out.

On the flagstone walk leading to the front door, a scattering of newspapers, flyers. The mailbox is stuffed with mail no one seems to have taken in for several days though you will not have registered *Eight days!* at this time.

Perhaps by this time you will concede that, yes, you are feeling uneasy. Guilty, and uneasy.

Knowing how particular your husband is about such things as the maintenance of the house and grounds: the maintenance of neatness, orderliness. The exterior of the house no less than the interior. Recognizing that appearances are trivial, and yet: appearances can be signals that a fundamental principle of order has been violated.

At the margins of order is anarchy. What is anarchy but brute stupidity!

And so, seeing uneasily that the house seems to be showing signs of neglect, quickly you wish to tell yourself *But it can have nothing to do with me!* Five weeks you've been away and only twice, each time briefly, have you called me, and spoken with me. Pleading with me *Let me go, please let me go* as if I, of all people, required pleading with.

My valentine! My love.

You will have seen: my car parked in the driveway, beside the house. And so you know (with a sinking heart? with a thrill of anticipation?) that I am home. (For I might have departed, as sometimes, admittedly, in our marriage I did depart, to work in my office at the university for long, utterly absorbed and delirious hours, with no awareness of time.) Not only is the car in the driveway, but I have promised you that I would be here, at this time; that we might make our final arrangements together, preparatory to divorce.

The car in the driveway is in fact "our" car. As the house is "our" house. For our property is jointly owned. Though you brought no financial resources to our marriage and it has been entirely my university income that has supported us yet our property is jointly owned, for this was my wish.

As you are *my wife,* so I am *your husband.* Symmetry, sanctity.

This valentine I've designed for you, in homage to the sanctity of marriage.

On the drive from the airport, you will have had time to think: to rehearse. You will repeat what you've told me and I will try to appeal to you to change your mind but of course you will not change your mind *Can't return, not for more than an hour* for that is the point of your returning: to go away again. You are adamant, you have made up your mind. *So sorry, please forgive if you can* you are genuine in your regret and yet adamant.

The house, our house: 119 Worth Avenue. Five years ago when we were first married you'd thought that this house was beautiful — "special." Like the old residential neighborhood of similarly large houses on wooded lots, built on a hill overlooking the university arboretum. In this neighborhood known as University Heights most of the houses are solidly built brick with here and there a sprawling white colonial, dating back to the early decades of the twentieth century. Our house is dark red brick and stucco, two stories and a third part-story between steep shingled roofs. Perhaps it is not a beautiful house but certainly it is an attractive, dignified house with black shutters, leaded-glass windows, a screened veranda, and lifting from the right-hand front corner of the second floor a quaint Victorian structure like a turret. You'd hurried to see this room when the real estate agent showed us the house but were disappointed when it turned out to be little more than an architectural ornament, impractical even as a child's bedroom.

On the phone you'd murmured *Thank god no children.*

Since you've turned off the car's motor, the air-conditioning has ceased and you will begin to feel a prickling of heat. As if a gigantic breath is being exhaled that is warm, stale, humid, and will envelop you.

So proud of your promotion, Daryll. So young!

How you embarrassed me in the presence of others. How in your sweetly oblivious way you insulted me. Of course you had no idea. Of course you meant well. As if the fact that I was

the youngest senior professor in the humanities division of the
university at the time of my promotion was a matter of signif-
icance to me.

As my special field is philosophy of mind, so it's mind that
is valued, not trivial attributes like age, personality. All of philosophy is an effort of the mental faculties to discriminate between the trivial and the profound, the fleeting and the
permanent, the many and the One. Pride is not only to be rejected on an ethical basis but on an epistemological basis, for
how to take pride in oneself? — in one's physical being, in
which one's brain is encased? (Brain being the mysterious yet
clearly organic repository of mind.) And how to take pride in
what is surely no more than an accident of birth?

You spoke impulsively, you had no idea of the crudeness
of your words. Though in naïveté there is a kind of subtle ag-
gression. Your artless blunders made me wince in the presence of my older colleagues (for whom references to youth, as
to age, were surely unwelcome) and in the presence of my
family (who disapproved of my marrying you, not on the
grounds that you were too young, but that you were but a departmental secretary, "no match" intellectually for me, which
provoked me to a rare, stinging reply *But who would be an intellectual match for me? Who, and also female?*).

Yet I never blamed you. I never accused you. Perhaps in my
reticence. My silences. My long interludes of utter absorption
in my work. Never did I speak of the flaws of your character and
if I speak of them now it is belatedly and without condemna-
tion. Almost with a kind of nostalgia. A kind of melancholy af-
fection. Though you came to believe that I was "judgmental" —
"hypercritical" — truly you had no idea how I spared you.

Many times.

————

Here is the first shock: the heat.

As you leave the car, headed up the flagstone path to the front door. This wall of heat, waves of heat shimmering and nearly visible rushing at you. "Oh! My god." Several weeks away in mile-high Denver have lulled you into forgetting what a midsummer heat wave in this sea-level midwestern city can be.

Stale humid heat. Like a cloud of heavy, inert gas.

The heat of my wrath. The heat of my hurt. As you are my wife I spared you, rarely did I speak harshly to you even when you seemed to lose all control and screamed at me *Let me go! Let me go! I am sorry, I never loved you, please let me go!*

That hour, the first time I saw your face so stricken with repugnance for me. Always, I will remember that hour.

As if, for the five years of our cohabitation, you'd been in disguise, you'd been playing a role, and now, abruptly and without warning, as if you hadn't known what you would say as you began to scream at me, you'd cast aside the disguise, tore off the mask and confronted me. *Don't love you. It was a mistake. Can't stay here. Can't breathe. Let me go!*

I was stunned. I had never imagined such words. I saw your mouth moving, I heard not words but sounds, strangulated sounds, you backed away from me, your face was contorted with dislike.

I told you then: I could not let you go. Would not let you go. For how could I, you are *my wife*?

Remembering how on a snowy morning some months before, in late winter, you'd entered my study in my absence and propped up a valentine on the windowsill facing my desk. For often you did such things, playful, childlike, not seeming to mind if I scarcely noticed, or, noticing, paid much attention. The valentine came in a bright red envelope; absorbed in my work, somehow I hadn't noticed. Days passed and I did not notice (evidently) and at last you came into my study to open the envelope for me, laughing in your light rippling way (that did not sound accusing, only perhaps just slightly wounded) and you drew out of the red envelope a card of a kind that might be given to a child, a kitten peeking out of a watering can and inside a bright red TO MY VALENTINE. And your name. And I stared at this card not seeming to grasp for a moment what it was, a valentine, thrust into my face for me to admire.

Perhaps I was abrupt with you then. Or perhaps I simply turned away. Whereof one cannot speak, there one must be silent. The maddened buzzing of flies is a kind of silence, I think. Like all of nature: the blind devouring force to which Schopenhauer gave the name *will*.

Your promise was, at the time of our marriage, you would not be hurt. You would not be jealous of my work, though knowing that my work, as it is the best part of me, must always take priority over my personal life. Freely you'd given this promise, if perhaps recklessly. You would not be jealous of my life apart from you, and you would not be hurt. Bravely pledging *I can love enough for both of us!*

And yet, you never grasped the most elemental logistics of my work. The most elemental principles of philosophy: the quest for truth. Of course, I hardly expected you, lacking even a bachelor's degree from a mediocre land-grant university, to understand my work, which is understood by very few in my profession, but I did expect you, as my wife, to understand that there can be no work more exacting, exhausting and heroic.

But now we are beyond even broken promises. Inside our house, your valentine is waiting.

As a younger man only just embarked on the quest for truth, I'd imagined that the great work of my life would be a definitive refutation of Descartes, who so bluntly separated "mind" and "body" at the very start of modern philosophy, but unexpectedly in my early thirties my most original work has become a corroboration and a clarification of the Cartesian position: that "mind" inhabits "body" but is not subsumed in "body." For the principles of logic, as I have demonstrated by logical argument, in a systematic geometry in the mode of Spinoza, transcend all merely "body" limitations. All this, transmuted into the most precise symbols.

When love dies, can it be revived? We will see.

On the front stoop you will ring the doorbell. Like any visitor.

Not wishing to enter the house by the side door, as you'd done when you lived here.

Calling in a low voice my name: "Daryll?"

How strange, *Daryll* is my name. My given name. Yet I am hardly identical with *Daryll* and in the language of logic it might even be claimed that I am *no thing* that is *Daryll* though I am simultaneously *no thing* that is *not-Daryll*. Rather, *Daryll* is irrelevant to what I am, or what I have become.

No answer. You will try the door knocker. And no answer.

How quiet! Almost, you might think that no one is home.

You will take out your house key, carried inside your wallet, in your purse. Fitting the key into the lock you will experience a moment's vertigo, wishing to think that the key no longer fits the lock; that your furious husband has changed the locks on the doors, and expelled you from his life, as you wish to be expelled from his life. But no, the key does fit. Of course.

Pushing open the door. A heavy oak door, painted black.

Unconsciously you will have expected the interior of the stolid, old, dark brick house to be coolly air-conditioned and so the shock of overwarm, stale air, a rancid-smelling air, seems to strike you full in the face. "Hello? Daryll? Are you . . . ?"

How weak and faltering, your voice in your own ears. And how your nostrils are pinching at this strange, unexpected smell.

Rancid, ripe. Sweet as rotted fruit, yet more virulent. Rotted flesh?

Please forgive!
  Can't return. Not for more than an hour.
  It was my fault, I had no idea . . .
  . . . from the start, I think I knew. What a mistake we'd both made.
  Yes I admit: I was flattered.
  . . . young, and ignorant. And vain.
  That you, the most brilliant of the younger professors in the department . . .
  Tried to love you. To be a wife to you. But . . .
  Just to pack my things. And what I can't take with me, you can give to Goodwill. Or throw out with the trash.
  . . . the way they spoke of you, in the department. Your integrity, your genius. And stubborn, and strong . . .

If I'd known more! More about men. Like you I was shy, I'd been afraid of men, I think. A virgin at twenty-five . . .

No. I don't think so.

Even at the beginning, no. Looking back at it now, I don't think I ever did, Daryll. It was a kind of . . .

. . . like a masquerade, a pretense. When you said you thought you loved me. Wanting so badly to believe . . .

And that sound: murmurous and buzzing, as of muffled voices behind a shut door.

"Daryll? Are you — upstairs?"

Telling yourself *Run! Escape!*

Not too late. Turn back. Hurry!

Yet somehow you will make your way to the stairs. The broad front staircase with the dark cranberry carpeting, worn in the center from years of footsteps predating your own. Like a sleepwalker you grip the banister, to steady your climb.

Is it guilt drawing you upstairs? A sick, excited sense of what you will discover? What it is your duty, as *my wife*, to discover?

You will be smiling, a small fixed smile. Your eyes opened wide yet glassy as if unseeing. And your heart rapidly beating as the wings of a trapped bird.

If you faint. Must not faint! Blood is draining from your brain, almost you can feel darkness encroaching at the edges of your vision; and your vision is narrowing, like a tunnel.

At the top of the stairs you pause, to clear your head. Except you can't seem to clear your head. Here, the smell is very strong. A smell confused with heat, shimmering waves of heat. You begin to gag, you feel nausea. Yet you can't turn back, you must make your way to the bedroom at the end of the corridor.

Past the charming little turret room with the bay window and cushioned window seat. The room you'd imagined might somehow have been yours, or a child's room, but which proved to be impracticably small.

The door to the bedroom is shut. You press the flat of your hand against it feeling its heat. Even now thinking almost calmly No. *I will not. I am strong enough to resist.*

You dare to grasp the doorknob. Dare to open the door. Slowly.

How loud the buzzing is! A crackling sound like flames. And the rancid, rotting smell, overwhelming as sound that is deafening, passing beyond your capacity to comprehend.

Something brushes against your face. Lips, eyes. You wave it away, panicked. "Daryll? Are you — here?"

For there is motion in the room. A plane of something shifting, fluid, alive and iridescent, glittering: yet not human.

In the master bedroom, too, venetian blinds have been drawn at every window. There's the greenish undersea light. It takes you several seconds to realize that the room is covered with flies. The buzzing noise you've been hearing is flies. Thousands, millions? — flies covering the ceiling, the walls. And the carpet, which appears to be badly stained with something dark. And on the bed, a handsome four-poster bed that came with the house, a Victorian antique, there is a seething blanket of flies over a humanoid figure that seems to have partly melted into the bedclothes. Is this — who is this? The face, or what has been the face, is no longer recognizable. The skin has swollen to bursting like a burnt sausage and its hue is blackened and no longer does it have the texture of skin but of something pulpy, liquefied. Like the manic glittering flies that crawl over everything, this skin exudes a dark iridescence.

The body has become a bloated balloon-body, fought over by masses of flies. Here and there, in crevices that had once been the mouth, the nostrils, the ears, there are writhing white patches, maggots like churning frenzied kernels of white rice. The throat of the humanoid figure seems to have been slashed. The bloodied knife lies close beside the figure, where it has been dropped. The figure's arms, covered in flies, are outstretched on the bed as if quivering, about to lift in an embrace of welcome. Everywhere, dark, coagulated blood has soaked the figure's clothing, the bedclothes, the bed, the carpet. The rotting smell is overwhelming. The carrion smell. Yet you can't seem to turn away. Whatever has gripped you has not yet released you. The entire room is a crimson wound, a place of the most exquisite mystery, seething with its own inner, secret life. *Your husband* has not died, has not vanished but has been transmogrified into another dimension of being, observing you through a galaxy of tiny unblinking eyes: the buzzing is his voice, multiplied by millions. Flies brush against your face. Flies brush against your lips, your eyelashes. You wave them away, you step forward, to approach the figure on the bed.

My valentine! My love.

Bad Habits

They came for us at school. They didn't explain why. In their faces was the warning *Don't ask!*

Uncle S., Aunt B. Almost we didn't recognize them, their faces were so changed.

Hurriedly they took us from school. In the corridor the principal stood staring. *What is? Family emergency? Why . . . ?*

Adult faces of alarm, disbelief. Adult faces you scrutinize, anxious to know your fate.

A. was the youngest, he tried not to cry. There was T., he was eleven. There was D., thirteen.

Tried. Not. To cry.

Uncle S. was driving. Aunt B. was staring straight ahead.

In the backseat, D. sat between us. D. was our older sister and held our hands tight.

Like in a roller-coaster car, you are strapped in and unable to escape, rising with excruciating slowness to the crest of an impossibly steep hill then plunging down, down, down! Down, down, down! Screaming.

Don't ask! Don't ask!

A. was whimpering and wiping at his nose. A. knew Mother was dead.

T. was staring out the car window. T. believed it had to be Father, they were going to the hospital to see Father who'd had a heart attack at work.

D. shut her eyes. Trying not to think of what awaited us at the house. Trying not to think that the house had probably burned down. Trying not to think that both Mother and Father were probably dead. Trying not to feel a thrill of excitement, how special it would make her at school: an orphan.

In the front seat of the vehicle, Uncle S. and Aunt B. conferred in lowered voices. The words were indistinct but the tone was unmistakable: urgent.

A decision was made. Uncle S. turned onto our street. Except after a few blocks the street was barricaded.

Uncle S. demanded to be let through. Uncle S. showed a police officer his driver's license. Camera flashes were aimed at Uncle S., who held his hand in front of his face. Uncle S. was pleading. Uncle S. spoke in a cracked voice. We heard Uncle S. say *No I am not his brother, I am hers.*

Uncle S. was allowed to drive through the traffic barricade.

Something had happened on our street. Almost you would think there had been a fire or an explosion. Neighbors stood on their lawns shading their eyes, staring. Strangers milled in the street and on sidewalks. There were many uniformed police officers. There were photographers running beside our car. Yellow tape had been posted around our house.

Yellow tape had been posted around our house! Out to the very edge of the grass our father kept trimmed short and free, or almost free, of nasty crabgrass and dandelions. Out to the very edge of our property where there was a three-foot-high chain-link fence that Mother kept mostly covered in climber roses, in the summer.

Our house looked so strange! Yet it was not changed, that we could see.

Everywhere we looked seemed strange. A blinding light of many flash cameras. Strangers' faces like masks of stretched skin. A din of voices, we could not hear.

Aunt B. instructed us *Keep your windows rolled up! Keep your heads down!*

Uncle S. turned the car into our driveway where the strangers were not allowed to follow. Police officers stood on the walk leading to the side door, by the carport. Quickly then, Mother appeared. Quickly then, Mother hurried to the car. Mother was hunched over shielding her face with her hands.

Mother crowded into the backseat with us. Mother lifted A. who was the youngest onto her lap. Uncle S. shut the car door that Mother was too weak to shut. *Take me away! Out of here! Oh god.*

So we knew: what had happened that was bad had happened to Father.

By a circuitous route we were taken to Uncle S. and Aunt B.'s house that was miles away. Yet in the street, on the lawn and in the driveway strangers were already there, waiting.

Reporters. Photographers. TV camera crews. A single police vehicle, parked in the driveway.

There they are! His wife! His children!

Aunt B. began to scream. Uncle S. cursed. In the back seat of the car Mother clutched at us, all three of us, as if trying to shield us even as she buried her tear-streaked face in D.'s hair.

Uncle S. protested the presence of trespassers on his private property but still they came rushing at us. Still they came clamoring after us. The police officers did not seem sympathetic. Mother clutched and pulled at us as we hurried into the house. Already we knew to duck our heads and shield our faces with our hands. Already we knew to run bent over, trying to ignore the cries pitched at us like stones.

Ma'am! Will you say a few—

—your husband innocent, d'you think?

—guilty? Do you think?

—are you surprised?

—did you suspect?

—any hint, in his behavior?

—marital relations . . . ?

Inside the house we hid. We hid upstairs. The windows of the house were always shut. The window blinds were drawn. Always. The house was not safe. Mother lay in bed with the covers over her head. We could hear Mother praying. *Oh God dear God help. Help him, help us. Help this to be a mistake.* Even upstairs the window blinds were drawn always. We hid in our beds. We were not allowed to watch TV. The house wasn't safe. There were strangers on the street. On the street, strangers had a right to congregate. There were television crews: WBEN-TV, WWSB-TV, WTSM-TV. A. could not sleep alone. Yet A. was likely to wet the bed. T. could not sleep. D. could not sleep. We were given food. We were in a room together. We slept like puppies together. We asked where Father was. We were told Father was away. We could hear voices outside the house. A TV helicopter circled overhead. Mother hid beneath the covers. For a long time Mother was silent. Mother began to cry. Mother began to scream. Mother was in a state of shock it was explained.

In a state of shock, poor woman will never recover.

Has got to be a mistake. Could not possibly . . .

Married to the man for fifteen years, what a . . .

. . . silly woman, not to know. Not to suspect.

The children! Think of the children.

Bad Habits' children? Or . . .

We were not allowed to leave the house. We were not allowed to play outside. We were not allowed to return to school. We were told that our presence would be "distracting." We were told that nothing we had done was bad or wrong or nasty or evil but still we were not wanted back at school. Mother made us kneel with her. *Pray! Pray to God for mercy.* D. refused to kneel. D. refused to pray. D. begged to be allowed to return to school. D. had just been elected to the student council when we'd been removed from school. D. had just been elected to represent her eighth-grade homeroom on the student council. D. screamed it was unfair. D. screamed she hated Father. Mother began to tremble. Mother began to shake. Mother had chest pains and could not breathe. Mother was not yet forty years old but had chest pains and could not breathe and had to be taken by ambulance to a hospital. We were not allowed to visit Mother in the hospital. We were not allowed to visit Father at the place he was being kept.

We were taken to another house. We were followed. A WXCT-TV van thundered alongside the vehicle in which we were riding. TV cameras were aimed at us. Bullhorn voices shouted. Microphones were shoved at us. *Were you surprised at your dad's arrest? Do you believe your dad is innocent? Do you love your dad? Was your dad a strict disciplinarian? Will you attend the trial? Do you feel sorry for the strangled children? Do you pray for your dad? Is there a favorite memory you can share with our TV viewers, of your dad?*

We were living now with Grandpa and Grandma. This was a different house in a different city. It was a different time. We had not seen Father in a long time. When we asked about Father we were told *God's will* and *Don't ask!* Mother was with us again. Mother had returned from the hospital. Mother smelled of the hospital. Mother wished to hug and kiss but we shrank away from her. Grandpa and Grandma were Mother's parents. Grandpa and Grandma were very old. Grandpa covered all the windows of the house on the inside with aluminum foil so that strangers could not peek in at us. Grandma drew the blinds down on all the windows. It was never daytime only night. The TV was for adults. The newspaper was for adults. We were taken to church here. We were allowed to go to church here with Grandpa, Grandma and Mother. It was not our old church but the same prayers were said. The same hymns were sung. The same Bible verses were read. The same sermons were preached. In our old church, Father had recently been elected president of the church council. In our new church, the minister prayed for Father and for Father's family. Mother was *the wife of,* we were *the children of.* There were fewer photographers now but still we had to be vigilant, for strangers rushed at us when we least expected them. Grandpa became very angry. Mad as a hornet, Grandma said of him. Grandpa refused to go outside without a hat on his head. Grandpa began to cover his bald, dented head with aluminum foil in the shape of a little cap before he put his hat on to go outside. Grandma kept all the blinds on all the windows drawn. Grandma could no longer knit or crochet for her arthritic hands trembled. Grandma was found wandering in the neighborhood in her nightgown, barefoot. Grandma was heavily medicated for a condition called dyskinesia. We were very embarrassed of Grandpa and Grandma and wished they would die soon. We wished we could move back to our old house and return to our old school like before and maybe what had happened to Father had not happened yet. We wished!

Bad habits. We were acquiring bad habits.

We did not remember Father very clearly. Sometimes entering a room one of us saw his shadow on a wall, looming to the ceiling. Sometimes in the middle of the night one of us heard him prowling downstairs muttering to himself. There was a gassy-bad smell of Father in the upstairs bathroom sometimes. There was a memory of Father in Mother's weepy eyes.

It is all a bad dream, children. A terrible mistake. I pray for this revelation and so should you.

We hated Mother! We loved Mother but could not bear the hospital smell.

We were forbidden knowledge of Father because it would be "too upsetting," "distorted," "exaggerated" for us but of course we came to know certain facts. We knew that Father was frequently on TV and in the newspapers because in all the Midwest no one was more famous than Father. No one was more acknowledged than Father. No one was more talked of, discussed. No one was more prayed-for by Christian congregations. No one was more reviled. When the old people were napping we slipped from the house. Even A., who did not want to be left behind. In the 7-Eleven we stared at newspaper headlines. A tabloid magazine cover. Front-page photographs of

Father who was "Bad Habits." Here was a man we might not have recognized immediately, older than we recalled, unshaven, eyes glittery and shrunken beneath grizzled eyebrows, a downward twist to his rubbery lips like a smile of secret merriment. "BAD HABITS" INDICTED ON 19 COUNTS OF HOMICIDE. ALLEGED SERIAL KILLER STANDS MUTE AT ARRAIGNMENT. 12-YEAR RAMPAGE OF TORTURE, MURDER, TERROR AND TAUNTS BY "BAD HABITS": WHY? UTILITIES WORKER, 53, LONGTIME LOCAL RESIDENT, ARRESTED IN SADISTIC MURDERS. NOTORIOUS "BAD HABITS" REVEALED AS HUSBAND, FATHER OF 3, EX-BOY SCOUT LEADER AND "DEVOUT" CHURCH OF CHRIST MEMBER. Suddenly D. began to laugh. T., who'd been staring with widened eyes, began to laugh. A., who wasn't sure that this was Father anyway, gave a cry of anger and knocked over the newspaper rack sending all the papers flying and we ran out of the store before the astonished clerk could stop us.

Bad habits of that summer.

D., who'd been vain about her hair, began plucking single hairs from her head. One at a time, D. scarcely noticed what she did.

T. began to bite his nails. Thumbnails first, then fingernails. Sometimes in his sleep. Waking to spit out bits of nail. Nasty!

Poor A., the nose-picker. He'd been apt to pick his nose before Bad Habits came into our lives, now his fingernails could not seem to stay away from his face, poking into his nostrils, savaging the soft interior skin of the nostril, provoking nosebleeds.

Prowling the house by night. Prowling the house.

Searching for the room where Father's shadow might be waiting.

Slipping from the house while the adults slept. Rummaging through neighbors' trash. Behind the 7-Eleven.

SERIAL KILLER UNREPENTANT: "GOD'S WILL"?

BAD HABITS HINTS TO POLICE: MORE VICTIMS' BODIES?

DNA MATCH LINKED TO SEMEN AT CRIME SCENES: SEX PERVERT?

There were court hearings. There was to be a trial. Mother was brave and hopeful for she believed, if there was a trial, Father's name (which was our name) would be cleared. *The evil cloud will lift. The nightmare will be over.*

We were made to pray with Mother. We did not expect the nightmare to be over.

We were the children of Bad Habits. For us the mystery was *Why had Father chosen those he'd chosen?*

It was the key to everything! If we could only know *why*.

Yet in secret we liked it, that Father refused to cooperate with his captors. It was said of Bad Habits that he was an "enigma" — "the face of evil." When he was questioned, Bad Habits remained "mute." Bad Habits showed "no remorse." We came to believe that it might be meant for us, the children of Bad Habits, to crack the code of his silence.

A way of Father communicating with us, as he'd rarely done when, in another lifetime it seemed, we had lived together as a family.

Poor Grandpa died of a sudden stroke, the aluminum foil head covering could not save him. Poor Grandma became too infirm and confused to live without nursing care. Mother wept, committing Grandma to a facility. Yet Mother did not despair, blaming Father for the unhappiness visited upon us.

One day, I will bring Grandma home to live with us. One day, your father's name will be cleared.

Mother took us to live in another city, with more distant relatives. Mother was grateful and taught us to be grateful. We would never complain. We would execute our household duties in the home of Uncle G. and Aunt C. as instructed. We would eat meals in the kitchen and clean up after ourselves without fail. D., the eldest, would oversee T. and A., her younger brothers, when Mother was not present. In this new household we were, at the start at least, more hopeful. We did not know that Mother was being assured by the attorney representing Father that a plea of not guilty on all counts was the wisest legal strategy since evidence linking Father to Bad Habits was purely (if massively) circumstantial. We did not know that Mother was being encouraged to hope and to "continually pray" for the best outcome by the minister of our former church and numerous members of the congregation who were stubborn in their belief that Father could not be the man who'd terrorized his hometown intermittently for twelve years. And so we did not know that Mother's optimism, which influenced our own, was perhaps unjustified. We were grateful that in this new household Mother did not monitor us so closely and even spoke, vaguely but enthusiastically, of enrolling us in a local school in the fall.

Still we slept, as restless and agitated as creatures being eaten alive by fleas. Still we slipped from our beds, prowled the nighttime house like feral cats. Dolores, Trevor, Albert: children of Bad Habits.

Dolores wished to believe *We can be like other kids. Nobody knows us here.*

Yet Dolores wished to crack the secret code of Bad Habits's silence. *Why had Father chosen those he'd chosen?*

Trevor and Albert could not assist her much. Trevor maintained a belief that Father maybe wasn't Bad Habits, exactly. Bad Habits was someone who'd taken over Father in some way, like a carjacker? Maybe that was it? Albert was too young to know what to think, what not to think, what was real and what was bad dreams, why poor Albert picked his nose until the nostrils bled, staining his fingers.

Sometimes even Dolores wasn't certain if she was real or (somehow) a girl in others' dreams. In weak moments thinking that now that we were living in Uncle G.'s house, which was a much larger and far airier house than our grandparents' house, we'd become caught up in Uncle G.'s dreams.

Or maybe Father's dreams?

Dolores discovered that the house in which we were now living was approximately three-hundred-fifty miles from the detention facility in which Father was incarcerated. Dolores believed that, by night, thoughts flew more rapidly and more easily across such spaces, than by day.

Bad Habits was a son of the Midwest. The Great Plains. Bad Habits had straddled the Mississippi River in his twelve years of rampage: eleven victims had lived on the east side of the river, eight on the west. Dolores believed *There is meaning in this!* Plucking hairs from her head, anxious and zealous to learn what the meaning might be.

Trevor pointed out that we'd lived on the east side of the Mississippi River and so what? *Like, it was an accident. No big deal.*

It happened that Uncle G., who was a light sleeper, was beginning to be wakened by Bad Habits's children prowling the house by night. Uncle G. wasn't happy with such behavior though Mother tried to explain that we meant no harm, and would not do it any longer. Still it happened, Uncle G. heard creaking on the stairs, footsteps in the downstairs hall. Cautiously he made his way downstairs, switching on a light to expose our furtive, feral-cat faces: *What are you doing awake at this hour? Go back to bed!*

A glisten of fear in Uncle G.'s eyes.

Father's shadow had not yet appeared in Uncle G.'s house. We could not find it and did not wish to find it, yet felt the compulsion to search.

It was summer. There was no school. We were not such freaks to be home all the time while other children were in school. We worked hard — very hard! — even Albert, who was small boned for his age, and tired easily — at our household tasks, and ate all our meals in the kitchen and cleaned up after ourselves tidy as hungry mice, yet we began to hear Aunt C. complain of us to Mother behind closed doors.

Your children. Bad habits. Can't you control?

Mother came to us, wept over us. Mother embraced us, kissed us, prayed *Jesus let my children be spared. Help my children to be good. Jesus come into their hearts, save them from sinful ways.* Mother smelled of something ashy and harsh, not the hospital any longer but a smell to make our nostrils pinch.

Sometimes, seeing our eyes on her, staring at the wild-haired, stark-eyed wraith-woman she'd become, Mother gave a little cry of hurt and seized our shoulders in her talon-fingers, shook shook shook us until our teeth rattled in our heads.

Bad! How dare you! This is a test God has put us to.

Our bad habits began to run together. In the way of our dreams running together. For it happened, Trevor picked his nose as well as bit his fingernails. Dolores bit her nails as well as plucked at her hair. Albert began to bite his nails, pluck hairs from his head, leak urine into his bedsheets even as, helplessly, he picked his nose until the tender nostrils bled.

It began to happen that in one of the upstairs bathrooms a faint gassy-bad odor began to be detected. Against the far wall of a room entered without caution, a man's shadow looming to the ceiling began to appear.

Dolores hid away. Dolores drew up lists. While her brothers played in the backyard, kicking a soccer ball, imitating the actions of normal boys by running and squealing like deranged little dogs, Dolores printed columns of names in her school notebook. Thinking *I will be the one to break Bad Habits's code.*

None of us could recall Father very clearly now. Before Bad Habits.

Gloating, Dolores thought *I will see Father, and tell him: that I know why. Only me!*

But when Mother went to visit Father in the detention facility, none of us were allowed to accompany her. Not even Dolores, who was thirteen years old and tall for her age.

Not yet! Soon. In her promises Mother was distracted and flurried. Since Mother was too nervous to fly, or to take public transportation, Uncle G. volunteered to drive her, but did not wish to see Father himself.

Descending the stairs with her suitcase, which she insisted on carrying herself, Mother slipped, twisted her ankle and nearly fell headlong down a half-dozen steps. *Oh! Oh!* Mother cried like a wounded bird. But she quickly recovered.

When Mother returned from the visit, exhausted and unsteady on her feet, she pushed past us without a word, hurried upstairs and locked herself in her room. Uncle G. refused to speak of the visit. Consequently we learned from eavesdropping on the adults that Mother had not been able to speak with Father for Father had been "distant," "cold." We learned, too, the shocking news that Father's attorney was entering a plea for him of not guilty by reason of insanity, which was an admission of guilt and which could not possibly be true, for Father was not insane.

Just stunned by circumstances, overwhelmed and confused, Mother believed. Like all of us.

We were incensed. Even Albert, who scarcely recalled Father any longer. *Our father is not insane!*

A half mile from Uncle G.'s house was a municipal park. Part of the park was playing fields, picnic groves, wood-chip trails. A larger part of the park was a wetlands nature sanctuary covering several hundred acres, much of which was wild, teeming with birds, insects, snakes. Trevor's nails were bitten down into the flesh of his fingertips, which made nose-picking arduous and exasperating, and so distended were his nostrils, he shrank from seeing his reflection in the mirror. Trevor drifted into the park dreaming of how he would lose himself in the wetlands and never be found until his bones were picked clean and white by vultures. Thinking vaguely *He will be sorry then. For what he has done to us.*

It wasn't clear whom Trevor meant. In fact Trevor had drifted beyond the access road to the nature sanctuary and was squatting in the grass watching boys playing soccer a short distance away on an open stretch of land. Next day, Trevor returned. And the next day. The boys were Trevor's age and a little older. They were husky rowdy energetic boys who shouted as they kicked the soccer ball from one end of the playing field to the other, laughing and cursing in imitation of older adolescents. They began to be aware of Trevor watching in yearning. Suddenly Trevor was astonished by jeering voices *Your father is a bad man! Go back to hell where you came from!*

Trevor stayed away from the park for several days. When he returned, the boys were waiting for him. Ambushing him with pebbles, sharp stones. Rushing at him shouting *Freak! Freak! Go back to hell!* and Trevor turned to run, struck on the back, on the side of the head, bleeding from a cut over his eye.

A strange comfort in this, Trevor realized. To know that you are hated, ostracized utterly. And nothing you can do about it.

Why? Why? was a question for Trevor to ponder more frequently, in the oblivion of summer.

Mother was nearly recovered from her nervous collapse after the visit to Father. Mother was determined to take us on nature outings. Long ago before she'd met Father and had what she called "my babies" she'd been an avid bird-watcher with friends who rose early, tramped in marshy places to see migrating birds through binoculars. Several times that summer Mother led us on nature walks into the wetlands but our outings ended disappointingly soon, for Mother tired easily and we were moody, sullen, anxious and distracted by our bad habits of picking, biting, plucking at ourselves, which followed us everywhere we went, like frantic shadows.

Yet again, Trevor returned to the park. To the soccer playing field. The boys were astonished and outraged to see him, squatting in the grass as before. When they ran at him, Trevor rose in a crouch and threw a jagged chunk of concrete the size of a hubcap at the nearest boy. Fortunately, the concrete struck the boy's shoulder and not his jeering face where Trevor had aimed.

A shriek of pain, a trickle of bright blood. *Now you know* Trevor laughed.

Hiding in the basement of Uncle G.'s house. Behind the furnace until a patrolman came to the front door with a warrant from juvenile court for Trevor's arrest.

Bad boy! Bad habits.

Some days, Dolores believed she was close to cracking the code.

Other days, Dolores despaired of ever cracking the code.

In secret, Dolores had assembled the names of Bad Habits's (known, alleged) victims. These she listed in columns. Her notebook was filled with columns. Where before she'd become the daughter of Bad Habits, Dolores had had little time for intellectual pursuits, hadn't been a particularly thoughtful or sensitive girl, certainly not a girl to ponder the inscrutable motives of others, now Dolores spent most of her time alone, brooding. Tirelessly she printed columns of names in her notebook, always in new arrangements. The first had been a column simply listing names of victims in the chronological order of their deaths, dating back to August 1993 and ending in March 2005:

Suzanne Landau	Melissa Patch
Tracey Abrams	Alice Taub
Duane Fitch	Carrie Miller
Gladys Zelmer	Sallie Miller
Eli Nazarene	Dennis Miller
Willis Rodman	Bobbie Dix
Donna May Emory	Allan Sturman
Alfred Myers	Molly Sturman
Thomas Flaxman	Ginny Hahn
Steven Etchinson	

Other columns reflected alphabetical order, names in ascending order of ages (youngest seven months, oldest sixty-two years), means of death (strangulation, stabbing, "blunt force trauma"), whether singly or with other victims, whether indoors or outdoors, distance from our house (the farthest was ten miles, the nearest only a few doors away on our side of the street), which side of the Mississippi River, months of the year, days of the week and so forth.

Some of her findings Dolores shared with Trevor. For Trevor, too, yearned to know *Why?*

It was maddening to us how the media continued to report that police could discover "no logic" to Bad Habits's actions and deemed him "senseless," "randomly vicious." There was heated debate in the media about Bad Habits's alleged insanity. We did not accept it that Father was insane as we did not accept it that Father had led an "ordinary," "average," "Midwestern small city" existence, though we could not have said what Father's truer life had been.

In our church it was said *The kingdom of God is within.*

In the public world, Father was a man named Benjamin S. Haslet Jr. He was fifty-three, five foot nine, weighed one-hundred-eighty pounds. He had been a "competent" public utilities worker, a "devout" member of the local Church of Christ, a former Boy Scout leader, a husband, father. Sources not wishing to be named spoke of his reputation for being "difficult to know," "withdrawn," "minding his own business." Dolores twined single pieces of hair around her fingers and plucked them from her scalp that was reddened and stinging. Coin-sized bald spots glimmered through what remained of her hair. She'd begun to wear a scarf over her head when she left the house but for days at a time Dolores didn't leave the house, preferring to brood over her notebook, neatly recopying, reprinting columns of the names of Bad Habits's (known, alleged) victims, in ever new arrangements.

At last, in the waning days of summer, we were taken to visit Father!

Remember to look hopeful, children. Smile at Father all you can.

There was to be no trial after all. Father had pleaded guilty. Father was now in a maximum security prison for men in the southern part of the state, less than two-hundred miles from Uncle G.'s house.

It was believed that Father's attorney had coerced him into pleading guilty to nineteen counts of homicide and to providing the police with names and descriptions of other victims for which Bad Habits had not claimed credit, dating to January 1988, in exchange for a sentence of life imprisonment instead of death by lethal injection. Everyone who knew Father believed this, or nearly everyone. Mother insisted he'd pleaded guilty to bring the tragic case to a close. To bring peace to the survivors of the victims. *But one day Father's name will be cleared. I know this.*

We were excited about seeing Father but we were anxious and frightened, too. Our bad habits kept us sleepless for nights in succession and by the time we arrived at the prison we resembled scrawny plucked chickens. Mother nudged us to smile and wave at the nearly bald middle-aged man on the other side of a Plexiglas partition, though our eyes so stung with tears we could barely make out his features. Of our months of nightmare dreams this was the strangest, as it was the one we could not have predicted: this vast noisy room with a high ceiling in which ugly iron beams were visible as in the underside of a bridge. The space was the size of a school gymnasium and noisy as a cave in which voices echo, re-echo and are magnified. We could not have anticipated so many visitors. Nearly all were women and children. There were vending machines near the entrance to the room, and these were popular. There were many guards. The inmates wore khaki-colored prison uniforms and those with hair had short, shorn haircuts. Mostly they were younger than Father by many years. Few wore eyeglasses like Father. They were not unusual-looking men. They were men you would see anywhere. Father was one of these except older and quieter. The way Father's mouth drooped, it did not look like a mouth that uttered words with much ease. Mother could not speak directly with Father but over a phone. Though we were only a few feet from Father, we had to speak with him over a phone. As Mother spoke in her animated, eager way we saw Father's eyes drift from her and onto us with a look of vague surprise and discomfort. As if he'd forgotten who we were! For months Father had had no word for us, his children. It had never been suggested that we might speak with him on the phone. Mother had conveyed to us Father's words for us: *I love you* and *God's will be done*. Even Albert had wondered if these were Father's authentic words.

Tabloid photographs of Bad Habits exuded an air of mystery and dread, for the notorious serial killer had appeared larger than life, covering an entire page. His forehead had appeared high and glaring with a kind of menacing light and his sunken eyes were "piercing." In person, Father was one of the less clearly defined inmates in the room. Mother did most of the talking, for Father had little to say. As at home Father had frequently murmured and grunted in a vague response to Mother's conversation, so in prison. Mother had aged a decade in the past several months yet bravely she'd dressed as if for Sunday, in cheerful colors. With a shaky hand she'd applied a mascara brush to her eyelashes and her tremulous mouth was a pert coral pink. Mother's eyes snatched at Father's through the Plexiglas partition but Father's eyes did not seek out hers. Though Father's chest hunched inward he'd gained weight in his midriff, which looked bloated, and there was a settled, fleshy contentment to him we had not recalled. His skin was the hue of faded parchment. A coarse gray stubble glinted on his jaws. Twists and clumps of loose skin hung beneath Father's chin. Behind his glasses, his eyes were shrunken and without luster, lightly threaded with blood. His nose was larger than we recalled, like a putty nose, with a filigree of broken capillaries. In the car on our drive to the prison Dolores had whispered to us her theory of why Bad Habits had killed the individuals he'd allegedly killed: the secret was that certain of the victims corresponded to us and to Mother. For instance, one of the first victims was named Gladys, which was Mother's middle name; and another of the victims had the surname Miller, which resembled Mother's maiden name, Muller. Another of the female victims had been thirty-nine at the time of her death, which had been Mother's age at that exact time. There had been a nine-year-old boy killed in a particularly savage assault at the time Trevor had just turned nine. There was a child Allan, who corresponded with Albert. Clearly, Dolores was mirrored in Donna and Duane. Tracey and Thomas were obvious matches for Trevor. Bad Habits had the identical initials as Benjamin Haslet! Here was the elaborate yet utterly simple answer to

Why? But the man in the baggy prison uniform, shoulders slumped and chest collapsing into his belly, bored gaze drifting past our heads, did not seem capable of such complex calculations. He did not seem capable of any of the acts of Bad Habits. He appeared distracted, like one who wishes to return to watching TV. Mother's eyes shone with tears. Impulsively, though perhaps it was a premeditated gesture, Mother brought her fingertips to her lips and pressed them against the Plexiglas at about the level of Father's downturned mouth. Mother now alarmed us by handing the phone to Dolores, who fumbled to take the receiver from her and could only mumble inaudible words. Next, Mother handed the receiver to Trevor, who mumbled similarly inaudible words, and next the receiver was held out to Albert, who shrank from it with a look of terror. An expression of annoyance flickered in Father's face, but he said nothing. He seemed now to know us, at least to know who we were in relationship to him. He might have said *A man's seed is sucked from him, to take root where it will.* But he did not, for Mother was weeping now, saying *One day your name will be cleared, Benjamin. I know this. I have faith.* Before we left, Mother insisted that we all kneel in prayer. Father took his time kneeling, for his knees were stiff. Mother led us in the Our Father. Our lips moved numbly. A yawn played about Father's lips and his eyelids drooped with a peculiar sort of contentment. Bad Habits was no more. Father was no more. Inmate Benjamin Haslet Jr. would spend the remainder of his life in a segregated unit of the prison facility. Three times a day he would receive meals on a tray shoved through a narrow slot in his cell door. He would eat, he would sleep. He would watch TV, he would read his Bible. He would be visited by the prison chaplain who would pray with him. All that he'd done had been taken from him. He'd been a younger man, but no more. *No reason. There was none. Something to do with my hands. A hobby. A test for God. If He was watching.* As we left the visiting room we turned to look back but already Father was being escorted away by a guard, his back to us.

We moved from our uncle's house but remained in the area. Within a few months, Mother would change our family name. We would not see Father again. One autumn morning Mother roused us early, to hike with her in the nature sanctuary. Birds were migrating. Warblers, robins, red-winged blackbirds. Trees quivered with the poised bodies of hundreds of starlings. There was a harsh smell of brackish water, organic rot. There were mudflats where turtles sunned themselves. There were shore birds picking in the mud. There were dragonflies, butterflies drifting like the most random of thoughts. Mother had discovered a trail through the wetlands. It was hardly more than a deer path but it was a trail. *There is another side* Mother said. *We can get to the other side.* We began our hike through the marsh. We hiked through the marsh.

Feral

1.

She was a good mother. Always she'd been a good mother. She had loved her son. She would not cease loving him. Only those few minutes she'd been distracted. Only seconds!

2.

The child was six years, three months old when what happened to him, happened.

Derek was healthy, big boned and inclined to fleshiness, with a soft rubbery feel to his fair skin that had given him the look, when younger, of a large, animated doll. His hair was silky brown and his moist warm brown eyes blinked frequently. His smile was sweet, tentative. He'd been named Derek (for his mother's now-deceased father), which didn't at all suit him, so his parents began calling him Derrie from the start—"Derrie-darling," "Derrie-berry," "Derrie-sweet." He had the petted, slightly febrile look of an only child whose development, weekly, if not daily, is being lovingly recorded in a series of albums. Yet, surprisingly, he wasn't at all spoiled. His mother had had several miscarriages preceding his birth and by the age of thirty-nine when he was finally born, she joked about being physically exhausted, emptied out, "eviscerated." It was a startling, extreme figure of speech but she spoke with a wan smile, not in complaint so much as in simple admission; and her husband kissed and comforted her as they lay together in their bed by lamplight, reluctant to switch off the light because then they wouldn't be able to see their baby sleeping peacefully in his crib close by. "God, yes, I feel the same way," her husband said. "Our one big beautiful baby is more than enough, isn't he?"

And so, for more than six years, he was.

3.

If he would see me again. If his eyes would see me.

If he would recognize me: I am your child, born of your body, of the love of you and Daddy.

If he would tell me: Mommy, I love you!

They were devoted parents, not young but certainly youthful, vigorous. They were Kate and Stephen Knight and they lived in the village of Hudson Ridge, an hour's drive north of New York City on the Palisades Parkway. Hudson Ridge, like other suburban communities along the river, was an oasis of tranquil, tree-lined residential streets, custom-built houses set in luxuriously deep, spacious wooded lots. At the core of the village was a downtown of several blocks and a small train depot built to resemble a gazebo. The Hudson

River was visible from the ridge, reflecting a steely blue on even overcast days. But there were few overcast days in Hudson Ridge. This was an idyllic community, resolutely *non-urban*: its most prestigious roads, lanes, circles were unpaved. Black swans with red bills paddled languidly on its mirror-smooth lake amid a larger, looser flotilla of white geese and mallards. Kate and Stephen had lived in New York City, where they'd worked for eight years, before Derek was born; determined that this pregnancy wouldn't end in heartbreak like the others, Kate had quit her job with an arts foundation, and she and Stephen had moved to Hudson Ridge — "Not just to escape the stress of the city, but for the baby's sake. It seems so unfair to subject a child to New York." They laughed at themselves mouthing such pieties in the cadences of those older, status-conscious suburban couples they'd once mocked, and felt so superior to — yet what they said, what they believed, was true. In the past decade, the city had become impossible. The city had become prohibitively expensive, and the city had become prohibitively dangerous. Their child would be spared apartment living in a virtual fortress, being shuttled by van to private schools, being deprived of the freedom to roam a back-yard, a grassy park, neighborhood playgrounds.

So ironic, so bitter! — that it should happen to him here.

In Hudson Ridge, where children are safe.

In the members-only Hudson Ridge Community Center.

4.

Had there been any premonition, any forewarning? The Knights were certain there had been none.

Derek—Derrie—was very well liked by his first-grade classmates, particularly the little girls. He was the most mild-mannered and cheerful of children. At an age when some boys begin to be rowdy, prone to shouting and roughhousing, Derek was inclined to shyness with strangers and most adults, even with certain of his classmates, and older children. As a student he wasn't outstanding, but "so eager, optimistic," as his teacher described him, "he's a joy to have in the class-room." Derek was never high-strung or moody like his more precocious classmates, nor restless and rebellious like the less gifted. He was never jealous. Despite his size, he wasn't pushy or aggressive. If at recess on the playground other, older boys were cruel to weaker children, Derek sometimes tried to in-tervene. At such times he was stammering, tremulous, clumsy, his skin rosily mottled and his eyelashes bright with tears. Yet he was usually effective—if pushed, shoved, punched, jeered at, he wouldn't back down. His flushed face might shine with tears but he rarely cried and would insist afterward that he hadn't done anything special, really. Nor would he tattle on the troublemakers. Almost inaudibly he'd murmur, ducking his head, "I don't know who it was, I didn't see." His first-grade teacher told Kate that Derek possessed, rare among children his age, and among boys of any age, a "natural instinct" for jus-tice and empathy. "His face shines so, sometimes—he's like a baby Buddha."

Kate reported this to Stephen and they laughed together, though somewhat uneasily. Baby Buddha? Their little Derrie, only six years old? Kate shivered, there was something about this she didn't like. But Stephen said, "It's remarkable praise. No teacher of mine would have said such a thing about me, ever. Our sweet little Derrie who had so much trouble learning to tie his shoelaces—an incarnation of the Buddha!" They joked about whose genetic lineage must have been responsible, his or hers.

Yet it worried Kate sometimes that Derek was in fact so placid, amenable, good-natured. Just as he'd begun to sleep through an entire night of six, seven, eight hours while in his first months, so he seemed, at times, dreamy, precociously indifferent to other children taking advantage of him. "It doesn't matter, Mommy, I don't care," Derek insisted, and clearly this was so, but was it normal? At games, Derek didn't care much about winning, and so he rarely won. If he ran and shouted, it seemed to be in mimicry of other boys. Watching him trot after them, eager as a puppy, Kate felt her heart swoon with love of her sweet, vulnerable child. *My own heart, exposed. My baby-love.* She perceived that Derek would require protection throughout his life and it was her innocent maternal vanity to believe that so good, so radiant, so special, so blessed a being would naturally draw love to him; and this love, like a mantle of the gods, shimmering gold, would be his protection.

5.

Yet what happened to Derek happened so swiftly and mysteriously that no one, it seemed, could have protected him. Not even Kate who was less than thirty feet away.

"The accident"—it would be called.

"The accident in the pool"—as if amplification were needed.

How many times Kate would repeat in her numbed, disbelieving voice, "I'd been watching Derek, of course. Without staring at him every moment, of course. And then, when I looked — he was floating facedown in the water."

Kate had brought Derek to swim in the children's pool at the Hudson Ridge Community Center as she did frequently during the summer. The warm, sunny July morning had been like any other, she'd had no premonition that anything out of the ordinary would be happening, and the accident would never have happened if there hadn't been, purely by chance, another commotion in the pool at the same time: a nervous, tearful, ten-year-old girl, the daughter of friends of the Knights, had jumped off the end of the diving board and gotten water up her nose and was crying and thrashing about, and the life-guard had hurried into the water to comfort her, though she wasn't in any danger of drowning; Kate, too, had hurried to the edge of the pool to watch, her attention focused on this minor incident, and on the attention of other mothers at pool-side; whatever happened to Derek, at the opposite end of the pool, had passed unnoticed. Derek had been swimming, or rather paddling, in his not-very-coordinated way, in water to his waist, and (this might have happened: it was a theory Kate would not wish to explore, lacking proof) an older boy, or boys (who'd bullied Derek in the past, in the pool) might have pushed him under, not meaning to seriously injure him (of course, Kate had to believe this: how could she face the boys' mothers otherwise?) and he'd panicked and swallowed water, flailed about desperately and swallowed more water, and (in theory, it hurt too much to wish to believe this) the boy, or boys, had continued to hold his head under water until (how many hellish seconds might have passed? ten? fifteen?)

he'd lost consciousness. His lungs filled with chlorine-treated water, he began to sink, taking in more water, breathing in water, beginning to drown, *beginning to die.*

The boy, or boys, who'd done this to Derek, if they'd done it (Kate had no proof, no one would offer proof, Derek would never make any accusation), were at least ten feet away from him when Kate saw him floating facedown in the glittering aqua water, his pale brown hair lifting like seaweed, shoulders and back several inches below the surface. "Derek! Derek!" — she ran blindly to leap into the pool and pull at his limp body, desperately lifting his head so that he could breathe: but he wasn't breathing. His eyes were partly open but unfocused, his little body was strangely heavy. She was hearing a woman's screams — hysterical, crazed. At once the lifeguard blew his whistle, came to haul the unconscious child up onto the tile and began immediately to apply mouth-to-mouth resuscitation; but Derek didn't begin to breathe, and didn't begin to breathe; Kate stood, dripping wet, staring down at the pale, unresisting body that was her son, her Derek, uncomprehending, as if she'd been struck a violent blow on the head yet hadn't fallen, her eyes open, stricken with disbelief. *This can't be happening. This is not happening. This is not real.* Then she was being helped, stumbling and sobbing, into the rear of an ambulance. One of the paramedics, a red-haired girl who looked hardly older than sixteen, was comforting her, calling her Mrs. Knight. They were speeding to a hospital in the next suburb, *and Derek died, in the ambulance he died, heart ceased to beat* yet in the emergency room Derek was resuscitated, heart galvanized into beating again, and he began again to breathe, it would be said *He was saved! Brought back to life.*

Kate had had no time to assimilate either of these facts. The first, that Derek had died, she would see (she would be made to see, by Stephen) was absurd and illogical; he'd ceased breathing temporarily, and his heart had ceased beating temporarily, but he hadn't *died*. It was the second, that he'd been saved by medical technology, "brought back to life," that she would focus on; everyone would focus on, her husband, their families, relatives, friends; for this was the truer of the two facts, the more logical, reasonable.

6.

"Your son will assimilate the accident into his life, as healthy children do. He's made a complete physical recovery and he'll begin to forget the trauma if you don't give him cause to remember" — so Kate and Stephen were advised by the emergency room physician who'd saved Derek's life, and whose special practice was, in fact, crisis medicine. Of course they saw the wisdom in what the man said.

Stephen believed they shouldn't speak of the accident to Derek at all unless he brought up the subject. Kate wondered if that might be too extreme — "What if he dreams about it? Has nightmares? We can't pretend it didn't happen." Stephen said, "We won't pretend anything. We'll let Derek lead the way."

Since the accident, Kate noticed that Stephen called the boy Derek, in a faltering voice, as if the very name hurt him to utter. Kate, by contrast, had to suppress emotion when she spoke of Derrie, and when she spoke to him; she was always being surprised when she saw him, for she'd somehow imagined him much younger, frailer. It was an effort for her to realize that he wasn't four years old any longer, or three — he was six, and husky for his age. She didn't dare hug him as desperately as she wished, a dozen times a day, for the doctor had counseled against this, and Derek himself gave no sign of welcoming it; since coming home from the hospital, he was quiet, subdued, withdrawn. "I'm okay, Mommy," he told her, not meeting her anxious gaze. And, "Mommy, I hated that water anyway."

When Stephen was home, Kate managed quite well with Derek, she believed. But when they were alone together, as they frequently were, she had to resist the almost physical craving to grasp him in her arms and burst into tears. *My baby. My darling. I love you. I would die in your place. Oh forgive me!* For she couldn't shake off the conviction that the boy knew very well how his mother was responsible, however indirectly, for what had happened in the pool.

What had almost happened in the pool.

It was a jarring surprise to Kate to learn, belatedly, that Derek hadn't liked the pool — he'd "hated" it. Naively she'd believed he'd loved it, as the other children did; though, looking back, she recalled how shy he'd been at first of wading out into water that came to his knees, how slow to play in it, splashing like other, younger children, as if in imitation of "having fun." *He'd tried to like the pool, the Community Center, for my sake. That's it.* A wave of shame swept over Kate. She would never tell Stephen this. How she'd been blind to her own son's dislike for the water, for the rowdy companionship of other boys in the water; how selfish she'd been, basking in the privileged atmosphere of the Hudson Ridge Community Center, which was easily the equivalent of an affluent suburban country club, where she could swim herself if she wished, play tennis, visit with her women friends. Not seeing how her six-year-old son was vulnerable to hurt as an exposed heart.

She told Derek he didn't have to go back—"Not ever, honey."

Stooping to kiss his forehead. (He didn't seem to want to be kissed on, or near, his mouth.)

Recalling with horror that crazed scream. A woman's scream—hers. Echoing continuously in her ears, when she paused to listen. She wondered if Derek, though unconscious, lying on his back on wet tiles, had heard it. *Yes of course. He heard. He knows.* For that was what death must be: raw, shrieking, confused, violent. Not peaceful at all.

7.

Days passed. A week. Two weeks. Since what had almost happened hadn't happened.

Derek was pale, quiet, subdued—"not himself" yet. The slightest noise from outdoors or in the house made him jump like a startled animal, his eyelids fluttering, his small body going rigid. His eyes were continually moving, shifting in their sockets. His breathing was quick and shallow, his skin appeared hot. He couldn't settle down to read, to play with one of his games, to watch a video—if Kate entered a room, he soon slipped from it noiselessly. He didn't seem to be hiding in the house, yet—where was he? Kate was forever trailing about calling, "Derrie? Sweetie?" in a calm, cheery voice that betrayed none of the anxiety she felt. Fortunately, Stephen knew little of this. Stephen was away most of the day, didn't return home until early evening weekdays, when Derek made an effort, or so it seemed to Kate, to be more normal. Yet even at these times he didn't like to be touched. As if being touched hurt his sensitive skin. As if being kissed was repugnant. Kate had an idea, a wild and unsubstantiated idea, that Derek feared his parents' mouths — he stared at them, at their mouths, or so it seemed to her, with a look of apprehension. "Honey? What's wrong?" she asked, in her most matter-of-fact voice. Invariably, Derek would shrug and shake his head. He might mumble, "Nothing." Or, irritably, "Mommy, I'm okay."

Kate's heart ached, regarding her son. Whatever had happened to him? Wherever, in those few minutes his heart had stopped, had he gone? That place he'd gone to, no one else could follow him. She heard again that terrified and terrifying scream — her own. Sometimes, alone in the house, when Derek was in the backyard, Kate jammed a towel against her mouth and screamed, screamed. *No! No! Don't let my son die.* She believed that this initial response, raw, anguished, primitive, was the natural response; behaving normally — as if nothing had happened, or almost happened — would be unnatural. Of course, she told Stephen nothing of this. He wasn't one to dwell on the past in any negative way.

He'd never reproached Kate for not having seen Derek slipping, or being pushed, underwater. He'd never reproached Kate for almost allowing their son to drown in three feet of water.

We'll let Derek lead the way.

Kate understood that this was wisdom. A vigorous, healthy-minded male wisdom. Yet sometimes, as Derek's mother, she couldn't resist feeling such emotion, she was left shaken, bereft. For she'd lost her little boy, after all. Where Derek had been so warm, spontaneous, quivering with energy before the accident, pushing himself into her arms to be hugged and

kissed, affectionate as a puppy, now he was stiff, watchful, unsmiling. Had he forgotten how to smile? Was it too much effort
to smile? The very posture of his little body communicated
Don't! Don't touch. He'd lost weight, those extra ounces that
had filled out his face, now his face was angular, his jaw more
pronounced. And those restless, shifting eyes. "Won't you look
at me, Derrie? Is something wrong?" Kate spoke with innocent
maternal concern, smiling. If she was frightened she gave no
sign. Gently, she grasped Derek's shoulders and squatted before
him as she'd done hundreds of times in the past and she saw that
he was staring at her now, as if without recognition; his eyes
were so dilated, the pupils so starkly black, bleeding out into the
iris, she shuddered, thinking *These are an animal's eyes.*

As if reading her thoughts, Derek shrugged out of her
grasp. He was breathing quickly, shallowly. He muttered, his
lips curling back from his teeth, "I'm *okay,* I *said.*"

He ran out of the kitchen, and out of the house. One of his
hiding places was somewhere beyond the garage, in a tangle of
briars and wild shrubs that bled out, unfenced, into a wooded
area owned by the township, where there was no path. Kate
was left behind in her awkward squat, legs aching, eyes stinging with tears. *But I'm your mother. I'm Mommy. I love you. You
love me. You've always loved me. You have to love me!*

8.

After the initial flurry of concerned calls from family, friends,
neighbors, the Knights' telephone was silent. Kate, who'd always been sociable, no longer had the energy to call her women
friends. For she would have had to rehearse her words to get

them just right. "Yes, what a shock it was! But it's over now, Derek is fine. He'll be back swimming before long, you know how boys are, he'd only just swallowed some water, thank God we live where we do and the ambulance arrived within minutes and there was never any real danger." No, she hadn't the energy.

When Kate asked Derek which of his friends he'd like to play with so that she could make arrangements with their mothers, as she usually had, Derek shrugged and said he didn't want to play with anyone. Kate said, "Not even with Molly? Sam? Susan?"—naming his closest little friends, but Derek impatiently shook his head no. He turned to walk away from Kate without a backward glance and she would have called after him except she feared rejection.

Except she feared his eyes: so dilated, a glassy, impersonal black.

He doesn't recognize me, really. Unless I speak to him, touch him. Force myself upon him as his keeper.

Unbelievable that, only a few weeks ago, that child had so often run laughing into her arms, saying, "I love you, Mommy! I love you, Mommy!" It was as if in fact he'd died, the child Derrie had died, and this other being had taken his place, a stranger.

But this was nonsense, of course. Wasn't it?

Kate dared not speak of such a notion to Stephen, who continued stubbornly to behave as if what had almost happened hadn't happened. That was Stephen's way: he wouldn't have succeeded so definitively, and at so relatively young an age, in his Wall Street brokerage house if he'd been less decisive, ambivalent. When he returned home from New York in the early evening he wanted peace, he wanted domestic family happiness of the kind to which he, like Kate, had become unknowingly addicted; in his expensive wool-silk suit he'd drop to one knee, arms outstretched, and cry out to Derek, "How's my boy? How's my big boy?" Stephen's face crinkled in fatherly ebullience and his voice was loud, like a TV turned up high. From an adjoining room, Kate flinched to see how Derek stiffened at his greeting, where once he'd rushed to throw himself into his daddy's arms and be lifted into the air like a Ferris wheel. Now Derek looked not at Stephen exactly but in Stephen's direction, head turned away, eyes shifting in their sockets, with the wariness of a cornered wild animal. Yet Stephen persisted, "How's my Derrie-boy?" The quieter and more reluctant Derek was to be wooed, the more determined was Stephen to behave as if nothing was wrong, seeking out the boy to hug, forcibly if need be, and kiss, and fuss over, like any loving daddy returning home eager to see his little boy. Until one evening, Kate, in the kitchen, heard what sounded like a scuffle, a child's cry and Stephen's louder, sharper cry, and when she ran to investigate, Derek had fled outside and Stephen, white-faced, incredulous, still squatting, was staring at his right forefinger, which was oozing blood — "He bit me. He bit me to the bone."

9.

"He isn't the same child. He isn't Derrie."

"Don't be absurd. You're becoming morbid-minded. He's still in a state of shock."

"He isn't. You've seen his eyes. He bit you."

"He reacted without thinking. It was a reflex."

"An animal reflex."

Stephen was silent. Of course, he'd seen those eyes. It was all they saw now, in the child's presence or in his absence: those eyes.

Staring, implacable, unreadable, nonhuman eyes. Grotesquely dilated, even in daylight. A horror in such eyes.

I don't know you. I don't love you. You are nothing to me.

10.

That Saturday they took Derek to the Hudson Ridge pediatrician who'd been treating him for years, since babyhood, and the man examined Derek and could find nothing wrong with him, and it did seem, in the examining room, that Derek was more cooperative than usual. Though he shrank from being touched, and resisted looking into the doctor's eyes, and responded only laconically to the man's friendly queries. But his eyes appeared less dilated and his pulse and blood pressure, the doctor said, were normal. The Knights didn't tell him about Stephen's bitten finger, about which Stephen in particular felt shame, nor did they tell him what a difficult time they'd had that morning getting Derek into the car.

Like bringing an anxious dog or cat to the vet, Kate thought.

Stephen's bitten finger, which had given him a good deal of stabbing, worrisome pain, had been treated by another doctor, a stranger, to whom he'd explained the circumstances of the biting with some embarrassment. After a week of antibiotics, Stephen's finger was healing and Stephen refused to discuss it with Kate but, as Derek's daddy, he'd learned not to forcibly embrace his son and smother him with kisses as in the old days.

In private, Derek's pediatrician asked his parents if Derek ever spoke of almost drowning, and they said no, never; and if he dreamed of it, or had nightmares, they weren't aware. Kate said, with a brave smile, "He's changed, as you can see. He seems older. More self-contained. Not a little boy anymore." Stephen said quickly, edging out Kate, as if fearing she might say too much, and too emotionally, "My impression is, he's forgotten. Children don't dwell on the past. He seems to have outgrown lots of things this summer — games we used to play together, habits of speaking, behaving. Of course, he's growing. He'll soon be seven. He isn't a baby any longer." Stephen spoke with the air of one confirming a principle: Derek's strange coolness toward his parents was to be interpreted as something positive, a sign of health, growth. Kate listened and made no comment. She suspected that the pediatrician knew more or suspected more than he was willing to say; but he wasn't willing to say it; nor were Derek's parents willing to hear it; the visit would end with friendly handshakes, as always. Two days later a nurse called from the pediatrician's office to report cheerfully that Derek's lab tests were all negative, and Kate said brightly, "What good news. Thanks!"

Perhaps that was all it required, then, to be a happy, normal mother: to behave as if one were a happy, normal mother. As if there were no reason to behave otherwise.

11.

Stephen conceded: "When Derek returns to school, he'll be more himself, I'm sure. The summer has just been too long for him."

For the first time in years, the Knights hadn't traveled in August to either Colorado or Maine, to stay with relatives. They'd reasoned that the commotion of travel, the busy, bustling atmosphere of households including other children, would have been upsetting for Derek just then. Neither wished to think that Derek's presence, in the midst of other, normal children, would have been deeply distressing to everyone. Neither wished to think that Derek would have resisted their efforts to travel together, as he resisted their efforts to interest him in brief outings and excursions close to home. He preferred to be alone, in his room with the door shut (but not locked: Derek's door had no lock) or, more often, outside. Where he might wander back into the woods, increasingly out of the range of Kate's strained voice. "Derrie? Derrie? *Derek?*"

In time, Derek drifted home of his own accord, when he wished. Wherever Kate might search for him, he wasn't; where Kate didn't think to look, he'd suddenly appear. Often he came up behind her in the house, noiselessly, and she gave a cry of alarm, turning to see him. He almost smiled at Mommy's alarm. *Those eyes. Feral eyes. He doesn't know me.* It seemed to Kate that Derek's teeth were more pronounced, his lower jaw longer and more angular, like a dog's snout; he sniffed the air, conspicuously; his very eyeballs had grown tawny, as if with jaundice, and the dilation was often so severe as to comprise the entire iris. The surface of his eyes was slick and glassy, reflecting light. Once, Kate came upon the child in his darkened room on the second floor of the house, crouched by a window, in a kind of trance. Was he staring at the moon? At the night sky churning with shreds of cloud, vaporous tendrils of light? She could hear his quick, panting breath; she saw that his mouth was moving, his jaws spasming as if he were very cold, or very excited. She would have gone to him to touch him, to comfort him, except something warned her *Don't! Don't touch* and she backed away, in silence.

Stephen stayed later and later in the city. Often didn't return home until 9 P.M. when, in theory at least, Derek was in bed, asleep.

Rarely did the three of them eat meals together now. Derek preferred to eat by himself, hungrily, lowering his head to his plate, eating with his fingers. Hamburgers, near-raw at their centers, oozing blood. He drank milk greedily, from the container, hunched inside the opened refrigerator door. Kate thought *It's good, he has his appetite back. It must be good.* How difficult for her, offering this strange child food at arm's length, to recall how once she'd fed him lovingly by hand, spooning baby food into his birdlike, yearning little mouth; how ecstatic she'd felt nursing him. Her milk-swollen breasts, her tender nipples, and the infant blindly locating the nipple, sucking with unfocused eyes — how happy she'd been. How addicted she'd become, without knowing it. *Love, baby-love. What hunger.* Now, remembering, she felt a stab of revulsion. Her breasts that were no longer warmly taut and swollen with milk ached; the nipples burned as if Derek had bitten and chewed them. Almost, Kate could remember blood trickling from her cracked nipples, tinged with milk . . .

I can't. Can't let myself. Must stay sane. I am the child's mother.

Like Stephen, Kate had been hoping that when Derek returned to school in September he'd change for the better, but that wasn't the case. Where Derek had once loved school, now he seemed to hate it. Where he would run about excitedly in the morning, eager for Kate to drive him, now he hung back in his room, or disappeared (where? — into the basement, behind the furnace) so that Kate had to hunt him down, calling his name, pleading with him. Where once he'd come home from school chattering with enthusiasm about his teacher, his classmates, his studies, now he was sullen and refused to talk at all. Suddenly, in second grade, he seemed to have no friends.

Kate was called in to speak with Derek's teacher and with an assistant principal to discuss Derek's poor grades, his poor deportment in class, his boredom, his listlessness, his defiance, his "antisocial behavior." All this was new, stunningly new to Kate, who'd taken for granted, since Montessori school, where her Derrie had been one of the sweetest, most well-liked children, that she was a mother blessed by good fortune; a woman late to motherhood, conspicuously older than virtually all of the other mothers, but blessed. Even envied. Now, all that was changed. *Did I want to think it might be my imagination? Mine, and Stephen's? Our haunted-eyed feral son.* In early October there was a threatening incident at school, Derek baring his teeth as if to bite another child, and in mid-October there was a biting incident, Derek actually biting another boy, sinking his small but surprisingly sharp teeth into the other's hand and drawing blood. For this, Derek was suspended from school for two weeks. (At the school, Kate professed shock, utter shock; her son had never done anything like that before; the other boy had been bullying him, he'd said; the other boy had in fact threatened *him*; that must be the explanation. Derek sullenly refused to discuss the incident. He didn't at all mind being suspended from school. When Kate and Stephen asked him how he could do such a "terrible, animal" thing, Derek merely shrugged and muttered what sounded like "hate 'em.") It was advised that the Knights arrange for Derek to see a child therapist immediately, as well as hire a tutor for him; and of course they agreed, of course they would do all they could. They were American parents of a moneyed, educated class, they would do everything humanly possible to help their child, to return him to the normalcy of the species. *He's our only son. We love him so. We don't understand. We are innocent. It's just a phase. A phase of growth. He isn't a baby any longer. What can we do? He drowned, what was human in him drowned. What is human is gone. What was ours is gone. Where?*

Yet: years later—when Derek was lost from them, long disappeared from their lives, when they were in fact no longer married, polite strangers to each other, and this politeness tinged with the melancholy of an old, unspeakable grief—Kate would recall with a physical stab of pain how, only a few days after Derek had returned sullenly to school, she'd thrown herself into a flurry of enthusiasm trying to arrange a party for his seventh birthday. That dark, windy November afternoon, between sips of red wine, bravely telephoning the mothers of a dozen of Derek's second-grade classmates to invite them to the party; as in a nightmare of rejection and humiliation, no one wished to come; even those mothers Kate considered her friends had no interest in accepting the invitation. Their responses ranged from sympathetic and embarrassed—"I'm truly sorry, Kate, but Molly is terribly busy now, I'm reluctant to schedule one more thing for her on that Saturday, but thank you"—to curt, nearly rude—"Thank you, but I don't think a birthday party for your son is a great idea right now, at least not for Andrew to attend." Yet, grim, smiling, the tart red wine coursing through her tight veins like liquid flame, clamps of panicked pain at her temples, Kate continued to dial numbers. It was hard for her to believe. *It's real, then. But how can it be real, he's only a little boy?*

At that moment, tramping through the woods behind the house in a chilly, windy drizzle that he preferred to the warmth of the house. And to her.

12.

The first tutor hadn't worked out, nor the second. Derek had spat at the first, a nineteen-year-old math major from SUNY–Purchase; the second, a friendly middle-aged woman who taught at the community college, he'd bitten on the back of the hand—not hard enough to break the skin, but almost. *Your son is sick. Disturbed. Needs help. You must know.*

Nor had the therapist worked out. Derek had gone berserk when they'd tried to urge him into the car for a second session, he'd guessed where they were taking him though they'd told him with vague smiles that it was nowhere he'd be hurt, only helped; still he'd known instinctively, could sniff the panic lifting from their skins, his darting, dilated eyes quick to detect fear in their eyes, so he'd pummeled, kicked, raked his sharp broken fingernails across Kate's forearm, shouting he hated them, hated them both, as Stephen tried to calm him, "Derek! No! Goddamn you, Derek!"—but the child wrenched free of his father's awkward hands to escape, running in a crouch, like a terrified wild animal, through the back lawn and into the woods where Kate followed him, for Stephen had turned away in disgust, Stephen had had enough for that day, it was the child's mother tramping through the unfamiliar woods cupping her hands to her mouth calling, "Derrie? Der-rie?" trying not to betray the desperation she felt, telling herself this was a game, this might be interpreted as a game, she had to win back the child's trust, that was it.

But wasn't his mother watching him, a six year old? In a swimming pool.

How could it have happened? In a few feet of water. And the child's mother only a few feet away.

Her attention distracted? Imagine!

How can she live with herself, a woman like that? Letting her own child drown.

These cruel gloating voices murmured about her as she stumbled through the wet underbrush, sobbing, her heart beating painfully, in reproach. She was panicked she might become lost in this no-man's-land: the township kept a ten-foot swath for telephone and electrical poles but otherwise the area was overgrown, a virtual jungle. Somewhere beyond a gravel access road there was the Hudson Ridge reservoir, Kate believed; but in which direction? For forty minutes she searched for the fleeing child calling, "Derrie? Honey—" and then, suddenly, there he was: only about fifteen feet away, watching her. His head was oddly lowered and his eyes fixed on her, his mouth stretched in a strange twisted smile. Or was it simply a grimace of his lips, the muscles in a spasm. Kate cried, "There you are, honey! Please come home with me, we're so sorry. Your daddy and—" Kate heard her bright ebullient voice, she forced herself to smile for perhaps this was a game after all, hide-and-seek in the woods, and nothing un-usual had happened back at the house. She and Stephen were guilty of poor judgment perhaps, they were well intentioned but blundering; the thing was to win back the child's trust. Smiling, Kate reached out happily for Derek's hand but he stood unmoving, staring at her with those dark, dilated eyes and the warning passed through her mind as if in the impersonal voice of another *Don't! Don't touch! He will attack* and so she knew not to force his hand, but simply to guide him back home, he was surprisingly tractable, though sullen, unresponsive. She was exhausted by this time, though as they made their way back to the house Kate chattered nervously, an American-mom voice she'd acquired from TV, unnatural to her, yet a revelation, offered to Derek so that he might believe, if he wished to believe, that, from Mommy's side, nothing had changed—"Sweetie, you know I love you. You *know*." It was a secret what he knew, of course. The inanity and futility of her words swept over her. Yet she refused to surrender to silence, for she was the child's mother, and she did love him, or what remained of him, or what she could recall of him, and in the kitchen that was so cheerily lit, clean, shining surfaces as in a TV advertisement, she gave the boy his supper, setting a plate before him at the Formica-topped table, standing at a little distance to watch in appalled fascination. As he ate. She realized that he'd come home with her, he'd allowed her to find him, because he was hungry; because, in the wild, he hadn't yet found the food he required.

13.

That night, or another. Lying awake. Separate from each other. Not touching.

Their bodies now shrank from touch. The accidental brush of the other's heated skin — almost, this was repugnant. Indecent.

For of their touch years before, their kisses, their embraces — what had come into the world? What creature born of their heedless yearning? They could not bear to think.

It was a night in midwinter, no it was a night in early March — the house quaking with wind and a smell of rain and winter-rotted leaves. It was not a night Kate could identify for she'd endured similar nights so many times, nights of fitful sleep, heart-pounding sleep and hours of wakefulness protruding like bleached, misshapen boulders out of eddying dark water, and now Stephen was nudging her, asking if she heard? — the stealthy sound of footsteps in the hall outside their room, Derek was prowling by night, slipping away as he'd been forbidden, yet to barricade him in his room, lock the door with a padlock, nail the windows shut, would be to admit he had to be penned in, a captive animal, so Stephen was nudging her shoulder as if to wake her in the pretense he didn't know she was already awake, as he'd been, "Do you hear, Kate? It's him." As if it could be anyone else.

And Kate, whose solace was now in sleep, groggy hours of day-sleep when she was alone in the house, fitful patches of night-sleep, where the feral eyes were strangely absent and it was the lost baby Derrie, the plump-cheeked little boy gazing at her with eyes of love, rose immediately with her husband, yes she would go with him, to follow Derek and bring him back, as she'd done herself, not once but a number of times, they fumbled with their clothes and on the stairs vertigo lifted from the darkness below but Kate refused to give in, Kate was going to be brave, strong, stubborn, she was the child's mother, she must take responsibility and would take responsibility, and at the back door as they hurried they saw a small, lithe, fleeing figure dart from the shadow of the house toward the woods — "There he is!" It was a night of high, windblown shreds of cloud passing the moon's bulbous face, a pocked, lewd face it seemed, a winking face, and no stars surrounding it, oddly, and there Derek ran in a crouch like a wild animal familiar with the terrain, and they ran in his wake, already breathless, panting, for they were in their forties, middle-aged and too old for parenthood, this was their punishment for daring to bring life into the world, raw unheeded life not theirs to protect. They cried, "Derek! Derek!" — but the March wind blew away their cries in mockery. The fat-faced moon leered down at them in mockery. In the marshy woods smelling of rot, in the sinkholes that wetted their feet within seconds, through underbrush tearing at their clothes, pricking their skins, through briars, thorns, branches whipping against their faces, they stumbled a half mile, or was it a mile? to the muddy gravel access road, across this road sighting Derek, or a figure they believed to be Derek, scuttling, crouched close to the ground, sharp eyes penetrating the darkness as theirs could not, except as the sky opened to marmoreal brightness as the moon glared through webs of broken cloud, and they were panting, shivering, desperate to follow the fleeing child, now losing him, now sighting him, and at last they emerged in a grassy space seeing him a distance ahead, Kate recognized with difficulty the eastern edge of the reservoir, a body of water commonly seen only from the road, and only from her car as she drove to and from the village — but now she and Stephen found themselves there, at what hour of the night they couldn't know, long past midnight, yet hours from dawn, they

saw the water's surface ripple with wind like the skin of a nervous animal and in it filmy, rushing puzzle pieces of sky and
the winking moon, and on the farther side amid tall whipping
cattails—Derek wasn't alone.

There were others with him. Small, lithe figures like his,
and several taller figures. Who these were, male, female, their
faces, their eyes, they could not see, were fearful of seeing;
they heard low murmurous voices, unless it was the wind, they
heard—was it laughter? They dared not venture forward.
They clutched hands like frightened children. "Don't let
them see us! Be still." Their hearts beat with a shared terror,
for what would happen to them if they were seen?

The Hunter

At the phone booth outside the Kwik Shoppe on Route 31, Spedwell, New Jersey, there she stood bathed in light. My eyes knew to follow such light. Hair shimmering-pale, falling to her hips. Face turning to me like a crescent moon. Quick shy smile. She would say *It was meant for us to meet, that was why I smiled.* For she had dialed the number of one who had failed to answer and if he had answered she would not have turned, restless and anxious, her eyes lifting to mine across the oil-stained pavement where I stood beside my pickup about to climb inside. Ignition key in my hand.

In that instant in such a way our lives were joined forever.

Hannah her name was: an old name. Out of the past. A name you would see chiseled in gravestones, in the oldest churchyards.

I had known in that instant seeing Hannah across a distance of perhaps thirty feet that there was this about her, young as she was and her body lean as a boy's and the sparrow-bones of her shoulders, revealed inside her loose tank top, I wanted to caress, and to kiss, so fragile a sudden blow might shatter them. I had known that Hannah's soul was not a child's soul but predated her years on the earth as my soul is an ancient soul out of place in these times of godlessness and a mongrel mixing of the races.

Liam Gavin I was named, for I was of the hawk, a hunter of the sky. Liam Gavin my grandmother-born-in-Galway named me, for my young mother abandoned me at my birth to be raised by my grandmother. For my mother had not an old soul but a childish soul, careless and cruel. Shallow it was, and doomed to wear out quickly. When it was revealed to me that my mother had died before I was ten years old, I did not mourn her.

Liam Gavin, a hunter of the sky.

The hunter is one who never mourns.

Hannah was not a runaway as the tabloid papers and TV would claim. Hannah was not a girl of reckless behavior though it was true, she had journeyed hundreds of miles to me. From the flatlands of western Michigan she had come East, she said, wishing to see with her own eyes the Atlantic Ocean. (And I would take her to see the ocean, two hours' drive from Spedwell.) She was my angel and in my arms light as thistledown weeping for love, that love had blessed her at last. For at that first moment and at that distance across the pavement Hannah's poor, ravaged skin was not visible to me.

Scar tissue on her right cheek descending beneath her jaw from a dog attacking and biting her when she was seven years old. Ever afterward Hannah feared all dogs, even the smaller breeds, as she feared sudden movements or loud noises and the sound of a dog barking made her small heart beat rapidly. (This I would feel, more than once when I held her at such a time.) Ever afterward she said she placed her faith in God blessing her in moments of chance, for only by the purest chance that day did a woman in a neighboring trailer hear her screams, only by chance had the woman returned home early from work that day, to run into the lane to pry the rottweiler's jaws open and release the child's face that streamed with blood. And only by purest chance did Hannah turn to see me, and the light around me.

Hannah and Liam Gavin were our names then, together. As if always our names had been together like carvings in stone.

She came to live with me. My place I was renting in Spedwell. Upstairs, over the pet supply store with the dusty display window. Five minutes' walk from Luigi's Pizzeria where I worked. And Hannah wished to work, but was too young. But Hannah came by the pizzeria to assist me often. There was no harm in this, my employer did not object. On deliveries Hannah rode with me in the van to keep me company after dark. Walking with me to customers' front doors, ringing the bell. If it was Hannah with her long shining hair and smile like a candle flaring in the dark who handed them the pizza in its big flat cardboard box, the tip would be as much as one dollar more than if Liam Gavin had brought them the pizza instead.

Did Liam Gavin resent this fact?

Certainly I did not. For all facts exist to be considered, and utilized.

In small towns like Spedwell you see through lighted windows in the evenings. In summer, especially, when windows are open. Often a front door will be ajar, or fully open. Even if you wish not to see at such times, to resist temptation, your eyes lead you to see. For in a small town like Spedwell they don't trouble to pull down their blinds. There is quiet here mostly, and trust.

Hannah said, I love it that people see us together. I love it that they see Liam and Hannah.

It wasn't clear until we had been together for some weeks that Hannah did not always speak the truth. Small untruths I would catch her in. That she would deny, shaking her head like a deceitful child. Long hair rippling and the scar tissue on her face shiny as teeth. There were men she smiled at in the pizzeria when she believed I couldn't see her face. On the street, a car or a truck passing and Hannah would narrow her eyes, staring. Telephone calls she made in secret, that I had reason to know of. When I spoke to her of such things she denied them, always she denied what I knew to be true, which was an insult to me. The man she'd tried to call, that day by the Kwik Shoppe, was a trucker whose route was Newark to Atlanta, and I learned that Hannah had ridden with him in his truck before coming to live with me. And there was the mailman who parked his van at the curb and climbed the stone steps to the building where we lived, which was built on a small hill at the end of Main Street. Six days a week this mailman, a black man of no clear age, their skins are so smooth-dark and their behavior so friendly-seeming. This Negro with a thin black mustache like it was drawn in crayon on his upper lip.

Six days a week he would come to place mail in the row of mailboxes outside our building that were made of cheap metal and rusted and their locks long broken. It was rare that I would see him, for I was at work, but I understood that Hannah would see him, seated on the front stoop in the sun, her thin legs bare and pale and her feet bare, and there she would paint her toenails. My portable radio beside her. Hannah's deceitful face uplifted, her slow smile. The ugly scar on her face did not deter her from offering herself to even a black man whose odor would cling to her for hours.

Saying, Hi there. No mail for me today again I guess?

Never any mail for Hannah. Who had no last name.

Lonliness I would write *eats at the heart. All my life I have been lonly. But I have faith, this will change somday soon.*

Our teacher's name was Mrs. Knudsen. We were instructed to call her Mrs. Knudsen and when she said, at the third class meeting, Please call me Evvie, Evvie is my name, some of us were unable to make the switch. Because you don't want your teacher to be somebody like yourself. There is a need to believe that your teacher is somebody different from you.

Mrs. Knudsen she was to me then. Saying, This is very good work, Liam Gavin. The way you express yourself is clear and direct and your vocabulary is well chosen and what you say is always interesting. Except you have misspelled a few words, I will show you.

She showed me in her own handwriting that was so beautiful:

loneliness   someday

There were about twenty of us in the class. The number changed each time. Men were released from the facility, or somebody new signed up for the course. Improving Your English Skills it was called. Tuesday and Friday mornings at 10 A.M. This was Red Bank Correctional where my sentence was eleven months to two years but would be reduced to seven months for good behavior. For always in such places Liam Gavin is a cooperative prisoner, a Caucasian.

Word was out in Red Bank, the English teacher Mrs. Knudsen was a good-looking sexy woman, which was true in a way of speaking, but Mrs. Knudsen was not the type of good-looking sexy woman the average inmate at Red Bank would desire. For Mrs. Knudsen was not young. Later I would learn she was thirty-seven. She did not look anywhere near that old, but you could see she was not young. Her hair was graying-brown and looked like she had washed it and combed it through but nothing more, so it was frizzy and limp. Her face was solid and creased around the mouth from years of smiling. In the fluorescent lights you could see lines beside her eyes. Some days she wore a dark lipstick that did make her look sexy, her mouth like something you would wish to kiss, or to bite, but other days her face was pale and a little shiny as if she'd rubbed it hard with a rag. Most days she wore slacks and a turtleneck sweater or a shirt and jacket. It is likely that Mrs. Knudsen was instructed to wear loose clothing to come into the facility, which is intelligent advice. It is the advice I would give to any woman.

The thing you noticed most about Mrs. Knudsen was her laugh. A quick loud laugh like she was being tickled. You liked to hear that laugh. In a prison facility, nobody laughs much. But when we had our classroom "discussions" Mrs. Knudsen attempted a sense of humor to put her students at ease, treating us like you'd treat older high school guys, and it was true that most of Mrs. Knudsen's students were younger than her, in age at least. In Red Bank as in other state facilities there are few men beyond a certain age, most of us were younger. By young I mean under thirty. Many young Negro prisoners who know one another from the street and do their business in prison, or try. There are some men not from cities, though, but from small towns, or rural parts of the state, and these were mostly white men. I was one of these.

Improving Your English Skills was a course that ran all the time at Red Bank when they could get teachers to teach it. The teachers were volunteers. I took the course only when Mrs. Knudsen taught it. And only for ten weeks because my parole came through. For good behavior as I have said. In such places the guards are mostly white like me, and trust me. Mrs. Knudsen liked me, and trusted me, and I have reason to believe she wrote a good report on me for the parole board. This was clear, for when we met again, five weeks after I was released, by accident we met at the Medlar Mall, Mrs. Knudsen smiled at me right away and put out her hand to me as nobody ever did in Red Bank or anywhere, and said, Liam, is it? Hello!

Like it was such a surprise, and it made her happy. Like I was somebody she knew and had a fondness for.

The fiery light in Mrs. Knudsen's eyes. I was not sure that I had seen it before, in Red Bank. Beneath her loose clothes it had been hidden. I saw now that her eyes were warm and dark and hopeful.

Let me buy you a cup of coffee, Liam Gavin. You're looking very well.

You're looking very well is not something anyone would say to me, of the people that I know or work with. Yet when Mrs. Knudsen uttered these words, I felt very happy.

Starbucks! Not a place I would ever go. Yet Mrs. Knudsen insisted, and inside seated at a small table I inhaled the smells, I looked around and saw that it was okay, nobody was staring at me or wondering who I was. *You are not one of us, you don't belong here* — these sneering words I would have expected, yet did not register. For so many people look like me now. White guys in their twenties, even high school kids. Mrs. Knudsen had her way of putting me at ease, asked me questions in a kind of slow searching voice like teachers do, how was I, what was I doing now, did I have a job, did I have a family, where did I live? Saying with her smile that made creases sharp as knife marks beside her mouth, You were one of my best students, Liam. You were always so attentive. You sat so straight. You wrote such interesting compositions. You made me feel less . . . despair.

I was surprised to hear this. I didn't know where to look. The coffee mug in my hand was heavy, and shaky.

Mrs. Knudsen laughed, saying in a lowered voice sometimes yes, she did feel despair. There was embarrassment between us for you don't expect your teacher to say such a thing but there was excitement too at such a confession. Mrs. Knudsen's hand shook a little, too, holding her mug of coffee. There was a look like a girl's — daring, flirty, pushy — in her face I had not seen at Red Bank where Mrs. Knudsen had asked us to call her Evvie but mostly we had not, out of politeness and clumsiness we had not called her anything to her face. Where she wore loose clothes and no makeup most days, never looking like she looked now at the Medlar Mall, never in sexy trousers that showed the curve of her hips and a sweater tucked into the waist of the trousers, and her mouth shiny with lipstick.

In a scolding voice saying, Evvie, please call me! I call you Liam, don't I?

Evvie, I said. Ev-vie.

But the word was strange on my lips, like a foreign word I could pronounce but did not comprehend.

Mrs. Knudsen was telling me of her family. Her husband who was a very busy man she said, an accountant. Her son who was fourteen and no longer needed her. Not even to console him when he's feeling blue. He just goes to the computer, and the door to his room is shut. Everything is e-mail, e-mail, that damned e-mail. Of course I understand he's no longer a little boy, I understand that. I wouldn't want him to remain a child. I love him too much. My husband . . .

In this strange intimate way Mrs. Knudsen talked to me in Starbucks. Like we were old friends meeting after many years. She was leaning forward with her elbows on the table. She had three cups of coffee, and I had two without finishing the last. She asked if I was hungry and I said yes so she ordered chocolate chip cookies, which I ate trying not to drop crumbs onto the table. This first time we met in the Medlar Mall it would seem to be, if you'd seen us, by chance. Mrs. Knudsen would consider it so. She had no idea, I had moved to Medlar. When I was released from Red Bank I looked through telephone directories for three counties until I found the right Knudsen family. Medlar was not too distant, the parole board allowed me to live in Medlar so long as I had a job there, as I did. And so I moved, and so I came often to the Medlar Mall at different times of day. I did not drive past Mrs. Knudsen's house. I knew the address, and I knew where the street was, but I did not drive on that street. Nor did I telephone that number even to hear Mrs. Knudsen's voice. I would not do such a thing. I was on parole, and I knew better. Mrs. Knudsen knew better too, it was not allowed to see people from Red Bank outside the facility if they are on parole. I thought *She is forgetting this. She is pretending to forget.* The knowledge made me happy, for it was our secret between us.

After the Starbucks, Mrs. Knudsen asked if I needed a ride anywhere and I said yes, that would be good. So Mrs. Knudsen drove me a few miles north on the highway to the place I was staying in, that had been a motel but was converted now to one-room efficiency apartments. Mrs. Knudsen said it must be lonely here, this is a melancholy place and I shrugged and said, It's okay.

Close by was the Amoco where I worked. To get to the mall I took the local bus. Soon I would have a car. I waited for Mrs. Knudsen to say she'd like to see my apartment, see how I'd decorated it, but she did not.

But Mrs. Knudsen took my phone number. And two days later Mrs. Knudsen called me. For she believed I must be lonely, she said. I had told her that my family was scattered, which was true. She understood how hard it must be, on parole like I was. In Red Bank you did not inquire why another inmate was inside, nor did Mrs. Knudsen inquire why I had been sent there. In one of the papers I wrote for Mrs. Knudsen I spoke of my conviction for aggravated assault, a fight I had gotten into with a man I didn't know, and had not meant to hurt so bad as I did, in a bar in Trenton. This was two months after Hannah betrayed me but still I was in that mood, quick to flare up and wishing to hurt even a stranger who pissed me off by the way he looked at me. But of this charge, and whether my sentence was fair, Mrs. Knudsen never spoke, nor would she.

The next week, on Wednesday when I was working half day, Mrs. Knudsen took me to lunch at a restaurant in Pinnacle, and afterward to a bookstore called the Bookworm. In a big old frame house, and down in the cellar was the Paperback Treasure Trove, which smelled like a graveyard but Mrs. Knudsen seemed to like it, shelves of moldy old paperbacks for prices low as fifty cents, twenty-five cents, ten cents. Mrs. Knudsen picked out a dozen paperbacks for me saying, Oh Liam, you'll like this! and *this!*—you'll love this! excited as a young girl. It made me smile to see her. Some of these were young-adult books, *The Solar System, In the Age of the Great Dinosaurs, The Red Pony.* Biographies of John F. Kennedy, Babe Ruth, the first astronauts. In Mrs. Knudsen's warm brown eyes I saw the hope of something, like pain it came so strong. Her eagerness to believe something of me I could not comprehend, still less name.

The moldy old books I wanted to toss down in disgust. I was not fifteen years old. I was not a mental deficient. Instead I thanked Mrs. Knudsen for her kindness. For the books, and for the lunch. Mrs. Knudsen touched my wrist saying in a scolding voice, Now Liam, call me Evvie, please!

Between us there was that flare of light, so fierce you would not believe it could ever go out. But I have grown wary of such, and distrustful.

Liam Gavin I was named, yet there was a being deep inside Liam Gavin who could not be named. This being had never been baptized in any church. No woman had sung lullabies to him cradling him in her arms.

This being seemed to reside in my eyes, I thought. Sometimes in the region of my heart. Sometimes in my belly. And sometimes between my hard-muscled legs.

Between my legs, a fistlike thing that grew rigid and angry with sudden blood.

This thing had no name. It came of a time before there

were names, or even words. Before God spoke with a human tongue.

This woman, of all women, I did not wish to harm. In her arms I wept and she was forgiving of my weakness. As women are forgiving of weakness if it is a bridge to their strength.

A light played about her head that was small and sleek, hair cut short. She had had chemotherapy she said, her hair had been thick and had fallen out and when it grew back it was light and fuzzy, soft as a child's and of no color, like thistledown. So she cut it short herself with scissors, that she need not think of it any longer. As she ceased, she said, thinking of all vain things.

She was a potter and a weaver. So many created things were displayed in her house, you stared at them in wonder. Inside this house of bright colors like flowers, and a smell of clay and paint. And baking bread she made herself, and fed to me: coarse whole grain with nuts, raisins, sunflower seeds. Meals she prepared for me in stoneware crockery, wild rice, polenta. Liking to watch me eat, she said. For she had so little appetite herself, yet yearned to feed others.

Her skin was pale as parchment. Her very face seemed shrunken. Her eyes were ringed in shadow yet became alert and glittering when she worked. Speaking to me, if she was not tired, she lifted these eyes and I felt something turn in my heart, they were beautiful in a way no other man could see. For Liam Gavin has been blessed in this, to discern beauty where another man, careless and crude, could not see beauty.

I was not certain of her age. She might have been older than Mrs. Knudsen. Yet she might have been much younger. She was of a smallness different from Hannah. In my arms she required protection. I thought *Here at last is one who needs me more than life itself.*

Outside her windows were feeders for birds. I helped her hang the newest of these, from a corner of the roof. She thanked me and her eyes filled with tears like precious jewels. Inside her kitchen we would watch cardinals, chickadees, juncos, house finches, jays at the feeders, beating their wings in the air, lighting on the perches. These birds she would identify for me. The male cardinals' red feathers bright as blood, astonishing to see. If she was tired we would lie on her sofa beneath one of her handmade quilts in the late afternoon as the sun slanted in the sky and dusk came on and we would watch the birds unseen and hear their small cries. Sometimes we slept, the birds' cries mingled with our dreams. And sometimes we shared the same dream, of the two of us lying together beneath a handmade quilt watching birds at a feeder, their small wings flailing the air.

It was a happy time for me. My happiest time I think. But it was a strange time. For Olive was the only woman I had known who could peer into my soul as through a window. The others, it was a mirror they had seen. Their own faces they had seen, and adored.

My love who was so frail, as if her bones were hollowed out. Yet when I was trapped in one of my nightmares, she would wake me. She would grip my face that burned with fever between her small cool hands and she spoke to me as you would speak gently to a child, to wake him but not to frighten him.

Liam! Liam Gavin. I am here, I will always be here. You are safe with me.

When Olive was first missing, they came to ask me questions. For it was known, I was Olive's friend. I had been living in her house for five months. So many questions they asked of me, yet I answered these questions. I did not attempt to flee. You would suppose I was as puzzled as anyone was, and alarmed, that Olive had gone away. They asked how we had met, and I told them of how passing through this small town, Upper Black Eddy on the Delaware River, I saw an arts fair beside a church, and stopped, and marveled at the rich colors of certain of the vases and pots, and there were weavings of a kind I had never seen before, and such paintings! I could not look away but stared and stared.

I did not tell them the complete truth: that the pots, vases, weavings, by Olive or by others, scarcely interested me. What held my attention was a single small painting of a boy of about twelve, with my face.

An angular Irish face it was, strong boned, frowning, pale blue eyes and lank hair the hue of burnt copper, a shade lighter than my own had been at that time in my life.

Olive did not paint much any longer, she said, but formerly she had done portraits, and this was a dream portrait, as she called it, of one who had appeared to her in a vision, but was not known to her.

I did not tell them how I saw the small name written in the corner of the canvas: *Olive*. Of how I knew that *Olive* would be my fate, before I looked up to see the woman observing me from only a few feet away.

Softly this woman uttered one word only, as I turned to her.

You!

I did not tell the police officers such truths, for these were private and sacred to me. For I knew I would be misunderstood.

Numerous times I was asked what I knew of Olive Lundt—for that was her full name—and where I believed Olive might have gone, and I could repeat to them only that I did not know. That there were many things in Olive's life of which she did not tell me. For Olive was an artist and not an ordinary woman, and because of this she led a life of inwardness and secrecy. In Upper Black Eddy it was known that Olive often went away, by herself. She stayed with friends at the shore. She stayed with friends in the Poconos. In cold months she drove to Key West where she lived with artist friends. She had been married, years ago. She was not close to her family who lived in Rutherford, New Jersey. She had many friends but certain of these friends did not know of one another, for Olive wished it that way. That no one know very much about her. During times of sickness, she did not want her friends to see her. It might have been a time of sickness now, I told them. It might have been her cancer returning. When Olive would wish to be alone.

They did not want to believe me, for of all the persons they interviewed in Upper Black Eddy, Liam Gavin was the one they suspected. Or wished to suspect. Because I was a parolee, and had what is called a criminal record, and had shared a house with Olive. Yet these police officers were men like myself. Like the prison guards at Red Bank, they knew a certain kinship with me. I answered their questions honestly. I had made no attempt to leave Upper Black Eddy. I spoke without guilt. I did not speak with the air of one who has been hurt or betrayed. More, I spoke in stumbling bewilderment.

Wonderment. That Olive would depart one night without saying good-bye, and without explanation.

Would you take a polygraph test, I was asked.

I would! I would gladly.

At the start Olive was so trusting, she gave me her checks to cash. She gave me money to shop for food. Many times, Olive said, I could curl up in your heart, Liam Gavin.

Later I came to believe the woman was testing me. She was testing her faith in me. As if half wishing I might steal her money and disappear. For then she would have smiled saying *It was to be. I am meant to live alone.*

In the third month I was living in Olive's house, her son came to her. She had told me that she had a son but he had not seemed real to me. The boy was eight years old. At the time of Olive's cancer he'd been five and six and she couldn't care for him so he went to live with his father and his father's new wife in Tom's River in south Jersey. He was a quiet child, small boned like his mother. But sullen and guarded in my presence. I vowed I would win this boy's trust. I would win his love. I spoke softly in his presence. I took him canoeing at the boat rental in New Hope. I repaired his broken bicycle. Yet he would not smile at me, rarely would he speak to me. Soon in the household the boy became a seed or a small bone in my throat I could not swallow, yet could not cough up. I did not hate him. I took care to hide my impatience with him. For there was a hope in my heart at this time that I would love him, and I would be a father to him. For it was time for me to marry. Seeing me with her son, Olive said, I love you, Liam, that you love my son! The tragedy of his life is, his own father does not love him.

Olive did not seem to see that her son did not love me, there was this strange blindness in one who used her eyes so shrewdly in her work. I would come to perceive that this is the willful blindness of the artist, who sees only what she wishes to see. For Olive in her innermost heart lived not for others but for *her work* as she spoke of it.

There came the hour when the boy shrank from me even when I smiled at him, and I thought *He will have to die.* It was a calm thought, as a hawk, high in the air, sights its prey far below on the earth, and prepares to strike, swiftly and yet without haste. Then in my arms in our bed one night Olive began to weep, that the boy lay sleepless — she knew! — in his room, and she felt such guilt over him for she could not love him, as a mother should love her child. Oh Liam, Olive said, I gave him up, when I believed that I would die. I wanted to spare him. I pushed him from me. I made him live with his father and his stepmother, he has never forgiven me. He will never trust another woman in his life.

I had to acknowledge that this was so. I felt a rage of pity for him. This boy so like myself whose mother could not love him, who had turned her face from him. And I knew that I could not lift a finger against him.

After this, it happened that I began to test Olive by certain measures. I wished to know if she loved Liam Gavin, or if she loved *her work.* For she spoke of *her work* fiercely yet tenderly as if she both hated it and loved it, *her work* deep in her body as an eye in its socket, or a bone encased in flesh. *Her work* she valued beyond her son. Through clumsiness I overturned a tall earth-colored vase Olive had spoken slightingly of yet in that instant I saw her eyes flash fury at me, and I knew that she had pride in the vase, as she had pride in all her created things, though she spoke and behaved in humility. It was the first time any woman or girl had looked at Liam Gavin in such a way. My hand leaped out, the back of my hand striking Olive's parchment face. Astonished she fell backward, she was sobbing, shivering. Yet there was an exaltation in her, that at last a man had dared to strike her as she deserved. Yet I ran from the house through a marshy field to the edge of the river where in broken pieces like crazed eyes the moon was reflected and where some minutes later the woman came to me, to touch my arm gently. For I understood that she would come to me, she would not expel me from her house and her bed. I understood the woman's pride was such, she had convinced herself she was without pride.

She would send the boy back to his father, she said. As a way of placating me. For she thought it was the boy who had come between us. She would do this for me, telling herself it was for Liam Gavin and not for herself, that the boy was a burden to her, a hook in the heart, a reminder of weakness she had no wish to recall.

We were tender as new lovers that night. For I had not wished to hurt this woman, truly. She was so shrunken and frail: the bone of her skull nearly visible through her wispy child's hair. Forgive me, I asked of her, and she forgave me of course, it was a sign of the woman's strength to forgive a man's weakness. Yet in that instant when the vase had shattered at my feet I understood that Olive had no need of me. She was a potter, a weaver. She had *her work*. She was not yearning and hungry for love as Mrs. Knudsen had been. She had not the innocence of Hannah who was a child in deception as in love. In her heart Olive betrayed me every minute of every day for in her heart there was no room for any man.

Yet I did not act on this knowledge at once. The way of the hawk is to ascend, to contemplate his prey from a great height. The way of the hunter is swiftness, yet not haste. And there was a sweetness to our lovemaking, that required me to be so gentle, like lovemaking to a child, that excited me, and when I was angry, the excitement that passed between us, too, was sweet. When the fire coursed through my body, Olive dared to approach me, and hold me. Olive was strong enough for such, and took pride in it. Saying, You see, Liam, I am your lightning rod! I can save you from yourself. My love, you're safe here with me.

In the open snowy fields in winter, and in the pine woods you see these: a few soiled feathers, tiny birds' bones, sometimes bits of legs, beaks. Remains of such predator birds as hawks, owls. For predators must prey upon smaller and weaker creatures to survive. *It is our destiny.*

Hannah. Evvie. Olive. And others to come, since Liam Gavin has moved to the Delaware Valley, at the border of the states of New Jersey and Pennsylvania, through which the Delaware River courses wide and beautiful and reflective of the sky far above.

Not crude "left-behind" remains, but careful burials: deep! In the pine woods, where the mossy earth is damp, and soft.

This polygraph Liam Gavin passed with no effort, like the others.

The Twins: A Mystery

"What's on?"

Elderly, retired Dr. A—— takes up the black plastic remote control in his slightly palsied hand, steadies it with his other hand and presses POWER. Like a magician's wand, the remote control causes the blank glassy face of the TV set to come alive. At once there's an antic, not very convincing image on the screen. Dissatisfied, Dr. A—— switches channels, with stabbing gestures of the remote control in the direction of the set.

"Nothing. Nothing to challenge the intellect is ever on."

Grunting, Dr. A—— pulls from a shelf a plain black DVD, slides it into the DVD player; suddenly on the TV screen there is a familiar face. Two faces. Dr. A——, with a smirk, settles in to watch.

"Well. Better than nothing."

They were twins. Identical twins. They preferred to think of themselves as brothers merely.

To be childhood twins is adorable. To be adult twins is abominable.

And so they were twins—they were brothers—with a healthy, skeptical attitude regarding the mystique of *twinness*. They clipped out tacky articles from the tabloids—PSYCHIC TWINS stories, TWINS SEPARATED AT BIRTH stories—to send to each other.

In biological terms, they were "identical twins" because their DNA was identical. Their chromosomes were identical. In fact, they were mirror twins.

Meaning that their faces, otherwise quite ordinary (though somewhat asymmetrical) Caucasian male faces, if halved and paired, made a complete face.

If, for instance, you vertically dissected B——'s and C——'s faces and matched the right half of B——'s face with the left half of C——'s face, you would have a perfect match.

The parts in their hair fell naturally on opposite sides of their heads. B——'s left eye was weaker than his right eye, and C——'s right eye was weaker than his left eye. B——'s habit of smiling, lifting the left side of his mouth initially, was mirror-matched by C——'s habit of lifting the right side of his mouth initially. B—— was right-handed, C—— left-handed. (Though C——, a strong-willed boy, managed to teach himself to become ambidextrous. "To fit into a tyrannical right-handed world.") B——'s most severely impacted wisdom tooth, removed when he was twenty-nine, was just behind his upper left molar, and C——'s most severely impacted wisdom tooth, removed when he was thirty, was behind his upper-right molar.

Of course, their well-intentioned mother had dressed them as twins in their early childhood. Their father had taken numerous photographs of them as babies, as toddlers, as small boys, both clothed and unclothed, out of a fascination with their *twinness*, which he believed had its source in his ancestral genes.

Their mother gradually realized, as the boys grew, that
their *twinness*, so remarked on by others, made them uneasy.
She ceased dressing them as twins by the time they were eight.
They went to the same elementary school but were sent to
separate New England boarding schools. They went to separate New England universities. B—— was married first, at the
age of twenty-six; when C—— married, at the age of twenty-
seven, it was remarked that, contrary to the clichés of *twinness*,
he married a woman very different from his brother's wife.

At least that was the impression.

The brothers' wives made an effort to like each other. But
they made little effort to come together socially. It may have
been a disorienting experience for B——'s wife, for instance,
to find herself in close physical proximity to C——, the identical twin of the man with whom she was intimate; as C——'s
wife very likely mirrored this discomfort, their social occasions were awkward. And there was Dr. A—— overseeing family occasions. In time, B——'s wife encouraged her husband
to see C—— alone, for dinner; C——'s wife may have been
slightly jealous of the brothers' closeness, but not excessively.
B——'s wife may have been jealous of C——'s wife, but not
excessively.

B—— was a CPA. C—— was head of the local branch of
a well-known national insurance company. Neither had considered medical school, not for a single hour.

Was Dr. A—— bitterly disappointed at his sons' refusal to
honor him by entering his profession? Or was Dr. A—— only
moderately disappointed, and given to ironic asides in his
sons' company as a way of allowing them to know the contour

of his feelings, without knowing the depth? The brothers, during their evenings together, speculated endlessly on this subject, but inconclusively.

The fact was, B—— and C—— were mild-mannered individuals. As if by design each had become middle-aged in their late twenties. Their squirrel-colored hair thinned at the crowns of their heads, giving them a boyish, questing look. B—— wore wire-rimmed glasses and C—— wore rimless oval glasses. Their eyes required bifocals when they were in their early forties. B—— carried himself with the affable resignation of a man carrying a soft, not heavy but cumbersome bundle, like a bag of laundry. C——, who was determined to be the "athletic, active brother," made it a point to walk with a spring in his step, even when not observed by witnesses.

Their mother died, of a particularly virulent cancer, when B—— and C—— were forty-two years old. They grieved for her bitterly, but in mutual silence, not needing to speak. It was possible that identical spasms of pain gripped the brothers at the time of their mother's death, and that they endured identical nightmares on the anniversary of her death, and dreamed often of her, but they never spoke of it. They were stoic, they suffered inwardly. The prevailing fact that their mother had died and left them with their father was a source of perpetual concern of which, too, they never spoke.

For what was there to say? *If only he'd died in her place . . . ?*

When the brothers met, they never embraced but they shook hands warmly, and in the eyes of each the pain and continuing wonder of their mother's absence from the world shone. And a crushing awareness then of the prevailing fact of their father's continued existence. Then a tic of a smile began at the left corner of B——'s mouth, and a tic of a smile began at the right corner of C——'s mouth, and their mood changed.

The brothers were not maudlin individuals. They scorned the victim culture. Passivity, self-pity. They were intelligent, well-to-do men who firmly believed themselves immune to the social pathogens of the era.

Their father was living. And aging.

It was remarked by B——'s wife, as by C——'s wife, that their father-in-law Dr. A——, always a difficult and somewhat enigmatic personality, was becoming more difficult, and more enigmatic, with age.

Dr. A—— had finally retired as a physician, reluctantly, in his midseventies. Still, the old gentleman prided himself on being a highly paid consultant in his rarefied field of neurophysiology.

Since his wife's death, Dr. A—— expected his sons to telephone him at least once a week. It was his custom to telephone them on Sunday evenings, though not every Sunday evening; if Dr. A—— telephoned his sons, it would be on Sunday evening. The brothers soon came to realize that Dr. A—— telephoned B—— first, and then C——. Not once had he varied in this custom. If B—— wasn't home to take the call, he delayed calling C—— until B—— returned his call.

(Why? Because B—— was the elder of the brothers by eight minutes.)

Dr. A—— had long ago ceased to photograph B—— and C—— as twin specimens; yet he had long pitted the brothers against each other. ("Competition is the source of genetic excellence. 'Survival of the fittest.' Otherwise, society becomes dysgenic. Races sink into degeneracy, and die out.")

Only in late adolescence did B—— and C—— understand that their father was manipulating them into rivalries, and declared a secret truce between themselves.

"Our allegiance is to each other. Not to *him*."

When Dr. A—— began to remark that neither of his sons was showing "much evidence of virility, still less of fertility" (in a crude though elliptical allusion to the fact that neither B—— nor C—— seemed to be inclined to have children), the brothers maintained a dignified silence.

Still, B—— secretly believed that C—— was their father's favorite, and C—— secretly believed that B—— was their father's favorite. Each thought of the other, "He can do no wrong in Dad's eyes."

Dr. A—— may have grieved at his wife's death, but he'd made a remarkable recovery. A lifelong optimist, he was inclined now to a robust, cheery nihilism. B—— believed that his father was a depressive personality, C—— believed he was more inclined to paranoia, mania. Their wives thought the old man was "normal"—if eccentric. He was wealthy yet frugal in small, you might say spiteful, matters. The cut-rate funeral for his wife, for instance. ("What's the purpose of an expensive funeral other than to provide income for funeral directors? Tell me.") The family home, a distinguished old English Tudor set back from the street in the city's historic district, had grown shabby since Mrs. A——'s death, with an air of purposeful dereliction. Vivid green moss grew in clusters on the slate roof, thistles and tiny saplings like rogue thoughts began to sprout in the rain gutters. The asphalt circle driveway was festooned with myriad weblike cracks. Shades were often drawn on all the windows facing the street, so that the effect was of a multitude of blank, blind yet staring eyes.

The brothers were concerned: when Dr. A—— died, would they jointly inherit the old house? Or would Dr. A——, performing a scenario of his secret devising, leave the house, perhaps even the bulk of his estate, to one brother, excluding the other?

For this reason alone, B—— and C—— dreaded their father's death, though they thought of it constantly.

One evening when the brothers were forty-nine years old, B—— glanced up from a book he was reading about Arctic explorations (B——'s amateur passion was for polar explorations, C——'s inclined to the American Civil War) with an expression of mild anxiety. His wife asked what was wrong and before B—— could reply, the phone rang. B——'s wife said, with a smile, "That's your brother." B—— said, "I hope not." He meant to be amusing, of course.

When B—— picked up the phone, however, there was C—— at the other end. Before C—— could say more than hello, B—— said grimly, "Something has happened to Dad, hasn't it? That's why you're calling."

C—— was silent, as if taken by surprise. He may have misinterpreted B——'s tone. He was often annoyed by what he called his brother's "aggressive sense of humor."

B—— said apologetically, "I'm sorry. Is something wrong?"

C—— told B—— that nothing was wrong, that he knew of. He was simply calling to say hello.

B—— doubted this. B—— said, "Did you say you'd heard from Dad?"

"No. Not me. Didn't he call you last Sunday? That's the last time I heard from him."

"Last Sunday? I don't think so. It was two weeks ago."

"Two weeks? Are you sure?"

"I think so, yes. Unless he called you more recently."

"He wouldn't have called me without calling you. You know that."

"I don't know that. I can't possibly know that."

"Well. Did you call Dad? Did you speak with him this week?"

"I called him, but he didn't answer. I called several times."

"I called, and he didn't answer. I assumed he would call this Sunday."

"You mean, last Sunday."

"Do I? No. I don't think so."

The line was silent. Each of the brothers was beginning to be upset. B——'s wife, standing in a doorway behind him, saw his shoulders stiffen and his hand rise to stroke his thinning hair in a way that touched her heart. C——'s wife, observing her husband in a similar posture, frowning, running a hand through his thinning hair, felt a stab of resentment, jealousy. For no one meant so much to C—— than B——. No marriage could mean so much to C—— and B—— as their *twinness.*

The brothers conferred, with mounting concern. It was determined that neither had spoken with their father in more than two weeks, though each had called, dutifully. Since Dr. A—— scorned such devices as answering machines or voice mail, there was no way to leave a message for him.

B—— said hesitantly, "Dad has been fatigued lately. He hasn't been himself."

C—— said, "Who is he, then?"

B—— laughed. "Got me."

C—— said, "I'm serious. *Who is he?*"

Again the brothers were silent. Each had a dread thought.

When they spoke, each spoke at the same time: "We'd better go to the house. Immediately."

In separate cars, from their separate homes on opposite sides of the city, the brothers drove to Dr. A——'s house. B——, who'd quit smoking (but kept a pack of mentholated cigarettes in the glove compartment of his car, in case of emergency), fumbled to light a cigarette, his first in nearly a year. When he arrived at their father's house, there was C——, standing on the front walk, smoking a cigarette and smiling strangely. Like B——, C—— had quit smoking recently. C—— said, "I rang the doorbell, and I knocked. I tried to look in the downstairs windows."

B—— said, "Dad would be upstairs. Probably."

"In the bedroom. Probably."

B—— and C—— tried the doorbell another time, and knocked on the heavy oak door. No answer. So far as they could see, the house was darkened downstairs. Shades were drawn over the windows that were filmy, almost membranous, with years of accumulated grime.

"Dad's deer rifle. You didn't think we should take it from him."

"How could we 'take it from him'? Dad wouldn't have allowed us."

"We might have taken it, without asking. To prevent something like this."

The brothers had begun to speak heatedly, without looking at each other. Neither could clearly recall which of them had first suggested "taking Dad's deer rifle," nor could he recall where the rifle might be kept; or even if their father still owned it. The old man had not gone hunting in more than a decade. Two decades? He'd been disappointed, in his sardonic way, that neither of his sons had cared to go hunting with him more than once, not even as adolescents. To have so much as mentioned the deer rifle to Dr. A—— would have been awkward and offensive so the brothers had said nothing, finally. Now B—— saw C—— pass a shaky hand over his eyes. C—— was looking pale, distraught. *He has been here already. He has seen, and he knows.* When C—— glanced up at B——, he winced, as with pain or guilt.

B—— said suddenly, "You've been here already, haven't you? You know what's happened to Dad."

C—— protested, "Are you serious? No."

"That's why you called me, isn't it?"

"What? You called me."

"That was last week. Last time. Tonight, you called me."

"I did not. This is ridiculous. I was reading when the phone rang."

"*I* was reading when the phone rang."

B—— was staring at C——. His heart had begun to beat rapidly. He was thinking that they were barely brothers any longer, let alone twins. He said, trying to keep his voice calm, "Well, have you?"

"Have I what?"

"Been here already? Earlier today? So you know what's— what's waiting for us upstairs?"

C—— said, his voice shaking, "Have *you*?"

B—— made a gesture of supreme exasperation, disgust. C—— made a similar gesture, cursing under his breath. Both brothers were on the weedy sidewalk leading to the rear of the house. They were shocked to see that large chunks of slate and mortar had fallen from the roof of the house into the overgrown lawn. A flock of noisy starlings beat their wings over-head. There was a smell here of something clotted and backed up, like sewage. The father's regal old black Lincoln Continental was parked half in, half out of the garage as if it had run out of gas at just that moment. The rear half of the car was covered in coarse birdlime.

At the back door of the house, which opened into a narrow entryway and into the darkened kitchen, both brothers hesitated. Was the door locked? (It was.) Who would be the one to smash the window, reach inside and turn the knob? (For if Dr. A—— was waiting inside, in perfectly good health, he would be furious with his intrusive sons.) C—— urged, "Go on. Do it." B—— urged, "You. You're Dad's favorite."

"The hell I am. You're the 'elder.'"

"You're the 'baby.'"

"Look, Dad has always favored you. Admit it."

"Dad has always favored *you*. I'm not blind."

"*I'm* not blind."

B—— came close to jostling C——, nudging him with his elbow as a boy might do, not to hurt but to assert power, rectitude. C——, panting, stood his ground as if daring his brother to touch him.

At last, B—— acted. He smashed the window, not with his fist but with a pair of heavy, badly rusted gardening shears lying on the rear porch.

"All right. You first."

"*You* first."

As soon as the brothers entered their former home, which seemed hardly recognizable now, the smell struck them like a wall.

(A smell of—what?)

(Rot? Decay? Organic decomposition?)

(A smell of death?)

B—— murmured faintly, "Oh Christ."

C—— whispered, "God . . ."

Like frightened children the brothers entered the kitchen. The room was considerably larger and shabbier than they recalled. The ceiling must have been twelve feet above their heads, the badly worn linoleum was sticky against the soles of their shoes. In the sunken sink, which more resembled an old-fashioned washtub than a kitchen sink, disorderly stacks of dirtied dishes soaked in fungoid-gray water.

B—— said, "He must have been mad. He was planning this."

C—— said, "If you thought so, why didn't you say something? You spoke with him last."

"I didn't speak with Dad last! You did."

"If you knew he was suicidal . . ."

"I didn't *know*. But I think you knew."

This time the brothers brushed against each other, as if accidentally. A sensation like translucent blue flames ran over their arms, where they'd touched, and seemed to ignite a similar fierce, near-invisible fire in their brains. Both were panting but trying to breathe shallowly through their noses, sickened by the smell.

They had no choice but to push forward. Their father would be upstairs. They entered the shadowy back hall and approached the stairs. Here the smell was even stronger, wafting downward like mist. Something scuttled away along the carpet with an air of indignation.

B—— said, half-pleading, "You have been here already, haven't you? You can tell me."

C—— made the airy, exasperated gesture of dismissal another time, and B—— caught his arm. "Just tell me. The truth."

C—— said, "I was not here. But I think you were, and you were afraid to discover him, by yourself. So you called me."

"I said *I did not call you*! You called me."

"And you're the one with the key. The beloved 'elder.' The favorite son."

"That's crazy. I don't have a key. You know that Dad didn't entrust keys to this house to anyone."

"Do I? I know that? On whose authority, yours?"

C—— spoke sneeringly, though he was sickly pale, and obviously very frightened. By this time both brothers were ascending the stairs, which creaked beneath their weight. They moved with painful deliberation, as if the pull of the earth's gravity had suddenly trebled. The air on the staircase and at the head of the stairs was humid, shimmering. It was all the brothers could do to keep from gagging. Now B—— was gripping C——'s arm at the elbow, and C—— didn't throw off his hand.

Slowly they made their way along the upstairs hall, which was darker than the downstairs hall, and longer than they recalled. They passed their former rooms: the doors appeared to be nailed shut. At the far end of the hall was their parents' sumptuously furnished bedroom, the master bedroom as it was called, which had been forbidden to B—— and C—— as children. If the door was open, and their mother called them inside, they were welcome to enter (and what a delight it was to enter!), otherwise not. Now the shut door was a reminder, and a rebuke to the brothers' childish, unspeakable desires.

"He's inside. I know it."

It was B——'s duty, he supposed, to push the door inward. But he could hardly lift his arm, which was as heavy as lead. C——, breathing quickly and shallowly beside him, made a feeble effort to turn the knob.

Somehow, they managed to open the door. Each pushed the palm of his shaking hand against it, and the door swung inward.

There, comfortably lying on a leather chaise lounge, a knitted coverlet spread over his arthritic knees, Dr. A—— was watching television. In his uplifted right hand, like a wand, he held the black plastic remote control. For a long moment, suspended as if the old man had pressed PAUSE on the control, Dr. A—— stared at his middle-aged twin sons, and his middle-aged twin sons stared at him. No one could speak.

Then Dr. A—— said, with scarcely concealed disgust, "So. You're too busy to call your elderly widower-father, but you've come intruding into his house, uninvited. What were you thinking? Hoping? That 'something had happened to Dad'?"

Both B—— and C—— began to stammer apologies.

"Dad, we thought—"

"Dad, we tried to call you—"

"You hadn't called us, Dad—"

"We were worried, Dad—"

"We were very w-worried—"

"Sons, go. Leave me. The sight of you revulses me. I don't doubt you've come sniffing around for your inheritances. But you've come too soon, by years."

Dr. A—— lifted the remote control and pressed FAST-FORWARD.

The brothers were downstairs in the kitchen, breathless and confused. For a dazed moment B—— couldn't recall: had they just entered the house? He'd just smashed the back door with the gardening shears? C—— was wiping his forehead, which was damp and clammy as the skin of a dead man. He removed his glasses to wipe the steamed lenses. It seemed to C—— that their father had forced them out of the master bedroom, yet he couldn't remember his father actually touching him.

B—— said in a hoarse whisper, "You led me into this! You've made a fool of me. Dad will never forgive me."

C—— protested, "Why is it my fault? You wanted to come here. You broke in the door."

"*You* broke in the door. Damn you!"

"You thought he was dead, not me. You kept saying—"

"You knew! This was a trick you and Dad concocted. To humiliate me."

"But you kept saying he was dead. You were the one who wanted to take the deer rifle from him."

"And you were the one who thought we shouldn't even mention it, though Dad has obviously been suicidal for years."

"He isn't suicidal, we just saw him. Didn't we just see him?"

"We haven't been upstairs yet, how could we see him?"

"Yes. We've been upstairs. He expelled us, he sent us out of the room. He's furious with us both, and it was your fault."

Suddenly the brothers were quarreling. They took no care if their father could hear them, their voices were young and aggrieved. It might have been the very day, the very hour of their mother's death. Their grief was fury, their hearts beat like furious fists in their chests. Tears spilled hotly from their eyes, with a rank, salty taste like blood. B—— was fumbling to snatch up a steak knife that looked to be about eight inches long out of the stagnant water in the sink. But C——, the more athletic and active of the brothers, with quicker reflexes, yanked open a drawer beside the stove and took out a bread knife of at least ten inches, not sharply honed, rather dull, but adequate for his purposes, for he meant only to defend himself against his crazed elder brother. The knife flashed, stabbing B—— about the shoulders and arms, as if it had acquired a demonic life of its own. B—— cried, "Stop! No!" The brothers struggled like a drunken couple trying to dance. The music in their heads was deafening, the sticky linoleum floor tilted giddily beneath their feet. B——'s hands were suddenly lacerated and slick with blood, but he managed to pick up one of the kitchen chairs, a vinyl-covered metal chair with tubular legs, and he swung it clumsily at C——'s face, which was contorted with hatred. The slippery bread knife went flying, across the Formica-topped table and onto the floor. Both brothers lunged for it. On the TV screen, so accustomed to professionally choreographed knife-fighting scenes, their antics were clumsily, unintentionally comic despite their desire to murder each other; yet they managed to snatch up the knife, each brother's fingers on it, B—— was grappling with C——, C—— was grappling with B——, the knife flashed and flew in an arc and was brought up with stunning swiftness and finality into the soft abdomen of one of the brothers, as if gutting a fish. The brothers were now slipping in blood. On their hands and knees, slipping in blood. The bread knife was being drawn, sawed jerkily back and forth across a neck, except because the blade wasn't very sharp, an inhuman strength was required.

Quickly, Dr. A —— pressed REWIND.

The telephone rang just as B —— was glancing up worriedly from *Great Doomed Expeditions: The Yukon*. His wife said, with a smile, "That's your brother." B —— said, "I hope not." He meant to be amusing, of course.

Stripping

Stripping the filthy things off. The stained things. The smells. Onto the floor with the filthy stripped-off things. Onto the floor with the stained things, the smells. Beneath the shower's nozzle. Hot hot as you can bear. Hot water streaming over shut eyes. *Why h'lo there! H'lo you do I know you?* Teasing smile. Taunting smile. *Think I do know you don't I?* Stripping off the smell of her. Onto the floor with the filth and the smell of her. And in the shower in the rising steam roughly soaping your hair that is strange to you, so greasy, spiky like the coarse fur of a beast. Soaping your torso, armpits. Your torso an armor of flesh covered in coils of wire. Your armpits bristling with wire. Washing away the body smells. And your filthy hands. Scratched knuckles, wrists. Broken fingernails and dried blood beneath. Draw your nails hard across the bar of soap, clean out the blood. Soap slipping from your clumsy hand you stoop to retrieve, grunting, the weight of your head suddenly heavy and pulses beating in your eyes, hearing her cry out in the terror of recognition *No no why? no let me go! why?* as hot water streams down your face like liquid fire *Why hurt me, why? why hurt another person* a riddle to echo in the shower's steam in the sharp needles of water erupting from the nozzle turned downward toward your face. The soap is luminous white like an object floating in a dream, you must not lapse into a dream but must carefully wash scrub cleanse yourself, lather away the blood and skin particles beneath your fingernails broken against her skin, repulsive to touch and smell, the sharp piercing cries, quivering eyelids and bleeding mouth gaping like the mouth of a fish drowning in air *No no oh let me go let me   Why are you doing this?* flecks of dead skin washing away, soapy water tinged with red swirling down the drain faint and fading and your powerful lower body eel-like lathered in soap, a luminous white gossamer of soap through which the wire-hairs protrude. If the body could speak *Yes I am lonely, it is my loneliness that must be revenged* this is why you were born, the simplicity of life-in-the-body, in-the-moment, the instincts of the predator cruising rain-washed streets as a shark might cruise the ocean open-mouthed seeking prey, cruising the nighttime city, in the distance the sound of a train whistle, melancholy and fading as the cry of a distant bird. Pleading for her life though such a debased life! Pleading for her life but this is life. No need to force her, on her knees she sank willingly. *I know you   think I know you hmmm?* Her soul was a frail fluttering butterfly. Her soul was soiled white wings beating. Her soul was torn wings, broken wings bravely beating. Her soul was a sudden sharp smell of animal terror. Saliva at the corners of the contorted mouth. In the ruin of the abandoned house. Crumbling bricks, rotted floorboards. Underfoot lay a child's mitten stiff with filth. Underfoot a torn calendar, stained newspapers. Stumbling in the dark laughing, dared to take your hand *Come this way   You know the way I think you do   you teasing* taunting eyes glassy-festive, high on methamphetamine, picking her way through the filth to the mattress that was known to her, stained beforehand with her blood or the blood of someone very like her *Where've I seen you before   have you seen me*   smiling as if laughing inside, where her soul was filth and it came to you in a wave of disgust like filthy water in your mouth that maybe she was known to you, in your memory known to you, in an earlier life you had been a schoolteacher until the school was barred to you, the children's eyes sharp as beaks pecking, maybe the woman had been a child once in your classroom in St. Ignatius Middle School in an earlier life before the school was taken from you and all seemed clear to you suddenly *Yes I am lonely, it is my loneliness that feeds me* beneath the shower in the sharp-stinging needles of water, such pleasure, such happiness, now the filthy things have been stripped off, the stained things and the smells and blood swirling down the drain and gone and the fragrance of soap in your nostrils, the simplicity of the naked body armored in flesh covered in wire-hairs thrumming with life, with heat *My loneliness I have come to love* this is why you were born, strip all else away and this is it.

The Museum of Dr. Moses

1. 1956

"Mommy!"

The things flew at me out of the sky. I thought they were darning needles stabbing my face. Some were in my hair, and some had gotten inside my pink ruffled sundress Mommy had sewed for me. I was trying to shield my eyes. I was four years old, I knew nothing of self-defense, yet instinctively I knew to shield my eyes. A stabbing, stinging, angry buzzing against my face, my cheeks, my tender exposed ears! I screamed, "Mommy! *Mommy!*" And there came Mommy to rescue me, only just happening to worry about where I might be, having wandered off behind my grandfather's hay barn; only just happening, as she would say afterward, to tilt her head to listen attentively for the cry of a little girl that might easily have been confused with the sharp cries of birds or cicadas or the half-feral tomcats that lived in the barn.

"Mom*my!*"

She heard. She didn't hesitate for a moment. She ran, swift and unerring as a young girl, though she was thirty-two years old and had not fully recovered from a miscarriage the previous spring, and was not in any case a woman accustomed to running. She heard my desperate cries and was herself panicked and yet had enough presence of mind to tear a bath towel off my grandmother's clothesline with which to wrap me, roughly, efficiently, as if putting out flames. Mommy shielded me from the wasps with both the towel and her bare, vulnerable flesh. She was being stung herself, a dozen times, yet tried to comfort me as I screamed in pain and terror — "It's all right, Ella! Mommy's got you." She half-carried me, half-ran with me out of the orchard, away from the pear tree disfigured by a black knot and by a gigantic wasps' papery gray nest attached like a goiter to the tree trunk overhead at a height of about nine feet; away from the crazed cloud of wasps that had erupted out of nowhere.

Long afterward my mother would say with her breathy, nervous laugh that she hadn't felt much pain herself, at the time. Not until later. For nothing had mattered except rescuing me.

"My mother saved my life, when I was four years old."

This was a statement I would make often, to new friends, or to people who, for one reason or another, I hoped to impress. *I was so loved once. I was a very lucky child.*

"My mother gave me life, and my mother saved my life. When I was four years old."

Is this true? I wonder: could a child die of multiple wasp stings? I think probably, yes. I think a child could die of the shock of the stings, the trauma of the assault as well as the wasps' venom. Perhaps an adult woman could die of such an assault, too.

2. The Summons

Twenty-two years later, driving north to see Mother, from whom I'd been estranged for the past decade and to whom I hadn't spoken for several years, I was thinking of these things. Driving north to the town of my birth, Strykersville, New York, and beyond Strykersville into the abandoned farmland and foothills of Eden County, I told myself, as if to comfort myself, the familiar story: four-year-old Ella exploring Grandpa's pear orchard, wandering far from the adults seated on the veranda of the old farmhouse, attacked suddenly by wasps that seemed to fly at her out of the sky; screaming, "Mommy!"—and Mommy running desperately to save her. It was a fairy tale with a happy ending.

(But where in this story was Daddy? He had not yet left us. He must have been there, somewhere. Or had he, too, wandered off from the adults on the veranda, in another direction? Maybe he'd even gotten into the car and driven away, into Strykersville, restless for a change of scenery. An hour's diversion in a local tavern. There was no Daddy in my story, and never had been.)

Like all beloved family stories, this story had been enhanced over the years. It had been enlarged to include a description of Ella's pretty pink sundress with the ruffled bodice that she'd worn for the first time that day, and Ella's blond-gold hair prettily braided, by Mommy, into two shoulder-length plaits entwined with pink satin ribbons. It had been enlarged to include an acknowledgment of my mother's physical condition, which hadn't been robust. *Yet Ginny never hesitated. How that woman ran! And none of us had even heard Ella crying.*

Snapshots of those lost years show my older brother, Walter, and me smiling and seemingly happy, and Mommy more somber, though attempting her usual earnest smile; a youngish woman with an oddly wide, sensual mouth; her dark hair parted on the left side of her head in the overly prim style of the fifties. In a typical picture Mommy would be crouching between Walter and me, her arms tightly around us to steady us, or to prevent us from squirming; face blurred, eyes averted shyly from the camera. (Which had probably been held by Daddy, who liked mechanical things, and did not like his picture taken, at least with his young family.)

Poor Ginny. She hadn't been well . . . Because, it was vaguely said, of the miscarriage; because she'd never gotten over giving birth to the little girl, a thirty-hour labor; because of certain "female weaknesses." (Meaning what? In that era in which breast, cervical and ovarian cancer as well as more ordinary menstrual problems were mysteriously alluded to as "women's shame," it was difficult to guess what this ominous term meant.) And because, just possibly, though this was never uttered in my hearing, she had a husband with a quick temper and quick fists who'd tired of loving her during her first pregnancy. *But Ginny is so devoted. So forgiving.*

Forgiving! That was the primary reason I'd become estranged from my mother. Not just Mother had endured my father's crude, often dangerous behavior when Walter and I were growing up, but, after her divorce, when I was in high school, she fell into the same pattern with Walter. He'd dropped out of school and never kept a job for more than a few weeks, he was a "charming" boy but a chronic drinker while still in his teens. Mother pleaded with me to be more understanding. "Ella, you're too hard on your brother. Ella, he's *your brother*." And I would secretly think, embittered as only a good, dutiful daughter can be, confronted with her mother's weak, hapless love for one who didn't deserve it *No. He isn't my brother, he's your son.*

After my grandparents died, Mother inherited their farm. It was only eleven acres, yet a fairly large property by Eden County standards. This she'd sold piecemeal, year by year; she worked at various jobs in Strykersville to support her family (receptionist for our family dentist, saleslady at Strykersville's department store, substitute junior high school teacher—a nightmare job she'd dreaded), and I'd taken part-time jobs while still in high school; but Walter drained our meager savings, my damned brother was always the issue, and when Mother paid a $2,500 fine for him after an accident he'd had driving while intoxicated, an accident in which the other driver was seriously injured, I stopped speaking to Mother. *You've chosen between us. Good!* I was disgusted with family life and with small-town life. I left Strykersville at the age of seventeen, attended the State Teachers' College at Oneida on a scholarship, worked at part-time jobs to support myself for four years, and was proud of my independence. I associated Strykersville with the past and I had no nostalgic yearning for the past, I'm not a sentimental person. For what is sentiment but weakness, and usually "female weakness"? *I am not one of you.*

I lived now outside Philadelphia. I had a good, if demanding, teaching job in a private school. I told myself that I didn't miss my mother, and I certainly didn't miss my brother who'd disappeared into America sometime in the midseventies. I had friends, and I had lovers—to a degree. (No one has ever gotten too close to me. Except for my mother, which is the reason I don't entirely trust anyone.) If the subject of family came up, I explained that I was estranged from mine. That had a dignified, nineteenth-century sound. But one evening, with an older woman friend, I began talking about my mother who'd saved my life, and I became emotional. I began telling my friend of the knitting, embroidering, sewing my mother had done, so many beautiful things over the years; she asked if I had any of these things and I said yes, I'd taken a few articles of clothing when I'd left home, a knitted cashmere coat-sweater, a long-sleeved silk blouse, a wool jersey vest with mother-of-pearl buttons. My friend examined these items and marveled over them — "Your mother is a wonderful seamstress. And she's never sewn for money?" I shrugged indifferently. Possibly I had not wanted to feel emotion. "I don't really wear this kind of clothing," I said. "It isn't my style." My friend was peering at the inside of the silk blouse, holding it to the light. "See this fine stitching? This is the Fortuny stitch. And this exquisite lace hem. What an interesting woman your mother must be!"

I looked, and saw, yes, the stitching was fine, and intricate, but what was the point of it? And the lace hem: why had my mother gone to so much trouble, to hem a blouse in lace, on the underside of the material where no one would ever see?

Driving north to Strykersville, a distance of several hundred miles from my home, I thought of these things as a way of not thinking of the present.

Driving north to Strykersville in the oppressive heat of August, after so many years, I thought of my mother as she'd been, as a way of not thinking of the woman she might be now.

She was fifty-four years old. To me, at twenty-six, *old*.

She was Mrs. Moses Hammacher now, she'd remarried abruptly, the previous March.

Wife of Dr. Moses!

After almost twenty years of being a divorced woman in a small town in which divorce was rare, yet a divorced woman whose husband was known to have been an abusive alcoholic, so that sympathy was entirely with my mother, and no one would have dreamed of criticizing her, my mother had suddenly, without warning, remarried: a locally known retired physician and Eden County coroner named Moses Hammacher, familiarly called Dr. Moses.

Dr. Moses! He'd been an old man, gaunt and white-haired, or so it had seemed to me, when I was in junior high.

Mother, how could you?

I had tried to call her. Finally, I'd written a brief letter to her, sending it in care of relatives to be forwarded. I had to assume the letter had been received by my mother, though — of course — Mother hadn't answered it. Since then I had not slept well. My sleep was thin like mist or spray, disturbed by strange echoing voices and muffled laughter. And my mother's voice sudden, pleading — *Ella? Come to me! Help me.*

In Strykersville, I drove across the familiar jarring railroad tracks and it was as if I'd never left. Though I had been imagining my hometown as unpopulated, for some reason, a ghost town, yet of course there was traffic on the streets, there were people on the sidewalks downtown, and probably I would recognize some of these people if I lingered. I did take note of the number of FOR RENT, FOR LEASE, FOR SALE signs; I saw abandoned, boarded-up houses. I drove past our old church, the First Presbyterian, to which Mother had taken Walter and me, before we were old enough to rebel; I drove past my old high school, which had been renovated and enlarged; I felt my heartbeat quicken in apprehension and dread. *Why am I here? She doesn't want me. If she wanted me . . .*

Mother had not invited me to her wedding, of course. She had not even informed me she'd remarried, I had learned from relatives.

The shock of it! The shame. Learning that your mother has remarried from relatives. And that she was now the wife of Dr. Moses.

I'd instructed myself before I began my trip that I would not do this, yet here I was driving around Strykersville, staring with rapt, lovesick eyes. Did I miss my past, truly? Did I miss *this*? I'd thought myself very shrewd—and very lucky—to have escaped this economically depressed region of Upstate New York as I'd escaped the confinements of my former life, and it seemed to me a risky matter, a sign of my own recklessness, that I'd been drawn back into it, like a moth blindly flying into a gigantic cobweb.

"Mother! Goddamn *you*."

For there I was driving slowly past our old brown-shingled house on Iroquois Street, with the flower beds Mother had worked so hard to keep in bloom, and the flowering Russian olive tree she'd kept watered through summer droughts, my eyes misting over with tears. The house now belonged to strangers, of course. I wondered what price Mother had gotten for the property, and where the money had gone: for according to my cousin Brenda, who'd been the one to give me information about Mother, she'd sold everything very quickly, including most of her long-cherished furniture, and even her car, after her "private" wedding to Dr. Moses Hammacher, and had gone to live with her new husband in his stone house in the Oriskany hills nine miles northeast of Strykersville. The doctor had had an office in Strykersville, in fact he'd had two offices, as a GP and as Eden County coroner; but he'd long since retired. My cousin Brenda believed that Dr. Moses—Dr. Hammacher—still saw some of his elderly patients; and that he'd turned part of his house into a kind of museum. "Museum?" I asked incredulously, and Brenda explained it was probably just an old man's hobby—"To give him something to do, you know, in his retirement." "But is this an actual *museum*? Open to the public?" Brenda said, "After the Fowler House was taken over by the County Historical Society, and all those old antiques, weaving looms, dressmakers' dummies, washboards and butter churns and whatever were put on display, Dr. Moses demanded money from the society to start a museum of his own. A history of medical arts in Eden County, which means, I suppose, a history of *Dr. Moses*! So the society gave him a small grant, to humor him, but he wanted more, and broke off relations with the society, and I guess he has this museum out in Oriskany, such as it is. Medical school things like skeletons and 'cadavers' made of plaster, old instruments, office equipment, things floating in formaldehyde . . . A few people went to see it out of curiosity when it opened about five years ago, but I never went." Brenda paused. She was conscious of speaking in an amused voice, and had suddenly realized that she was talking about my new stepfather. "Ella, I'm sorry. I'm sure . . . your mother is happy with Dr. Moses." But she sounded doubtful.

I said, miserably, "Why on earth would Mother marry *Dr. Moses*? He's old enough to be her father." *And my grandfather. But I don't want another grandfather.*

Brenda said sympathetically, "I can imagine you're upset, Ella. We all were, at first. I mean . . . your mother is so *sweet*. So *trusting*. And Dr. Moses is, well . . . a kind of strong-willed man, I guess. He must be in his mideighties yet he doesn't seem terribly old when you see him. Certainly his mind is sharp as always. Razor sharp. Maybe your mother needs some-one strong willed to take care of her." Was this a reproach? Quickly Brenda amended, "Ella, your mother told me, when I happened to run into her downtown, a few days before the wedding, that she was 'embarking on a new life' — she was 'very happy' — she and Dr. Moses were driving to Mexico, where she'd never been, on their honeymoon. She said she had been 'very lonely' — but that was over now. I'm sure that she married Dr. Moses voluntarily; I mean, I don't think he coerced her in any way. You know what your mother is like, Ella!"

Did I? Even when I'd lived with my mother, had I known her?

As if hoping to console me, now that she'd upset me, Brenda went on to say that Dr. Moses was still an individual of some reputation in the county. He still drove his fancy British car, a twenty-year-old silver green Bentley, which was like no other car in the county; he'd also acquired a Land Rover, plus an RV, of the kind popular with retired people. Still, he cut a gentlemanly, dapper figure in Strykersville, with his dignified derby hats in cool weather and festive straw hats in warm weather. He wore his trademark pinstriped suits, white starched cotton shirts with monogrammed gold cuff links, striped neckties. People respected him, though they tended to joke nervously about him as they'd always done. (I recalled how, years ago, my high school girlfriends made a show of shuddering and shivering as Dr. Moses passed by us on the sidewalk, tipping his hat and smiling his white-toothed smile, "Good day, girls!" His gaze, mildly defracted by bifocal lenses, lingered on us. We had to wonder who would wish to be county coroner and examine dead, sometimes badly disfigured and mangled bodies extracted from wrecks? And for virtually no salary.) This tall, white-haired gentleman had been both Dr. Hammacher, a well-to-do physician with a general practice, and Dr. Moses, the cheery county official who was invited into public schools in the district to give talks and slide presentations with such titles as "You and Your Anatomy" and "The Miracle of Eyesight." As Dr. Moses he exuded an air of civic responsibility like those fanatically active businessmen who ran the Strykersville Chamber of Commerce, the Rotary Club, the Loyal Order of Moose and other service organizations. I'd thought him older than my grandfather back in the midsixties when he came to our junior high assembly to speak on "The Miracle of Eyesight."

For this, an energetic talk that left the more sensitive among us queasy, Dr. Moses used a large plaster-of-paris eyeball as a prop; it swung hideously open in sections to reveal the veiny interior of the eye, uncomfortably suggesting a dissection. I felt light-headed, and resistant. Yet Dr. Moses must have made a strong impression on me since I remembered long afterward certain parts of the eye: the pupil, the cornea, the lens, the iris, the retina, the sclera, the aqueous humor, the vitreous humor, the optic nerve, the blind spot. Dr. Moses concluded his presentation by appealing to us, "So you see, boys and girls, the miraculous anatomy of the human eye alone teaches us that evolution—the blind chance of natural selection, survival of the fittest—is simply not feasible. No organ so complex as the human eye could have 'evolved' in a hit-or-miss fashion as the Darwinists say. Nor could it have evolved out of some primal protoplasm. It would have to have been, like our souls, *created*." Dr. Moses squinted at us through his shiny bifocals. "By a *creator*." How dramatically the man spoke! In our naïveté some of us may have confused white-haired Dr. Moses in his gray pinstriped suit with *creator*. "Are there any questions, boys and girls?" Our mouths wanted to smile, to grimace and giggle, but could not.

And now, as in a malevolent fairy tale, Dr. Moses had married my mother.

Dr. Moses was my stepfather.

Dazed, I heard Brenda's cautious voice. She was asking, "Ella? You aren't crying, are you?" and I said quickly, incensed, "Of course I'm not crying! I'm laughing."

3. In Oriskany

Strange to be driving here alone.

I stopped in Strykersville only briefly, and continued out into the country toward Oriskany. As I ascended into the hills I felt as if I were driving, under a strange half-pleasurable compulsion, into the past: there were farmhouses, barns, granaries I vaguely recalled, though a number of these were for sale or abandoned; there was the old Starlite Drive-In on the Oriskany Pike, a morose, funereal ruin jutting up above overgrown fields. About three miles north of Strykersville I crossed the high, humpbacked, rusted-iron bridge above Eden Creek that I vaguely recalled as one of the nightmare bridges of my childhood: below, the creek was diminished and mud colored, its gnarled banks exposed in the languid heat of August. Descending the steep bridge ramp I saw, nailed to an oak tree by the side of the road, a small, darkly weathered sign:

MUSEUM OF EDEN COUNTY MEDICAL ARTS
6 MILES

The museum of Dr. Moses existed! The next signs appeared at two-mile intervals, all of them small and undistinguished; finally, when the Oriskany Pike veered to the east, a sign at the crossroads indicated that the museum was a half mile away, on a gravel, single-lane county road. At the crossroads were a boarded-up Sunoco gas station and a dilapidated bait shop. Nearby was an abandoned farm; the land surrounding it had long since reverted to tall grasses, nettles, scrub trees. Yet the landscape here in Oriskany was starkly beautiful: the foothills miles away at the horizon, in a checkered pattern of luminous golden sunlight and shadow that moved slowly across it, like brooding thoughts, cast by isolated clouds. Though the air at ground level was hot, hazy, humid as an expelled breath, the sky overhead was a crystalline blue.

I turned onto the gravel road and drove a half mile. There was no mistaking Dr. Moses's house/museum for it seemed to be the only human habitation on the road, and the sign in the weedy front yard was prominent.

MUSEUM OF EDEN COUNTY MEDICAL ARTS
PROPRIETOR MOSES HAMMACHER, MD
HOURS DAILY EXCEPT MONDAY
10 A.M.–4:30 P.M.
FREE ADMISSION

There was something naive and touching about Dr. Moses's museum, I thought. The carefully posted visiting hours, the appeal implicit in *free admission*. For who would ever come to such a remote, dreary place? The house was tall, dignified, impressive; one of those gaunt stone houses built at the turn of the century, with steep roofs (because of the heavy, often damp snowfall south of Lake Ontario from November through early April); the gray fieldstone of which the house had been constructed looked bleak and stained. There were double bay windows and a narrow veranda. On the highest peak of the roof there was even a lightning rod, a relic of a vanished rural past, only just slightly askew. (And there was a TV antenna.) I parked my car in the cinder driveway, conscious of being watched. (A movement at one of the downstairs windows?) Though I'd written to my mother telling her I would be coming, I couldn't be sure that she'd received the letter, and that anyone expected me. Or would wish to see me.

Judging from the waist-high grasses surrounding the house and by the quantity of weeds in the driveway, there were few visitors to Dr. Moses's museum.

As I climbed out of my car I thought I saw again, fleetingly, a movement at one of the windows. Dr. Moses? Or— Mother? Frightened at what I might find inside, I smiled, and called out shyly, "Hello? It's me, Ella." I felt it might be a mistake to step boldly onto the veranda and ring the doorbell, though visitors to the museum would be expected to do this. "Ella McIntyre." As if my last name might be required! My hands were shaking badly by this time, and my throat was painfully dry.

After a moment the front door opened, and a figure appeared in the doorway. I smiled, and waved. "Hello! It's Ella."

Dr. Moses stepped out onto the sunlit veranda and regarded me in silence. I was startled that the man, in person, so closely resembled the Dr. Moses I'd been envisioning. Except that he wasn't so tall as I remembered, and his hair, though still surprisingly thick, was no longer snowy white but a faded ivory. He wore a starched white shirt, sleeves rolled casually to his elbows, and dark, pressed slacks. At a distance of twelve or fifteen feet he seemed to me quite handsome, an individual of some distinction, though obviously elderly. And he'd put on his head, in a gesture of hasty gallantry, one of his straw hats. His right hand was held at a stiff, unnatural angle, however, pressed against a pocket of his slacks as if against—what? A weapon? Not a gun, it wouldn't have been large enough. A knife, or a small hammer? A scalpel?

Cicadas screamed out of nearby trees. The heat lifted from the earth into my face. I was reminded of that attack of wasps out of the sky. I smiled harder, as a flirtatious child might smile at her taciturn, frowning grandfather. "Dr. Moses? It's your stepdaughter, Ella."

Suddenly, Dr. Moses's face melted into a smile. His teeth were still shiny white, and his eyes, behind winking bifocals, were appreciative, affectionate. "Ella, dear girl, hello! Your mother and I have been waiting for you."

It isn't possible, he remembers me? As a girl, years ago?
Dr. Moses has been awaiting me, all this time?

Gentlemanly Dr. Moses left my mother and me alone to visit in the parlor. Though we were shy with each other, self-conscious and awkward. I kept wanting to touch Mother, as if to prove she was *here*, and I was *here*, this wasn't a dream. I kept saying, dazed, "You look so young, Mother. You look so pretty."

"And you, Ella. You've grown into a . . . beautiful young woman."

We gripped hands, and stared at each other. I was feeling faint and I believed that Mother was deeply moved as well. Her thin fingers were icy, I'd noticed a mild palsied tremor in both her hands. Tears brimmed in her eyes that seemed to me strangely exposed, and enlarged, as if lashless. Several times she wanted to say more, but stammered and fell silent. Was she frightened? Of me, or of her own emotion? Or — of her husband? After Dr. Moses's initial, courtly greeting of me, whom he referred to as his "prodigal stepdaughter," he'd retreated upstairs, meaning to be inconspicuous perhaps, but his slow, circling footsteps sounded directly overhead; the high ceiling above creaked; Mother glanced upward, distracted. I was asking her simple, innocuous questions about her wedding, her honeymoon, relatives, Strykersville neighbors and friends, and she answered in monosyllables; I told her about my teaching job, my semidetached brownstone with its small rear garden, my regret that I hadn't seen her in so long. Some caution prevented me asking of more crucial matters. I sensed that my mother's mood was fragile. And a harshly medicinal, gingery odor pervaded the room, making my nostrils constrict; after only a few minutes I began to feel mildly nauseated. The parlor was furnished in period pieces of the late nineteenth century (not a single item anything I recognized of Mother's) and its two tall, narrow windows were shaded against the August heat; brass lamps with curiously leathery shades emitted a dim light. Truly I could not see Mother clearly, even at close range. *Ella! Help me.* I heard this appeal silently, as Mother squeezed my hands.

I whispered, "Mother? Is anything wrong?" but immediately she pressed her fingers against my lips and shook her head *no*.

Meaning *no*, there was nothing wrong? Or *no*, this wasn't the time to ask?

In her weak, eager voice Mother asked, "How long can you stay, Ella? We were hoping—a few days?"

A few days! I didn't believe I could bear more than a few more minutes, the smell made me so nauseated.

Yet I was smiling, nodding. "That would be lovely, Mother. If you and . . ." (I paused, for to call my stepfather Dr. Moses as we'd called him as schoolchildren seemed inappropriate) "and he—wouldn't be inconvenienced?" In the airless heat of the parlor I was nearly shivering. I was desperate to flee this oppressive place, yet I would not leave without Mother, if she needed me.

"But Dr. Moses expects you to stay with us," Mother protested, "—he's had me prepare a guest room. I've prepared your favorite dessert for dinner tonight. Dr. Moses is very eager to get to know you, Ella. I've told him about you." Mother spoke wistfully. (What could she have told Dr. Moses about me that wouldn't have given her pain?) I noted that Mother, too, called her courtly husband Dr. Moses. I wondered if such old-fashioned formality was a natural part of their relationship. For Mother was so much younger than Dr. Moses Hammacher, a girlish, indecisive personality clearly dependent on him, it would have been difficult for her to call him Moses, as if they were equals.

"I suppose I could stay. At least tonight . . ."

"Oh Ella, you *must*. Dr. Moses and I would be so disappointed if you didn't."

Dr. Moses and I. I didn't like the sound of that.

It was strange: I had not made any plans for the night. Vaguely I might have planned to return to Strykersville to stay with Brenda, or in a motel; next morning, I might have driven back to Oriskany to visit with my mother, if our first visit had gone well. But really I hadn't thought that far ahead, my mind was blank as a child's.

Overhead, the ceiling creaked. I glanced upward nervously.

"I was surprised to hear you'd married Dr. Moses, Mother. But of course I'm happy for you." I peered closely at her. *Should I be?* "Brenda has told me . . . you sold the house, and everything in it, and your car. It was a small, private wedding."

"Not a church wedding," Mother said, smiling regretfully. "Dr. Moses doesn't believe in 'superstitious religions,' as he calls them. But he does believe in a *creator*."

"He seems very . . ." Again I paused, desperate to think of the appropriate word. ". . . gentlemanly."

Mother laughed suddenly, and winced as if it hurt her to laugh. Tenderly she touched her face at her hairline. "Oh, yes. He *is*."

"And you seem so — happy. Together."

Was this true? I'd seen Mother and Dr. Moses for only a few minutes when I'd first arrived at the house. During that time, Dr. Moses had done most of the talking.

Again Mother laughed, and winced. The footsteps had ceased circling overhead. (Was Dr. Moses coming downstairs to join us?)

"I am happy, Ella. My life was empty and selfish before I met Dr. Moses. It was at the funeral of your great-aunt Helena May—you wouldn't remember her, she died at the age of ninety-seven. But Dr. Moses had known her. He claimed to have been a beau of hers. This was just last fall! Since then . . ." Mother stared at me with her exposed, lashless eyes. *Ella, please. Don't judge me harshly. Help me.* Her hands were visibly trembling. There was a tremor in her left eyelid. She was clearly a woman in distress, in thrall to a tyrannical male. Yet it was typical of my mother, maddeningly typical, that she would wish to defend him, in her weak, hopeful way, as for years she'd defended my father, and then my brother, as if she believed such loyalty was expected of her as a good woman. "I can help Dr. Moses, you see. With his work. He's such an idealist! And sometimes he isn't well. I don't mean in his soul, he has a strong, pure soul, but in his 'mortal coils,' as he calls his body. For he will be eighty-five years old in December. Such a youthful eighty-five! Still, he needs me. And I didn't need that house, or those possessions, or even a car. Dr. Moses has a car, and a Land Rover. He will drive me anywhere I need to go, and my needs are few. In fact we've gone on several journeys together, and have new trips planned: to Alaska, next summer, where Dr. Moses has been years ago, which he describes as 'beautiful, and so pure.' Sometimes, in remote places, where medical help isn't readily available, Dr. Moses volunteers his services; and people are so *grateful*. They've given him gifts, mementos." Mother was speaking rapidly, almost feverishly. As if wanting to convince herself as well as me. "Dr. Moses is a special person, Ella. He isn't ordinary. People whisper about him behind his back—and about me, I know!—but they're just jealous. I've helped him with the museum, you know. I'll be helping him when he expands it. I want to help him. He's so proud of the museum. He'll be showing you through it, before dinner. The County Historical Society insulted him, Ella! Giving him such a small grant. A man of his accomplishments! Dr. Moses deserves more respect from the citizens of Eden County, and he will receive it."

"How have you helped Dr. Moses with the museum, Mother?"

By giving him your money, obviously. What else?

Mother smiled mysteriously. The tremor in her eyelid was more visible. Her eyes brimmed with tears and, unexpectedly, she hid her face in her hands.

Earlier, when I'd first arrived, we'd embraced awkwardly, and shyly, scarcely touching. For Dr. Moses had been present. But now I hugged my mother hard, to comfort her, as she tried not to cry. I was shocked by how much weight she'd lost, I could feel her ribs through the filmy layers of her shirtwaist as she trembled in my arms. What most shocked me was that the medicinal, gingery smell wafted from her, like perfume.

"Mother, what is it? Tell me."

It was then that Dr. Moses entered the room, pushing open the door without knocking. Gently he said, "Ella, dear. You're upsetting your mother, you see. Which you don't want to do, if you value Virginia's health."

4. The Museum of Dr. Moses: First Visit

Dr. Moses was eager to show me the museum. By this time, I was very curious about what it might be.

On a table at the entrance was an opened ledger for visitors to sign. Surreptitiously I saw that the last visitors were a couple from Troy, New York, who'd been there on June 8, 1978. More than two months ago. Prior to that, someone had visited in April. "Not everyone signs the ledger," Dr. Moses said severely, seeing where I was looking. "Some visitors forget."

Immediately I took up the pen and signed.

Ellen McIntyre   Bryn Mawr, PA   11 August 1978

(Strange, how you wanted to please Dr. Moses! A childish wish to entice, out of that gaunt brooding face, the man's sudden approving, warm, fatherly smile.)

"Very good, Ella! Now Ella McIntyre is part of the museum's official history."

With the air of an impresario, Dr. Moses switched on lights and ushered me into a large, rectangular, cluttered room that had probably once been the formal living room of the old stone house. There were double bay windows, and an imposing marble fireplace. The twelve-foot ceiling was a filigree of cracks and the ornamental moldings at the top of the walls were outlined in grime. The space was airless and intense, as if most of its oxygen had been siphoned off. The medicinal-gingery odor I had smelled on my mother prevailed here, but was challenged by a stronger, sharper odor — formaldehyde? And there was the underlying odor of dust, mice, time that belonged to such houses. I felt light-headed, thinking of my poor mother trapped in this place, deluded into imagining herself the beloved helper of a vain, eccentric husband. At once, I could see Mother's touch in the museum: the dark crimson silk panels at the windows, which could be drawn over the venetian blinds by cords, made from the identical pattern of our living room drapes in the Iroquois Street house; several attractive hooked rugs of the kind Mother used to make to give to relatives and friends, like the one I'd had in my college dormitory room, of which I'd been proud; hand-sewn linen lampshades in that dignified hue called eggshell. "How ambitious this is," I heard myself say falteringly, for I felt that some immediate, positive response was required. "How — *interesting*." My nostrils constricted, I had to fight an impulse to gag. Dr. Moses took not the slightest notice of my discomfort, for clearly he was captivated by his own domain. Proudly he showed me a row of glass display cases that had obviously been dusted and cleaned very recently, perhaps that very day, for there were telltale lines of demarcation between grime and polished glass; I had a disagreeable vision of my mother, frail, unwell, hurriedly dusting and cleaning these cases under Dr. Moses's sharp-eyed supervision. In our house in Strykersville, Mother had kept things obsessively clean, in a perpetual anxiety of allowing dirt and disorder to intrude by the smallest degree; I'd had to resist such impulses in myself as an adult, understanding that they were insatiable, like addictions. Yet, I had to acknowledge, Mother had given this bleak, austere place a welcoming, even homey touch.

Dr. Moses said, "Some of these instruments are my own, and some I've acquired over the years. Decades! People may think that Dr. Moses is as old as the Oriskany hills but of course there were predecessor physicians in Eden County, dating back to the late 1700s." We were staring at primitive medical instruments: stethoscopes, wooden tongue depressors, forceps, suction devices, rubber enemas, small handsaws.

Saws! I laughed, pointing at these badly rusted things. "Is this why doctors used to be called 'sawbones,' Dr. Moses?" It was a sincere question, such as a bright child might ask. Dr. Moses chuckled, opening the display case and removing a ten-inch saw to show me. "Of course, the amputee would be strapped down onto a table. A limb would have to be removed if it became infected and gangrenous. If the patient was lucky, he or she would be rendered unconscious by a powerful dose of whiskey or laudanum." Dr. Moses indicated leather straps attached to an examining table, and hanging from a wall. I was feeling dangerously light-headed, but I tried to smile. The saw's teeth, stained by rust, or blood, or both, felt disconcertingly dull against my fingertips. "But you've never done such an amputation, Dr. Moses, have you? Not *you*." My question was nervy, almost coquettish. Dr. Moses seemed to be brooding on it as with finicky care he replaced the saw back inside the display case and shut the glass lid. Thoughtfully he said, "Not of any living person, I believe."

I'd been forgetting: Dr. Moses had been Eden County coroner for forty years.

On the wall before us were framed anatomical drawings, some primitive and crude, some finely rendered, and startlingly beautiful; among these were Leonardo's symmetrically ideal human being (male, of course) and several line drawings of Dürer. "Our ancestors believed that the immortal soul dwelled within 'mortal coils,' you see. But the question was: where?" Dr. Moses indicated a drawing of what appeared to be a dissected human brain, but I glanced quickly away. I pretended a greater interest in the miscellany of medical equipment Dr. Moses had assembled in his museum. So much! More wooden tongue depressors that reminded me of the

Popsicle sticks of my childhood, and tourniquet devices, and rubber contraptions resembling hot-water bottles; a rubber ball attached to a pronged hose — "To flush the wax out of your ears, dear." There were hypodermic needles of different sizes, one of them unnervingly long — "Nasty, yes. But death by rabies was nastier." There were thin transparent tubes suggestively coiled — "early catheters. Nasty, yes, but death by uremic poisoning was nastier."

I found myself staring wordlessly into a large display case of metal specula, several of them mounted with tiny mirrors, which made the pit of my belly — or the mouth of my uterus — contract in an involuntary spasm. Dr. Moses may have noticed me wince, for he said, in his kindly, firm voice, "Again, Ella! — the alternative to a thorough pelvic examination was often, for females of all ages, much nastier than any examination." I staggered away, into another aisle, wiping at my eyes. An entire section of the museum was devoted to childbirth but I wasn't in a mood to examine anatomical charts of pregnant bellies, embryos curled in the wombs of headless female bodies. Nor did I want to see close-up the "birthing table," with far-spread stirrups and gnawed-looking leather straps. A centuries-old odor of urine, blood, female suffering wafted from it. I murmured, "Dr. Moses, shall I go help Mother prepare dinner? I always used to help her when I was a . . ." But Dr. Moses, intent on leading me forward, didn't hear, or took no heed.

We were in a part of the museum devoted, as Dr. Moses explained, to more "personal" items. He'd begun his practice in Eden County in 1922, nearly six decades were represented here, so he'd had to be highly selective. On an antique sideboard were more modern, stainless steel instruments, scalpels and such, which looked razor sharp; I felt a shiver of dread, that Dr. Moses might lift one of these for me to touch, as I'd touched the saw, and I would cut myself badly. I felt relief on coming to an old-fashioned scale of the kind I recalled from childhood, and climbed up on it. Dr. Moses weighed me, frowning as he shifted the small lead weights back and forth on the rod. "What! Only one-hundred-eight pounds, Ella? Really, for your height, you should weigh twenty pounds more." Dr. Moses measured my height, bringing the steel rod gently down on the top of my head. "Yes. You're five feet nine. We'll have to fatten you up, dear, before you leave Oriskany!" Dr. Moses patted my head, my shoulder, my bare, slightly trembling arm. Close up, his handsome ruin of a face was a maze of miniature broken capillaries and his eyes, behind the bifocal lenses, were sharply alert, like darting fish.

Next we came to a vision chart, a display case of old-fashioned lenses and eyeglasses, and, to my delight, the gigantic eye. It was about the size of a large watermelon, lone and staring in a corner of the museum. Excitedly I said, "I remember this, Dr. Moses! Your wonderful talk at our school. We were all so — impressed." Dr. Moses had some difficulty opening the eye, parts of which seemed to have stuck together; the veiny interior was laced with cobwebs, which Dr. Moses brushed at irritably. (Whoever had cleaned the museum had not thought to clean the interior of the eye, obviously!) "But do you remember the lesson, Ella? Can you recite for me — ?" He pointed at the parts of the eye and with schoolgirl solemnity I recited: "The pupil, the cornea, the lens, the iris, the retina, the sclera, the aqueous humor, the vitreous humor, the optic nerve, the blind spot." Dr. Moses was genuinely surprised. He mimed applause. "*Very* good, Ella. No one else from that school assembly, examined at this time, would do so well, I'm certain." My face smarted pleasantly. I'd surprised myself, in fact. "Your mother has told me you were an honors student, and I can see she wasn't exaggerating, as Virginia sometimes does. A pity, though, you hadn't gone on to medical school. We might be a team, Ella."

I laughed, feeling my face burn. Truly, I was flattered.

But you're retired, Dr. Moses. Aren't you?

The rest of the museum visit wasn't so pleasant.

At the farther end of the room were shelves of bottles containing rubbery semifloating shapes: some were human organs, including eyeballs; some were human fetuses. These, Dr. Moses called his "specimens"—"mementos." Clearly, each bottle had a personal meaning to him; shelves were labeled according to dates, bottles were yet more meticulously labeled. The stench of formaldehyde was almost overwhelming here, but Dr. Moses took no notice. He was smiling, tapping at bottles. I'd averted my eyes, feeling faint, but soon found myself staring at a quart-sized bottle containing a shriveled, darkly discolored fishlike thing floating in murky liquid, apparently headless, with rudimentary arms and legs and something—a head? a heart?—pushing out of its chest cavity. "This poor creature, I delivered on Christmas night, 1939," Dr. Moses said, tapping at the bottle. I felt faint, and looked away. *Not a fetus. An actual baby.* I wanted to ask Dr. Moses what had happened to the poor mother, but he was moving on. You could see that the museum was Dr. Moses's life and that a visitor was privileged to be a witness to it, but in no way a participant.

It was then that Dr. Moses muttered, "What! What are these doing *here*?" I had a glimpse of what appeared to be human hands. Embalmed hands. Several were appallingly small, child sized. Dr. Moses blocked my vision, frowning severely; he gripped my elbow and led me firmly onward. I made no sign that I'd noticed the hands, or Dr. Moses's agitation. I was hoping that, if there'd been a mistake of some kind in the museum, Mother wasn't responsible.

The museum tour was ending. I was exhausted, yet strangely exhilarated. Almost, I felt giddy; drunken. The powerful smells had gone to my head. And Dr. Moses's mesmerizing nearness. *This man is my stepfather.*

Slyly Dr. Moses said, "Ella, dear: meet Cousin Sam."

With a snap of his fingers he'd set the skeleton to rattling and vibrating. I had to check the impulse to shudder, sympathetically. "Cousin Sam has been with me for a long time, haven't you, Sam?" Dr. Moses said. Naively I wondered if this was a commercial skeleton of the kind sold to medical schools or if Dr. Moses had constructed it himself, meticulously wiring and bolting bones together. It appeared to be the skeleton of a man of moderate height; its bones discolored with age and its skull dented; the eye sockets were enormous. The skull seemed to be listening to us with a monkeyish air of mock severity. Strands of cobweb drifted between the skeleton's ribs; something scuttled inside one of the eye sockets: a spider? I looked away, unnerved. Dr. Moses chuckled. "And these, Sam's relatives." Close by, on a fireplace mantel, was a row of silently staring skulls. These, too, appeared to be listening to us with mock severity. "Skulls resemble one another to the untrained eye," Dr. Moses said, "but to the trained eye, distinctions abound." He picked up one of the smaller skulls and turned it over so that I could observe its badly cracked cranium. I had to suppress the instinct to hide my eyes, as if I were looking at something obscene. "This is the skull of a young girl of about thirteen. She died, very likely, by a severe blow to the head. A hammer, or the blunt edge of an ax." I wanted to ask when the girl had died, but could not speak. "She died before your time, Ella," Dr. Moses said.

I managed to ask, "Where did you get these skulls, Dr. Moses?"

From the county morgue. From the county graveyard.

Dr. Moses smiled mysteriously. "Death is plentiful, Ella. There is no lack of specimens of the genus *Death.*"

The tour was over. It was time to leave the museum.

But I'd noticed double carved-oak doors at the rear of the room, and asked what was behind them. Dr. Moses said, "A new wing of the museum, the Red Room — not yet ready for visitors. Another time, Ella."

5. The Revelation

If I can endure this meal, I can endure anything.

And yet: I surprised myself at dinner, I was so hungry for my mother's food. I had not eaten since breakfast that morning, twelve hours before, and my hand shook as I lifted my fork. "Mother, this is *delicious.*" Despite the heat, and her apparent infirmity, Mother had prepared one of her heroic meals. Thinly sliced roast beef, delicately whipped potatoes, several kinds of vegetables, fresh-baked whole-grain bread. For dessert, my childhood favorite: cherry pie with a braided crust. Dr. Moses had an elderly man's finicky appetite but it was clear that he liked to be presented with a full complement of carefully prepared food. And though he drank sparingly, he also served red wine in fine crystal glasses.

A bamboo fan whirred and hummed over the dining room table, stirring the languid air and diluting the pungent medicinal odor. There were freshly cut crimson roses (from Mother's small, meticulously tended rose garden at the side of the house), scented candles burning in silver candlestick holders. The dining room was furnished in an early twentieth-century style but on the windows were flounced white silk drapes my mother had hand-sewn and I recognized the crocheted place mats as her handiwork. The thought occurred to me *Wherever my mother goes, she brings herself. It was wrong of me to leave her.* Throughout dinner Mother sat wanly smiling at me, and at her husband, but was virtually silent, as if she were very tired, unconsciously touching her hairline and jaw where it appeared to be slightly swollen. She'd put on lipstick, but no other makeup. She'd forgotten to remove her apron. Her silvery white hair had gone limp in the humidity. She ate and drank little, while Dr. Moses, fresh shaven and handsome in a taffy-colored seersucker jacket and yellow striped tie, turned his attention to me. It was "Ella," "Ella, dear," "dear Ella!" until I began to feel uncomfortable.

Dr. Moses told me he'd been born in Düsseldorf, Germany, in 1893. His parents had brought him to the United States, to the port of Boston, when he was seven years old; he'd gotten his medical degree from Boston University; in 1920, an adventurous young man, he'd emigrated to the wilds of Upstate New York. Initially, he settled in Port Oriskany. He married the daughter of fellow German emigrants. He moved to Eden County, to the town of Rockland, and then to Strykersville, where he would maintain his medical practice while buying this stone house in the Oriskany hills, living here happily ever since. "Solitude and beauty, in Oriskany," Dr. Moses said, lifting his glass to me. He paused. "We were not blessed with children."

"I'm sorry," I said uncertainly.

"Dear Ella, you shouldn't be! There have been many children in my life, children I've loved, and who have loved me."

For some reason, this statement, not boastful but matter-of-fact, made me very uneasy.

And what became of your first wife, Dr. Moses?

In the parlor, I'd noticed a stiffly posed sepia-toned photograph of a young, dashing, dark-haired Moses Hammacher seated in a Model T beside a plump, stern-browed young woman with a look of being tightly corseted; this woman, I assumed, was Dr. Moses's first wife. Naively I asked her name, and Dr. Moses said with surprising sharpness, "It isn't good manners, Ella, is it, to discuss a previous spouse in the presence of—" He indicated Mother, whose cheeks flushed with embarrassment at being so singled out.

Mother protested weakly, "Oh, I don't mind, dear! Her name was—"

"*I* mind." Dr. Moses struck his fist on the table. Our wineglasses shuddered, the lighted candles flickered in alarm. "She is not Mrs. Moses Hammacher *now.*"

Dr. Moses was breathing audibly. His eyes lurched behind his shiny glasses. Like guilty children Mother and I lowered our gazes to our plates. I wanted badly to reach over to Mother beneath the table and take her hand; I knew her fingers would be thin, chill, limp. Yet she would grip my hand, hard. *Help me, Ella! Take me from this terrible place.*

The remainder of the dinner hour passed in a haze of strain and apprehension, though Dr. Moses didn't lash out at Mother again, or at me. He resumed his cordial, courtly manner, telling me at length of his plans to expand the museum and to advertise — "statewide, beyond the narrow parameters of Eden County. Perhaps, in the preparation of a brochure, you might help me, Ella?" Startled, I may have smiled; I said nothing. As if to impress me, while Mother sat silent, looking very tired, Dr. Moses told me of his travels — his "frontier adventures" — in Mexico, the American Southwest, and Alaska, "among indigenous peoples." He'd retired as county coroner in 1964, and for several years afterward he traveled extensively every summer — "Following the horizon. The lure of the mountains. The very sky called to me." How lyrical Dr. Moses's voice, how yearning! Though I feared and distrusted Dr. Moses, knowing him now to be a domestic tyrant, and possibly a dangerous one, I found myself charmed by him, as I'd been in the museum. His sensual, powerful will. His sexual will. *Women have been captivated by him. And men.* A man who has exerted his will over others never relinquishes that will, or the wish to exert it, as he ages; his victims understand this, and succumb. The strength of the one draws the weakness of the other, as in a perverse magic. "On my travels, I've met many people, including young girls and women," Dr. Moses said, smiling wistfully. "I was a Pied Piper to them, bringing medical attention and care where there'd been little — but, of course, I never took advantage of their trust. Did I, Virginia?"

Mother woke from her mild, melancholy trance to smile quickly. "Oh, yes. Dr. Moses. I mean — no."

"Your mother has aided me invaluably in my museum, Ella. Since last fall. Did you know that, Ella dear?"

Was there some secret message being conveyed to me, in these words? Dr. Moses spoke with such certainty, fixing me with his singular, intense gaze. Was he suggesting that one day I, too, might aid him?

But how?

A strange, original character! After a glass or two of wine it didn't seem to me far-fetched to believe that Dr. Moses was more than an ordinary man. If circumstances had been slightly different he might have been an individual of public renown: a medical educator, a health official in the federal government, a TV personality. *He might have been my father.*

Seeing my stricken expression, Dr. Moses asked playfully, "Have you any questions, Ella?"

That question! Put to us junior high school students, with the effect of silencing us all.

Now, however, I asked a question I might have wished to ask at that time, if I'd had the vocabulary and the courage. "What compelled you to become a doctor and a coroner, Dr. Moses?"

Dr. Moses stared at me, brooding. "'Compelled'? Why do you say 'compelled'?" His white, wiry eyebrows frowned. "It has always been my own free choice, dear Ella. As it was your mother's free choice to become my beloved wife and help-mate, and yours to come here."

It wasn't that the kitchen of Dr. Moses's old stone house was brightly or even adequately lighted; but the overhead light was strong enough to allow me to see clearly, for the first time since I'd arrived, Mother.

She hadn't wanted me to help her with the dishes, of

course. She'd protested feebly. But I'd insisted, carrying plates into the kitchen, stacking them in the sink. It was then I saw that Mother wasn't at all well. Her face was swollen and discolored at the jawline; she walked slowly, favoring her left side; she appeared to be in pain. I took the dishes she'd been carrying from her, set them in the sink and placed my hands firmly on her narrow shoulders. I was several inches taller than Mother, who'd certainly shrunken in the past decade. In a lowered voice, I asked, "Mother, what is it? What has he done to you? *Tell me.*"

Mother was trembling, and could not speak. Her eyes pleaded with me. I touched her face with my fingertips as gently as I could, yet she flinched with pain. Though Mother tried to ease out of my grip, I managed to examine her face and discovered, at her hairline and behind her ears, scabby, scarred incisions and ugly black stitching. A face-lift? *Mother had had a face-lift?*

"It will heal, in time," Mother said quickly. "Dr. Moses wanted simply to 'restore my youth' to me. He'd seen me and remembered me, he said, from years ago, when I was younger, and—well, he wanted that woman as his wife. Ella, don't frown so, I agreed, of course! And it hasn't been terribly painful, really. Dr. Moses gives me pills. I've been able to sleep, most nights. And I do look younger, I think. Don't I?"

I was incredulous, appalled. "Dr. Moses gave you a face-lift? Here? In this house? But—it looks infected."

"It isn't infected, I'm sure," Mother said. "Dr. Moses examines it frequently. When the incisions have healed a little more, he'll remove the stitches. And the staples." She laughed, apologetically. She took my hand to guide it, and allowed me to feel rows of staples in her scalp, embedded in her very scalp like nails. Staples!

"Mother, this is terrible. This is barbaric."

"Ella, no. If I'm not healing well, it's my own fault. This lumpiness by my ears, I should be massaging it, Dr. Moses says. I'm not a very good healer, I never have been. After having my babies, I was weak, sick for months." Mother was pleading with me, standing close so that she could speak quietly, urgently. "I never did recover, I guess! But I love you, Ella, and I love Walter, and I—I don't regret having my babies, I *don't*. And I don't regret marrying Dr. Moses except I'm afraid of . . ." She paused, breathing hard. She was leaning against me, a frail, tremulous weight.

"Afraid of what, Mother?"

Mother shook her head wordlessly. *Afraid.*

The strange thing was: the barbaric face-lift had worked, to a degree. Mother's face had been tightened, the droopy jowls and flaccid flesh of middle age were gone; in the more flattering light of the parlor, she'd seemed quite attractive, pretty. I'd reacted in the most predictable and banal of ways, seeing her: I'd complimented her on looking young—"pretty." As if such attributes were of high value, worth the agony of a face-lift; as if youth and feminine prettiness were unconditionally superior to the dignity of age. Unknowingly, I'd reinforced Dr. Moses's selfish act. And I was this woman's daughter. "Let me take you out of here, Mother," I whispered. "Right now!" I would take Mother to the emergency room of the Strykersville hospital, I would have her wounds examined at once. I would protect her against her tyrannical husband . . .

But Mother resisted. In her weak, stubborn way.

Pleading, "Ella, please don't speak of this to Dr. Moses. *Please.*"

"Mother, of course I'm going to —"

She pressed her fingertips against my mouth. No!

"Dear, I beg you, *please.* Just for now. I do love Dr. Moses, you see. He has made me feel worthy, and desired. He has allowed me to help him in his work. His mission. He isn't always strong, at his age. Don't judge us harshly, Ella, as you are always judging others! I'm your mother."

I'm your mother.

But that was why I'd come to help her, wasn't it?

Mother said, in her anxious lowered voice, now gripping my hands in hers, "Dr. Moses calls me his 'helpmate.' Oh, I was afraid at first, but he gave me a potion to drink, and my fears dropped away — or almost. His first wife, he said, disappointed him. She had no *imagination,* and she had no *courage.*"

Mother was speaking wildly, desperately. I saw that I could not convince her to come away with me immediately; I would have had to carry her bodily, and fight off Dr. Moses. Tomorrow I would reassert myself. If Mother remained stubborn, I would confront Dr. Moses in person.

I relented: "Mother, all right. I'll wait until tomorrow."

Yet still Mother clutched anxiously at me. "Ella, you do promise? You won't speak to Dr. Moses tonight?"

Suddenly I was very tired, my head ached from the several glasses of rich, inky-dark wine my new stepfather had pressed on me. "Yes, I promise! Not tonight."

I knew, that night, I would dream of ugly black stitches in my own flesh, and rows of staples in my scalp.

6. The Museum of Dr. Moses: The Red Room

I am in the Museum of Dr. Moses. I, too, am a specimen.

In the middle of the night I was wakened by the end of a dream that, as it vanished, cracked and stung me like a whip. I sat up, heart pounding alertly, and switched on a lamp.

Silence. The old stone house, the steep-slanted roof above my head. In the night sky a pale, opalescent moon was partly shrouded by clouds.

I hadn't undressed, I'd only taken off my shoes. Lying on an unfamiliar bed in my damp, rumpled clothes. I had not intended to sleep but to lie awake vigilant through the night.

The guest room to which Mother had brought me, on the second floor, front, of Dr. Moses's stone house, had a single bay window framed by yellow chintz draw curtains; I'd recognized the design at once, and felt comforted. As a girl, I'd had similar chintz curtains in my room. In fact, I'd helped my mother make these curtains, laying out material on the living room carpet, measuring and scissoring. *My little helper!* Mother had called me.

Though I'd been uneasy about spending the night in Dr. Moses's house, when Mother brought me into this room and I saw the curtains, the matching bedspread and pillows, and, on the floor, a hook rug like the one I'd had in my college room, I felt a stab of happiness. "Mother, thank you." I'd wanted to hug her, but resisted the impulse for Mother was in pain. She smiled almost shyly, touching her swollen jaw. "I thought you might like this room, Ella. You'll be the first guest since I've come here to live."

In the hall outside, Dr. Moses stood uncertainly, wanting to say goodnight. He extended a hand to shake mine, an awkward, formal gesture, but I pretended not to notice, for I couldn't bear to touch him. "Goodnight, dear Ella!" I only murmured in response, and did not smile. His eyes lingered on my face wistfully.

Since Mother's shocking revelation, I looked on Dr. Moses with distaste, and fury. In his presence I'd been very quiet.

He knows. We are aware of each other now.

It was a childish gesture — I'd pulled a heavy mahogany rocking chair in front of my door. As if, if Dr. Moses wanted to enter in the night, this could keep him out. (The door had no lock.) But, I reasoned, if the door were pushed open, there would be sufficient noise to rouse me.

Now I myself dragged the rocking chair away from the door.

There was no bathroom in this guest room, I would have to use a bathroom in the hall Mother had shown me. "It will be yours, Ella. No one else will use it." Barefoot, I walked stealthily. In my rumpled shirt and slacks, hair disheveled, I would have been embarrassed to be seen by my hosts.

I'd brought with me an eight-inch flashlight, which I always carried in my duffel bag.

In the antiquated, poorly lighted bathroom, I examined my face in the mirror; gingerly I touched my forehead, cheeks, jaws, for I looked strangely puffy, especially beneath the eyes. And my eyelids were reddened. Had I been crying? In my sleep? I ran my fingers quickly through my hair, drew my nails across my scalp, searching apprehensively for — what? Staples? Small nails? Behind my ears, where I couldn't see, the skin was tender as if inflamed, but there were no stitches.

My mother's voice murmured *Ella, help me! Don't judge me.*

Boldly then I left the bathroom, and stood for a brief while in the darkened corridor. I knew what I must do, but hesitated before taking action.

The house remained silent. Except for the wind, and a thrumming, rhythmic sound of late-summer insects in the tall grasses and foliage close outside the house. The long corridor, running the width of the house, faded into darkness at its far end. I didn't know which was the master bedroom, but I believed it was some distance from my room. *He would not have wished me closer to Mother, to hear her cries in the night.*

I made my decision. I descended the stairs, which were covered in a threadbare carpet.

On the first floor, I made my way quietly and unerringly to the museum. Adrenaline flooded my veins! The heavy outer door was unlocked. Inside, I shut the door and switched on my little flashlight, which provided a narrow, intense beam of about fifteen feet, and made my way along the center aisle, past the glass display cases, past Cousin Sam dangling motionless before me like a mock-proprietor of the Museum of Dr. Moses, and at the double oak doors at the rear of the room I paused, and swallowed hard. *The Red Room. Not yet ready for visitors.*

It had been a warning, I knew. Dr. Moses had warned me.

Still, I pushed inside. I had come so far, and would not turn back.

The Red Room: so-called because the walls were covered in a crimson silk wallpaper. Once it had been elegant, now it was rather tacky, yet still striking, attractive. The elaborately molded ceiling had been recently painted white, there was even a chandelier, antique, once beautiful but now somewhat tarnished, its cut-glass ornaments glazed with grime. This room was smaller than the other part of the museum and the exhibits were crowded together, most of them not yet labeled. I found myself staring, at first without comprehension, into a glass display case containing human skulls; except, when I looked more closely, these were heads; human heads; somewhat shrunken, and the faces shriveled; they had swarthy, coarse complexions and straight lusterless black hair, their eyes still intact, though half-closed, sullen and unfocused. They were, or had been, the heads of aboriginal peoples — Indians, Mexicans, Eskimos. Adults, adolescents, children. Atop one of the cases, set down in apparent haste, was the miscellany of hands I'd glimpsed yesterday evening in the museum, whose presence had so offended Dr. Moses. The hands were clawlike, some of them blackened and missing fingers and nails, but otherwise perfectly preserved. Some were still wearing rings. I heard my small, naive voice — "These can't be real." In fascinated revulsion I touched the smallest hand, which must have belonged to a girl of about eleven. The fingers were utterly motionless yet seemed warm with life. As I nudged against the hand, the hand naturally moved.

"No!"

Unknowingly, I'd begun to speak aloud. The shock must have been so profound.

The flashlight beam seemed to be moving of its own volition, jerkily. My hand had begun to sweat, I could barely hold it. I was staring at a large, rectangular Plexiglas case in which luxuriant coils of lustrous, glossy hair were displayed. There must have been a dozen hair samples, ash blond, russet red, dark brown, dark blond, wheat colored, silvery gray, black threaded with gray . . . Unlike the embalmed heads and hands, these hair samples were beautiful to contemplate. The flashlight beam lingered on them. There did not appear to be remnants of scalp attached to the roots. Several of the samples were prettily braided with satin ribbons. Others were bow-tied with ribbons. The effect was festive, mesmerizing, as Christmas decorations. I wondered: did these locks of hair belong to girls I'd once known in Strykersville? Was it possible two of the matched braids had been *mine*?

He is a murderer. A demon. These are his victims.

Glass jars in which appalling things floated. Eyeballs, which stared without rancor at me, and through me. Organs I did not wish to identify: fleshy, fist-sized hearts, livers, female and male genitalia. Each jar was marked in a cryptic code, neatly inked on white adhesive labels: rq 4 19 211; ox 8 32 399. *Yet a code can be cracked like any riddle.* In my numbed state my mind worked rapidly as a machine: the numerals might refer to letters of the alphabet, the letters might be reversed. There was a logical intelligence here, a scientist's methodology.

The flashlight beam led me on. I was very tired and wanted only to crawl somewhere and shut my eyes and sleep and yet my eyes were opened, staring at fresh-skinned skulls mounted on poles, whose bones glistened wetly; lampshades of fine, fair human skin, meticulously handsewn; the facial mask of an attractive woman, skin peeled carefully from her bones, attached to a mannequin's egg-smooth, featureless face; sawed skulls, painted like bowls, displayed on shelves; dangling things that stirred with my breath, a Calder-like mobile of fingers, toes, noses, lips, female labia; what appeared to be a belt of linked female breasts, with protuberant rosy nipples. On a dressmaker's dummy was the skin of a big-breasted female torso, flayed and made into a kind of vest,

sewn onto a durable material like felt. Appalled, yet fascinated, I turned over the hem of the vest . . .

"Ella!"

The whisper came from behind me. Yet my heart was
beating so powerfully, I wasn't sure I'd heard. The flashlight
slipped in my sweaty hand and fell loudly to the floor. I
turned, panting, and crouched, but could not see clearly. An
indistinct figure stood at the threshold between the two
rooms. "Ella, no." I drew breath to scream, but could not. My
legs lost all strength. The floor beneath me opened suddenly
and I fell, fainting.

7. Morning

He is a murderer. A demon.

Morning! A shaft of sunshine fell across my dreaming face
like a laser ray. My eyes opened, I found myself lying on an
unfamiliar bed, in rumpled clothing. My head was twisted at
a painful angle as if in my sleep I'd been trying to scream. The
soles of my bare feet were sticky.

Quickly I got up. I could barely stand, I was dazed with ex-
haustion. I saw that I was in the room to which Mother had
brought me with the yellow chintz draw curtains—the guest
room. Except the curtains had not been drawn, morning sun
flooded hotly through the windows. Confused, I saw that the
heavy rocking chair had been dragged back in front of the door.

I fumbled, checking my bag: my little flashlight was
missing.

It was 7:20 A.M., I saw by my watch. I could not believe
that I'd slept the remainder of the night, after the horrors of

the Red Room. And so heavy, stuporous a sleep, my head ached violently and my mouth tasted of ashes.

I began to panic. I threw my things into my bag and prepared to escape. In the corridor outside my room I heard voices downstairs. My heart flooded with adrenaline. I knew of only one way out, down those stairs. As I descended, I heard Dr. Moses's voice grow louder, scolding. My mother's voice was faint, nearly inaudible.

They were in the kitchen at the rear of the house. I wondered if they were arguing over me.

I thought I heard Dr. Moses say, "You will *not*" — or maybe he said, "She will *not*."

I heard a screen door slam. Through a side window I saw Dr. Moses walking swiftly past, I saw just the top of his bare head, his thin stained-ivory hair. I recalled a small barn to the rear of the house, converted to a garage, and hoped that Dr. Moses was headed there.

I went into the kitchen where Mother was seated numbly at a table, in a dressing gown and slippers. The dressing gown was one I'd never seen before, champagne colored, made of a gossamer fabric and decorated with lace; the satin slippers were a match. *Her new husband bought that for her. For their honeymoon.* I felt a stab of revulsion at such knowledge. Mother's swollen eyes, lifting to me, were stricken with guilt.

"Mother, we're leaving here! I'm taking you out of this terrible place."

"Ella, no. I can't—"

"Mother, you *can*. We're leaving *now*. He can't stop us."

Yet I spoke angrily, desperately. I pulled Mother to her feet. She clutched at my arms. She said, pleading, "Ella, I can't. He would never let me leave. 'Whither thou goest, I will go.' He made me pledge these words when we were married. He meant them—'for eternity.'" In the bright sunshine I could see the ugly staples and stitches in Mother's scalp, above her hairline, through her limp, silvery gray hair, that had pulled her forehead taut, smoothing out the wrinkles to make her look young—"pretty."

"He's a demented, evil old man. You know what he is."

"He would follow us, and hurt us both. You don't know, Ella—"

"I know. I saw."

"You saw—what?"

"The Red Room."

Mother hid her face in her hands and began to cry silently.

"You judge us too harshly, Ella. You don't *know*."

"I know what I need to know, Mother!"

My mind was working rapidly but not clearly. I knew I should escape Dr. Moses's house—if I could—and notify police—and return to get Mother. But—what if he hurt her in the interim? What if he fled with her, took her hostage? Killed her? Like the others? I was too distraught to speak with him and pretend that nothing was wrong. He would see through any subterfuge, he was far too shrewd.

"Ella, what are you looking for?"

"Something—to help me."

I was rummaging through drawers. My fingers closed about a sharp blade, a steak knife; I saw that I'd cut myself.

"He's a murderer, Mother. He's crazy. He has killed people for his museum. We have to protect ourselves." I took the knife and hid it in my bag. My hand was trembling badly, smarting with pain. Mother stared at me. Her swollen face had taken on a passive, childlike expression. She was stroking nervously at the underside of her jaw. "Come on, Mother. *Please.*"

At last she allowed me to lead her through the house, to the front door. It was a desperate flight, no time for her to pack. No time to take anything! I'd hoped that Dr. Moses had driven out in one of his vehicles, but I hadn't heard the sound of any motor. My own car was parked in the driveway where I'd left it. I had to trust that Dr. Moses had done nothing to it, that the ignition would start.

"Ella, where are you taking my wife?"

Dr. Moses was waiting for us on the front porch. He'd circled the house as if guessing my intentions. His voice was coldly furious, threatening. He possessed little of his courtly charm: he'd become an old, ravaged, truculent man with glaring eyes who hadn't yet shaved, stubble glittering like mica on his jaws. He wasn't wearing his starched white cotton shirt, or his dapper straw hat. Instead he wore work clothes, gardener's clothes, soiled. On the trouser cuffs were earth stains, or bloodstains. *His butcher's uniform. And now he has come for you.*

Suddenly I lost all control. I pushed blindly at him. The astonished old man could not have been prepared for my ferocity, my desperation. "Murderer! Demon!" I shoved both my hands against his chest, I pushed him backward off the porch and he fell heavily down the stone steps, his expression stunned, bifocals flying. He fell hard against the front walk, striking his head, and groaned, and twitched, and convulsed, and made no more sound. I had a fleeting impression of blood at his nose, outlining his gaping mouth. Mother was whimpering, yet docile. I half-carried, half-walked her to my car. "You're safe, Mother! He can't hurt you now."

I hadn't had to use the knife, for which I would always be grateful.

8. Escape

He has died. He can't follow.
    An old man, his skull eggshell thin.
Was it true? I wanted so badly to believe so.

I drove south toward Strykersville, but would not stop there. I would not stop for hours, fleeing south out of the Oriskany hills, and out of Eden County, and into Pennsylvania. Mother in her dressing gown curled up beside me as I drove, drew her slippered feet up beneath her on the seat, like a child so exhausted by fear and strain that, at last, she has become relaxed, and sleeps innocently, not knowing what it is she flees, and whether it will follow.

Acknowledgments

The following stories appeared, often in slightly different versions, in the following publications:

"Suicide Watch," *Playboy* magazine, 2006.

"The Man Who Fought Roland LaStarza," *Murder on the Ropes*, edited by Otto Penzler (New Millennium, 2001).

"Feral," *The Magazine of Fantasy & Science Fiction*, 1998.

"Bad Habits," *McSweeney's*, 2005.

"The Twins: A Mystery," *Alfred Hitchcock's Mystery Magazine*, 2002.

"The Hunter," *Ellery Queen's Mystery Magazine*, 2003.

"Valentine, July Heat Wave," *Harper's Bazaar*, 2006 (UK) and *Ellery Queen's Mystery Magazine* (U.S.).

"The Museum of Dr. Moses," *The Museum of Horrors*, edited by Dennis Etchison (Leisure Books, 2001).

"Stripping," *Postscripts* (UK) and *The Year's Best Fantasy and Horror*, edited by Ellen Datlow and Terri Windling (St. Martin's, 2005).

"Hi! Howya Doin!" *Ploughshares*, 2007.